A Different Reality

Davey D. Jones

Copyright © 2023 Davey D. Jones

All rights reserved.

ISBN: **9798869649324**

A Different Reality

To my dear mother, Eirwen, and father, Bill

- thank you for Everything!

ACKNOWLEDGMENTS

I would like to thank all the following for their advice and encouragement: Dr Clive Lee, Peter Morrissey, Andrew Smart, Will John, Ryan Schachtel, my cousin - Myra Price, and last but not least, my brother Bert.

A special thanks to Eric Heyman – the artist who patiently changed the cover design again and again. And finally, a big thank you to Jordan Thorne for seamlessly digitizing the above artwork.

"Grief is the price we pay for love."

- Queen Elizabeth II

Chapter 1

I look down at my unconscious brother in the hospital bed and feel my chest tightening – this is all my fault. He looks so peaceful there, not like the last time I saw him - a look of sheer terror on his face as he ran away from… me.

The room is silent except for the rhythmic beeping coming from the machines monitoring Danny. The doctor and nurse look on. I see my distraught mum barely clinging on to her sanity and my guilt deepens. Next to her my friend Claire is studying me – her expression changes from suspicion to concern as she looks from me to my brother. The doctor flicks through Danny's patient records on the clip board baffled by what he sees.

'We just don't understand what has happened to your son,' he says, facing my mum. 'He's not in a coma, we see him moving in his sleep, but we just can't wake him up.' I catch Claire's furtive glance at me and immediately look away to hide my guilt. If they look carefully, they'll see that Danny is maintaining a very toned physique – especially for a nine-year-old laid up in hospital. The beeping from the heart monitor gets faster. 'Here it goes again,' the doctor says shaking his head. Images of wild horsemen chasing Danny wielding a blood-curdling array of weapons flash through my mind and I have to stop myself from screaming 'Run!' I glance at Claire who is looking on wide-eyed with worry, a feeling shared by the doctor, nurse and most acutely, by my mum.

* * * * *

Danny *is* running for his life. He ducks under a canvas screen and comes out on another row of market stalls and looks quickly left and right searching for the soldiers chasing him – an arrow thwacks into the market stall's wooden beam above his head. He darts across the path between the stalls and tunnels his way below tables and carts struggling to catch his breath as he scoots from one concealed place to another. He can hear them shouting, they are close. He's confused - what just happened? Danny doesn't have time to work it out - he desperately needs to find a place to hide.

The market-stall holders and shoppers look around trying to determine the cause of the uproar. The fact that they are wearing flowing robes and head scarves doesn't even register with Danny anymore. Some of the women wear veils and are escorted by burly bare-chested men carrying clubs, alert for any danger from passers-by. The people are all a beautiful caramel-brown colour with long dark hair. Most of the men have beards and carry deadly curved daggers tucked into cloth belts wrapped around their long-flowing robes. The sound of camels making their presence known doesn't register either. All Danny cares about is getting away from the soldiers who are armed with swords or spears and dressed in white tunics under bronze chest plates. Their muscular arms and legs have leather and metal shin- and wrist-guards. They are all wearing spike-topped bronze helmets which leave their bearded faces exposed – the armour, spearheads and swords sparkle as they catch the blistering Mediterranean sun.

He looks left then right and dashes across the passageway and rolls under a heavy wooden cart loaded with bales of something wrapped in great cotton blankets. He peers between the spokes of the wooden wheels as bronze-clad legs race by. If the soldiers catch him, he may lose his hand, even his head. If he's lucky, they'll sell him at the slave market, where he'll probably be worked to death. What just happened? he asks himself again as he wipes away the ever-present sand from his brow and spits some grains from his parched mouth.

* * * * *

The nurse is busy checking the equipment, looking for any fault which might explain these sudden increases in Danny's heart rate – as if he were sprinting. I put an arm around my sobbing mum's shoulders in an effort to provide some comfort, but the guilt and the task ahead almost make my knees buckle – I feel so weak, the task so hopeless. Danny's soul is stuck in a host in a different time and place – but I don't know where or when, I don't even know if his host is a boy or a girl, let alone what he or she looks like.

Danny is breathing really rapidly now; the pinging of the heart monitor sounds as if it isn't far off becoming a constant bleep. The doctor points out the twitching muscles and the eyes which seem to be searching below the eyelids.

'He appears to be having a dream, or more likely a nightmare judging by his rapid heartbeat, we'll try a sedative to bring his vitals to a safe level.' At this he glances at the nurse who starts to prepare a syringe. When the nurse is ready, she squirts a little out of the needle and looks at the doctor for the go-ahead – the doctor nods and the nurse hesitates before fiddling with the intravenous tube connection. Just as the nurse is about to inject Danny the monitor's bleeping slows down. And down. And down. I can't think straight. Is Danny dying? Wherever he is, 'whenever' he is? What's happening?

The beeping slows back to a regular beat and everyone in the hospital room breathes out a sigh of relief. Looking at the monitor, the patient notes and back at Danny lying motionless in his bed, the doctor shakes his head again in complete bewilderment. Then he looks at me and the worried look I have glaring at the syringe in the nurse's hand.

'Lewis, isn't it?' he asks me. All I can do is nod. A moment before I was on the verge of leaping across the hospital room and slapping the syringe out of the nurse's hand before she could give the sedative to my brother. I don't know what is going on, but I know that Danny probably needs to be alert and in control of all his senses; I don't know what kind of effect a sedative would have on him. To be honest, I really don't know much about the situation I've gotten my brother and I into. But I do know more than everyone in this room.

However, I can't say anything because it sounds nuts.

'Don't worry, Lewis,' the doctor continues, 'it was just a sedative to help calm your brother and help him out of his nightmare.' He looks at me for confirmation that I've understood, but all I can give him is another nod.

While my mother tries to keep her emotions from completely unravelling, I make a vow, I will save Danny. Whatever the danger, whatever it takes, I will bring him back to the here and now. Shame engulfs me and I close my eyes, once again seeing the fear in my brother's eyes – please God, give me a chance to see him again so I can ask for his forgiveness. The doctor escorts my mother out of the room while the nurse tucks the bedsheets neatly around Danny lying there seemingly peacefully asleep.

As we slowly recover from the earlier fright caused by Danny's erratic heartbeat, Claire leads me to a quiet place near the ward's drinks' machine. She quickly glances around to check there is no one within earshot, 'Lewis, how did this happen? What's going on?' I look at her and don't know what to say, where to start. My mum saves me from the awkward moment by suddenly appearing after her quick chat with the doctor.

'Are you both okay?' she asks.

'Yes,' we both answer.

'The doctor's gotta finish his rounds and stuff, so we have to come back for an appointment later with him and the neurologist, at 1 o'clock.' She looks at me and I nod. 'I've got a few things to do so can you meet me back here for the meeting?'

'Yeah, of course, Mum.' She gives us both a kiss on the cheek giving my arm a squeeze in the process and heads off. Mum is trying to soldier on, but her drawn face and sagging shoulders add to my worries – is she close to having a breakdown? I watch her walk off sorting out something in her handbag as she heads out of the ward.

The smell of disinfectant in this famous old London hospital is doing my head in – I usually like the smell of a place or thing that's clean, but now it just seems to burn my nostrils. 'Can we go to the park nearby, you know the one with the pond?'

'Sure,' Claire says, and so we turn and head for the exit. We walk to the park in silence, my mind unable to think straight – thoughts bouncing around in my head. We stop near the pond and then Claire faces me and says, 'So?' I'm still not sure how to explain what's been happening. Claire's expression looks a little sterner. 'I can't help you if you won't tell me what's going on,' she says looking at me straight in the eye.

I look at her but can't maintain eye contact. She's our buddy – Danny looks up to her like an older sister, Mum loves her and is always telling us how lucky we are to have such a good friend. When my dad disappeared two years ago on an aid mission somewhere in the jungles of Central Africa, it was hell. Not knowing if he was alive or dead almost drove me crazy. It actually felt as if my mind could literally break in half – like when we playfight at school and someone gets your arm behind your back and lifts your wrist up closer to your head, a half-nelson I think wrestlers call it. That feeling where your arm could snap at any moment is how my head felt. But Claire was always there for us – always seeming to know what to say and do – emotional intelligence, my mum calls it.

'I know that you and Danny have been up to something. These last few weeks I can tell you've been keeping something from me,' Claire continues. I quickly look back at her, she's looking at me with those penetrating hazel eyes. She may be willowy, but she has an intensity and formidable inner strength which make people think twice before having a go at her. When I look back at Claire, I can see she is exasperated. She flicks strands of her long wavy fair hair away from her eyes and waits for a response. I look at her and know I need help – and she is my best mate. My shoulders slump and I look down at nothing.

'Come on,' Claire says softly, 'let's sit on that bench under the tree and you can tell me all about it.' Then in a voice with power behind it but still soft, 'I can help you, Lewis, we can help Danny.' I allow her to lead me over to the bench in the park and then sit side by side looking over the pond with ducks occasionally quacking and flapping wings causing curtains of water to catch the sunlight on what others might describe as a beautiful day.

Where do I start? How can I tell her that after Dad disappeared, I was having nightmares that kept me from sleeping without sounding like a wimp? I had told Danny who was having the same nightmares not to tell anybody, or we'd never hear the end of the mickey taking. I'm thirteen, I shouldn't be waking up with tears in my eyes from bad dreams. Imagine if the boys in my rugby team heard that.

'I found a way to stop having nightmares,' I tell her. The look in Claire's eyes changes from concern to confusion.

'What? I don't get it. What's that got to do with anything?' she asks.

I try to think of a way to explain it so that I don't sound pathetic. 'You know when Dad disappeared on that aid mission in the jungle?' Claire nods, 'Well, Danny and I both had these recurring nightmares where it seemed like Dad was home again. He would turn up when Mum, Danny and I were having breakfast, smiling and laughing with presents or groceries in his arms – we would all cry with relief that he was okay. We kept having the same dreams, sort of, but in different situations; Dad would turn up while we were on holiday, playing footie in the park, at picnics, even coming into class at school. A little different but always with the same result – that feeling of sheer joy because Dad was back home safe, and all the family were together again.'

Claire looks even more confused, 'But... I still don't get what that has got to do with anything, I mean dreams...' I look at her imploringly and so she stops.

'I have to explain things right from the start or you won't understand how we've gotten from nightmares to Danny lying in hospital fighting for his life – maybe literally.' Claire nods for me to go on. 'It was horrible, I'd wake up convinced my dad was back with us and then realise it was just a dream; it was like hearing the terrible news that my dad was missing, possibly dead, for the first time – reliving that raw grief every morning, again and again. I felt exhausted, hollow inside – stunned. I dreaded going to sleep.' I pause and take a deep breath and look across the pond – the vivid memories bring back that heart-rendering pain. 'The worst thing was that I could see Danny was going through the same thing – and finding it even harder to deal with – I suppose being Danny's age made it tougher.' I can see that Claire is trying to work out where I am going with all of this, so I continue.

'One night I was having the same sort of dream where Dad shows up, but this time I realized that it was just that - a dream. It was weird, but I remember thinking in my sleep that I didn't want this nightmare to continue. Even in my sleep I felt exhausted, so I shouted "Stop!" like a director on a filmset. Everything in the dream stopped. If we imagine that my dream was a film, then it was set on the beach where Mum, Danny and I were drying off after a swim. Then Dad approached us smiling…' my voice catches in my throat and I feel Claire's hand giving my forearm a little comforting squeeze. 'I'm the "director" of this movie and know that I can change the storyline to how I'd like it. Everyone in the dream was frozen in place, waiting for my instruction. So I said to him, "Dad, you can't keep coming into my dreams – you're killing me." My words visibly hurt him, so I tried to explain myself, "I love you Dad, but seeing you every night coming home, when in reality you're not, hurts so much, I can't take it." That's when I realized the extent of my powers as director of my dreams.'

'What do you mean, what happened?'

'Well, I'm not only the director, but the screenplay writer as well, so I decide how people react and feel in every situation in my dream. I wanted my dad to understand where I was coming from and so he did. The pain disappeared from his eyes, and he said, "Good man, Lewis. You look after Mum and Danny till I get back, okay?" I nodded, and said, "Love you, Dad," - he looked at me with so much affection and said, "Love you, Lewis," then he turned around and walked away and everyone on the beach continued to play or do what they were doing before.'

I've been welling up as a result of recalling that moment. Claire puts her arm around my shoulders and gives me a hug. I try to discreetly wipe away the tears with my forearm.

'So, you can decide the way your dreams pan out…'

Claire is trying to sound cheery, 'You know that's pretty cool – you must have wicked dreams,' I look at her with one eyebrow raised. She looks suddenly flustered and rambles on, 'I mean, really cool and exciting dreams – in a good way.'

'Yeah, actually, they were – I started looking forward to sleep – it was like being the star of a film or game, every night – the ultimate escapism. I always won, beat the bad guys, and got what I wanted,' I cough as Claire now looks at me in the same quizzical way with eyebrow raised. What just happened there? I've never really thought about how pretty Claire is before, but - no, this isn't right, I shouldn't be thinking like this. Especially now.

Claire seems to share the same feeling of awkwardness and so blurts out, 'Can anyone do this? Can anyone stop having nightmares and be the "star of the show" in their dreams?'

I take a moment to think about the research I did in what seems like ages ago but was really only last year, 'No, I don't think so. I looked it up on the internet and hardly anybody mentions it. But eventually I did find one or two articles on it. It's called dream leaning.'

'What do I have to do again?' she asks.

'Basically, you pretend to be the director on a filmset. The film is your dream. You choose the actors and tell them how you want them to act in your dream. If you don't like a certain actor or character – you can tell them to go, and they just vanish. Once you get the hang of it, it's great. Eventually, you can even continue one dream from the night before if it's a dream you are really enjoying.

'Danny and I were having so much fun with our dreams – it was great; especially during the pandemic lockdowns: we were able to travel almost anywhere every night and escape that feeling of being imprisoned at home.' I look at Claire whose mind has drifted off as she seems to contemplate the wonderful potential of always having the dreams you want, following a storyline you've directed.

Then a cloud seems to pass over her face, and she turns to me and shakes her head slightly as she says, 'I still don't get how this has got anything to do with Danny.'

'Dream leaning is just the first step – once you can do that, you're able to go beyond just dreams, you-' I'm interrupted by my mobile phone going off, it's my mum. Oh no, I think I've messed up, and then I realize I still have time. She must be phoning to remind me that we have an appointment with Doctor Jeffries and the neurologist, 'the brainy doctors' my mum calls them, in about 10 minutes.

'Lewis, where are you?' my mum asks evidently walking and talking - I can hear that she's a little out of breath and the sound of hustle and bustle in the background.

'Sorry, Mum, I'm with Claire in the park – I'll be with you now.'

'Okay, see you in a bit.'

'See you, Mum.' I put the phone back in my pocket and get up from the bench. Claire is still sat there. She looks up at me questioningly.

'I've got to go to that appointment - I'll see you tomorrow, okay?' Claire nods. 'Oh, and Claire, um, thanks. Just talking about it makes me feel better.'

'Hey, that's what friends are for,' she says with a smile.

'But one thing - please don't tell anyone about this?' There's a tone of pleading in my voice which I don't like.

'Of course I won't. We'll work this out, whatever it is, Lewis – together we can do it.' She's a rock, I smile and head off. I glance back at her after a few paces. She seems lost in thought sat on the bench, gazing out over the pond.

Chapter 2

I haven't slept well and apparently, nor has Claire, so after tossing and turning most of the night, we ended up texting each other and arranged to meet for a milkshake before school. Spring is on its way; the blue skies and fairly warm temperature mean this is the first day of the year I don't have to wear a coat. As I walk to the café I try to order in my mind what I'm going to say to Claire – and remind myself I mustn't forget to ask her to bring Danny's dream diary to school tomorrow. I posted it to her when Danny went to hospital thinking the police might search my house looking for some explanation as to why my brother has fallen into a coma-like state, find Danny's diary, and then arrest me – it doesn't make sense, I know, but I've become so paranoid. I think I might be on the brink of losing my mind. Walking into the café I see Claire sitting in a quiet corner with two chocolate milkshakes on the table.

'Hey,' I say as I plonk my bag on an empty chair and sit down opposite her, 'How are you doing?'

'Tired, I couldn't sleep. I really don't feel like school today.' She then pushes one of the milkshakes over to me.

'Thanks,' I say and suck some up through the straw – this is the best milkshake in town. I sit back and we stare at each other.

Claire quickly scans the café and leans forward and in almost a whisper, 'Lewis, I still don't get how dream leaning can end up with Danny in a sort of coma in a bed in hospital.'

'Being able to steer your dreams allows you to reach another level, like in a game.'

'Sorry,' Claire looks lost. I try to think of a better way to explain it and realize I have to go back a step.

'We were enjoying leaning our dreams – we were actually having a laugh - some of our "film-making" was hilarious. We got people to do crazy things, or we lived like heroes or famous celebs, and...' I can't mention the movie stars and singers I've been dating.

Claire reads my thoughts, 'Never mind that – you can tell me about that another time,' she smiles, eyes twinkling briefly. 'Go on.'

'We started trying to influence our dreams by reading adventure stories which took us to different times and places. But then something strange happened.' Claire leans in, hanging on my every word. 'One night we watched Gladiator, it's a great film,' I see Claire nodding agreement, 'but probably too bloody for someone Danny's age. Mum was on night shift, so I was in charge. I could see my brother was a little freaked out by the film, so I tried to take his mind off it by just babbling away about nothing really. We had our milk, cleaned our teeth, and almost with relief we got to bed. The lights went out and I think we were both fast asleep before our heads hit the pillows.

'I seemed to fall asleep and straight into a dream. I was sort of drawn to this door which I opened and then stopped dead. It was the entrance to a desert under a starlit night – sand dunes drifting far into the horizon. When I eventually walked through what must have been some kind of portal and looked around, I realised that the starry night had these roundish "windows" framed by swirling luminous light-blue vapour floating all around me. Each "window" had a different scene going on – like paintings in a gallery. Inside one of these windows, I saw Romans, like in the film I'd just watched, having a feast in a clearing at the edge of a village surrounded by a forest on a beautiful sunny day. I walked towards the window to have a better look. Suddenly, I felt my body lurch forward as I was sucked into the swirling ring of vapour. It was like - and I suppose it's always the same – I feel like I'm trying to surf, standing on a rollercoaster. My arms flew out for balance as I shot through the darkness going around and around and upside down like riding along a giant corkscrew, then just before I felt I was going to be sick, everything went black.

'I woke up with a jolt, except I wasn't in bed, but lying on some grass looking up at the blue sky where a scattering of clouds were passing peacefully by. I just lay there for a moment, making shapes out of the clouds – faces, animals, and all sorts. It all looked so real. The sun appeared from behind one of the clouds and shone right into my eyes so that I had to look away. I remember thinking, "What's happening?" The ground felt cold, so I rolled over onto all fours and saw that I was wearing a creamy-coloured top that was open at the neck and reached down to my knees, tied at the waist with a bit of rope. It was really rough fabric – wool, I guess. The sleeves only reached my elbows and that was when I noticed that my arms were tanned with black hair, not fair.'

'Are you saying that you were a different person in your dream?'

'Well, yes and no.' This doesn't help her at all judging by the look she gives me. 'It's me, but I'm in someone else's body. I'm sort of residing in someone else's body for the duration of the dream.'

'Weird,' I hear her say under her breath. She looks away and seems to be trying to remember if she's ever been someone else in her dreams.

'Yeah, I suppose. I'll explain what I think is happening there later.' If she thinks this is odd, her mind is going to be blown away by the fact that my spirit travels to a different place and time and 'borrows a body' while I'm in that dream location. Maybe I have already lost my mind.

'What happened next?'

'I was in a meadow surrounded by forest. But this was different. More real. I could feel the cool breeze against my cheek. I could smell the meadow flowers and smoke from a wood fire somewhere nearby. When I looked at something, it seemed more distinct, if I walked the shadows would move just like in real life. When I stamped my foot, I felt the firmness of the ground. It seemed more vivid, less "swimmy". I looked around and thought I saw someone who walked like Danny disappearing into the edge of the forest on the far side of the glade I was in.

'So I followed. But then there was the sound of someone blowing a horn, like in the movies, and then, wham! The silence was shattered by the sound of shouting, screaming, metal clashing against metal, horses, yells, and other noises I couldn't identify – it sounded like a massive fight or battle had just started. So I did what I usually did in a dream that was turning into a nightmare and was about to yell "Stop!" but weirdly, someone else beat me to it. I couldn't understand what was going on - something was wrong. Someone else was trying to lean their dreams in my dream. And everything seemed so real, so noisy, so vivid. The noise was getting louder, then I recognised the sound of metal I'd heard a moment ago – it was the ring of swords hitting swords or shields. There were cries of pain, wailing, people pleading, angry shouts and mad laughter – it was horrendous.

'All of a sudden, the dark-haired boy I saw entering the woods earlier shot back out and ran right past me. In a moment we were both sprinting towards the forest away from the racket. When we got into the wood, we both found a tree to hide behind and looked back across the glade. The ground seemed to rumble, I looked towards the far treeline and saw these wild horsemen come streaming out. It was my turn to lead, so I grabbed the boy and ran. We were running for our lives through the trees, branches whipping painfully into our faces, but the terror following us gave us wings, we just ran, our hearts in our mouths. The sounds behind us seemed to be getting nearer – I could hear men shouting, horses whinnying, the sound of leather and other stuff jingling and creaking, they were getting close, really close, and then we came to a steep slope in the forest.

'We were both so scared we just hurled ourselves down the bank bouncing down through brambles and off tree trunks like rag dolls. We got battered. There was blood oozing from cuts on our faces and arms, our strange clothes were torn. But the priority was to keep hidden from the wild men. At the bottom of the slope there was a bush hiding a little cave-like hole. We scrambled into it and pushed branches and shrubs back in place and drew the roots hanging from the roof of the cave across to form a kind of screen.

'The horsemen followed us down the bank more carefully. Then they stopped near where we were hiding. They were quiet, just waiting. I was breathing so hard I thought they must hear me – so I tried to control my breathing by opening my mouth wide - in and out, gradually my breathing slowed until it seemed almost normal, but my pulse was racing. I glanced over at the boy, the wide-eyed expression plus the way he wiped his forehead with his forearm made my heart stop. I looked closer, studied the nervous expression on his face, and the way he looked around. And I remember thinking, "No, this can't be happening!" – I was sure that the boy I was looking at was Danny and that I had somehow brought him into this nightmare.'

'Hold on a minute, I thought you said the boy was dark-haired? Danny has fair hair, like you.'

'Remember I told you I was dark-haired because I was in someone else's body. So was Danny.' I can see she's a bit lost but finishing the story might help her grasp what I'm saying.

'So I whispered, "Danny?" The boy's head whipped around, and he looked at me with a look of fear mixed with surprise. "Danny," I said again so quietly it was barely more than a breath, "it's me, Lewis."

'"Lewis?" Danny's jaw dropped so his mouth formed a big O. I nodded. The look of relief on his face almost broke my heart. He shuffled quietly towards me, then cuddled up to me with his head on my chest and arms wrapped around me. "I'm scared," his voice trembled as he said it.

'As quietly as I could, I hugged him and whispered, "it's okay, we'll be all right."

'"They definitely came down this way." A man's voice broke the silence. "We better find them, remember our orders, no survivors." The man's horse raised its head and neighed. "Spread out, form line and head down that way." There were grunts of acknowledgement as the riders moved away from us in a line scanning the trees. I could see them more clearly then. They wore a mix of armour and leather. Some had steel helmets, others were bareheaded. They carried all sorts of weapons, long swords, bows, spears, and what I learnt later were maces – balls of metal with spikes on them attached to a handle. Up the slope we could still hear the sound of fighting. So basically, we were surrounded.' Just by recounting the story I can feel that cold fear taking hold of my body, the hairs on my arms are standing on end.

'What happened next?' It's strange, but the fact that Claire is listening so intently is very gratifying.

'We stayed where we were. I could feel Danny trembling, and the trickle of hot tears on my chest – but he never made a sound, just clung to me. Then, I guess the rush of adrenalin left us drowsy - we fell asleep and woke up in our beds back here – in this time and place.'

'Wow, that was some dream… hold on, are you saying that you and Danny were in the same dream?'

'That's the thing, it wasn't a dream.'

Claire's eyes narrow as she looks at me. 'What are you talking about, my head's about to explode – I…' she quickly scans the café again before looking back at me as she tries to work out the implications of what I have just said.

'When Danny and I woke up at home we were breathless. Danny asked me, "Were you just with me in the woods running away from those bandits?" I said, "Yes," and went to rub an itch on my head and winced at the pain shooting through my whole body. Then Danny tried to move and felt pain shooting through his body too. He looked at me, I looked back at him – both of us wondering the same thing. I checked my body for any bruises or scratches from the trees and brambles, but there weren't any. I felt like I'd had a full workout – you know, my muscles were aching like just after rugby training. But there were no visible wounds or scratches. Then something occurred to me, "Danny, did you shout 'Stop' in that dream?"

'He nodded, "But all that did was draw the bandits' attention to me - that's when I started to run – I realized they wanted to catch me or maybe kill me, and that I wasn't dream leaning anymore." He then looked at me intently, "Lewis, you won't tell anybody I was scared, will you?"

'I looked at Danny then and realised what a terrifying experience it must have been for him - it was for me; I can't imagine anyone facing that without falling apart, let alone a nine-year-old. So I told him, "You did well." He looked at me unconvinced. "How many people can think straight with a bunch of wild men on horses chasing them? You kept your cool when most people would have stood frozen with fear and then been ridden down by the bandits and probably killed. And that's also key, if you aren't scared of being killed by screaming horsemen with swords and axes, then you're a moron." I remember looking at Danny then and thinking, what have I done? I almost got my little brother killed.'

'Okay, hold on. Let me get this straight. You and Danny weren't in a dream – you both travelled to a different time and place - a Roman village, through a kind of window in space?' I nod. 'But both of you didn't have any visible injuries, because your "hosts" are left with the scratches and bruises?' I nod again. 'But you do have a sort of ache from a kind of muscle memory that travels with you through… through dreamland or whatever it is?'

'Yes, that's it exactly!' I'm relieved that Claire has come to the same conclusion as we did. But then I see the dubious expression on her face. 'You realize why we didn't say anything to you now, right? It sounds crazy – we thought we might be having some sort of family mental breakdown – not something you want to broadcast to your friends. But when we thought about it there were things that would seem to support the idea that…' I don't know how to say this. I peer around to double-check nobody is listening. I lower my voice. My throat is dry and Claire is obviously desperately trying to believe me but struggling. She needs me to say it. 'We've been actually travelling to different times, or maybe even parallel universes – I haven't worked it out yet. And that's where Danny is now.'

Claire is stunned into speechlessness. If her jaw drops any lower, it'll be resting on the table. 'You can't be serious? You can't really believe that?' Her voice is quite loud, so I shush her quickly and see that the waitress is approaching our table.

'I'm serious,' I say quickly before she reaches us. 'It's true.'

'Sorry, Lewis, that's just ridiculous.' Her response makes me livid, why can't she get it? I can feel anger bubbling up inside me – the same rage I had that night when I chased Danny before he went to hospital. I look away not wanting her to see how furious I am with her, then look at her straight in the eye.

'So you are cleverer than Einstein or Stephen Hawking?' I snap at her.

'What are you on about?' she responds equally annoyed.

'They both believed in parallel universes and the possibility of time travel, possibly the two greatest minds in science.'

'Yeah, right,' she responds sarcastically.

'Don't take my word for it, look it up. Then you might not act like such a smart a-'

'Can I get you two anything else?' the waitress asks.

'No, thank you,' I say trying to look relaxed and failing by the look the waitress gives me as she turns on her heel and heads off.

'We're going to be late for school,' Claire says as she collects her stuff and stands up. I'm so angry that she won't believe me, I just grab my bag and follow her out of the cafe. We walk to school briskly not speaking to each other. I take deep breaths, trying to calm myself. Deep down I know I must try and sort my temper out – it's not good for me – or anyone close to me.

* * * * *

Danny has been lying under the wagon for what seems like ages watching the legs of soldiers running back and forth shouting to each other and searching various stalls in the open-air market. Their voices fade as they continue their search elsewhere. His mouth feels like sandpaper – he needs to get a drink of water soon otherwise it feels like he's going to choke.

He tries to work out what just happened. Months ago, he had come to Carthage in his dreams and was enjoying the Arabian-nights' feel of the place when he saw her. The rest of the world seemed to revolve around this girl who looked like a princess from a Disney movie. On the few occasions he's seen her since in the bustling marketplace, he's marvelled at how the merchants, friends, and passers-by are drawn to her – always smiling, enjoying a bit of banter, and then moving on with a spring in their step. On those fortunate times when he sees her, he runs around the marketplace so that he can pretend to be casually walking directly past her. Unfortunately, he usually becomes so self-conscious it affects his walking and so he's convinced he must look like a puppet on a string when he actually waddles past. However, on some of these random-but-not-random walks past he's sure that, when he casts furtive glances at her, he catches her smiling at him.

Today he'd resigned himself to the fact that he might not see his 'dream girl', so Danny decided to just enjoy the bizarre experience: ambling around the marketplace breathing in the aromas of exotic spices, gawking at the locals with their Arab-style clothing, and studying the curious goods on sale.

He'd gotten a little bored and was just thinking about trying to find a place to sleep so his spirit could return to his real body in London when he saw her. As pretty as ever, radiating a carefree contentment walking with her sister, servant, and a couple of bodyguards. Even better, he noticed that her purse, tied to her belt, had slipped its knot and landed silently in the sand at her feet. He'd thought that this was his chance - he darted out, swooped the purse up in his hand, and said, 'Excuse me.' She turned at the sound of the voice and saw Danny looking at her holding her purse in his outstretched hand. She smiled, looking directly into his eyes. Time had seemed to stand still as they recognised kindred spirits - liking what they saw, a strange but pleasant warm feeling passing between them.

But then the moment was shattered by her sister screaming 'Thief' and pointing at him. Instantly, time sped up as Danny instinctively leapt back from the grasping clutches of one of the guards and ducked under the swinging club of the other – he stood up bewildered, and in a moment took in the scene: the wonderful girl was shouting 'Stop!' at the guards, the sister seemed to be concealing a mischievous smirk, and the guards just looked like rabid dogs let off their leashes. The attention of the crowd in the market was drawn by the commotion, eyes staring over and trying to ascertain what was happening. Then shouts of alarm, hands pointing at Danny, and men armed with spears and swords started to make their way through the crowds of shoppers towards him. Without thinking, he scurried under a camel and through some hanging curtains into the next row of market stalls. Frantically looking left and right, he saw a cat dart past him and under a wagon, he followed and ended up dashing from one place to another trying to find the best place to hide.

And now here he is lying in the sand under a wagon still not sure how he's ended up in this mess – he was only trying to help after all. If only he could just wake up in his bed back in London. Danny swallows trying to get some moisture into his mouth. He can feel his lips starting to crack a bit where they've dried out. Behind him, he hears some camels grunting and grumbling near the sandstone water troughs. Danny licks his lips and weighs up the risk, he must have been here for ages, so surely the soldiers will have given up the search by now. He can't stand it any longer and decides to sneak out carefully and gulp down as much water as possible before returning to his hiding place – the camels will hide his presence from searching eyes. Slowly, checking all around, he crawls out backwards and sneaks quietly between two camels at a trough.

The reflection in the trough's water makes Danny pause. No one would recognise him at home. Instead of seeing a fair-haired white boy, he sees a youngster with black hair and brown skin. Only his hazel eyes and the expression on his face seem familiar. He remembers Lewis telling him that when they explored places in their dreams, they occupied another person's body. This explained why nobody took any notice of them and why they could speak the local language. Not immediately though, it seemed to take a moment or two before, as Lewis described it, 'The brain goes through a sort of computer-like update where it needs time to upload new information'. People call him *Habibi* here in Carthage, and leave him alone, usually.

He forms a cup with his hands and scoops up some water, he refills and drinks more, but he has inadvertently spooked the camels who go into a panic causing them to bump, spit, and growl. They scatter as far as they can with their hobbled feet revealing Danny at the trough. A chorus of shouts and movement alerts Danny to the fact that the soldiers are on to him.

He looks around desperately. Danny sees a ragged scaffold against a perimeter wall up ahead – it doesn't look as if it would remain standing in a strong breeze, but he has no choice, it is the only escape route – he can hear the sound of the soldiers shouting to each other getting closer. His Dad's words flash in his mind, 'If you're going to ignore me when I tell you to stop climbing everything in sight, then just make sure you use three points of contact: that means that two feet and an arm, or two arms and a foot are supporting you at all times'. He sprints to the scaffold and starts scaling it like a monkey. He hears the rapid sound of something being spun followed by a hiss as a stone whizzes past his ears and bounces off the scaffold – he glances back and sees two soldiers swirling slings above their heads and firing stones at him. He reaches the top of the scaffold and is just about to step onto the top of the wall and freedom when he feels an explosion of pain in his arm which promptly goes numb and causes him to lose his grip - he feels himself falling…

Dido tries to work out what happened. The scrawny boy with the nice face had finally found an excuse to talk to her - why did her sister scream out that he was a thief? Surely it was obvious he was just returning her purse which had slipped the knot. And just now, she saw the soldiers chasing him again, so he climbed a scaffold but didn't make it to the top. The memory of his body falling from the scaffold through an awning, and then thumping into the ground brings tears to

Dido's eyes and causes her hands to tremble. Is he okay? She utters a quick prayer to the goddess Tanit that the boy isn't badly hurt.

Jezebel looks at her sister Dido, trying to hide her feelings of envy and loathing. Dido is her father's favourite, his 'golden girl'. A completely inappropriate expression as her sister has long raven-coloured hair which falls to her waist. The way that people are drawn to Dido's naturally happy demeanour enrages Jezebel further, her resentment manifesting itself in a smouldering hatred; she has made it her goal in life to spoil anything that might bring Dido happiness. Now Dido looks distraught as the soldiers pick up the unconscious boy's body and take it away – probably to the jail. Unless he's dead – it's hard to tell. If he's dead, he'll be thrown into the midden pits outside the city walls. She smiles to herself – yes, enjoy that sister.

Chapter 3

I look over at Claire as we walk to the hospital to visit Danny. I'm glad that the little spat we had this morning has been forgotten and we are back to normal. We're meeting Mum for our usual daily visit – it's been a few days since Danny wouldn't wake up, but it seems like an eternity. I wonder how he'll be when we get there.

We've arrived early, so we decide to wait for Mum in the concourse. I scan the café and see an empty corner away from anyone, so we grab a juice from the machine and sit at a table where I'll be able to see Mum when she comes through the entrance. Claire scrutinises me.

'Were you serious this morning, you weren't having me on?'

'100% serious,' I answer, disappointed that she still doesn't believe me – the only person I've confided in, and she looks at me like I'm some sort of lunatic. I can feel this morning's tension returning.

'Oh, come on Lewis. What are you talking about, going on about "finding Danny", and your spirit travelling to other times and places? You've got to see that this sounds unbelievably ridiculous. The sooner we live in the real world the sooner we can really help Danny. He's here, in a room at this hospital!'

'Some of the world's greatest minds believe in parallel universes and the possibility of time travel-'

'Yeah, you mentioned that this morning,' Claire says sceptically, looking away.

'If Stephen Hawking and Einstein were sat here telling you that parallel universes probably exist and that time travel is a real possibility, would you be so cynical?'

'Are you sure they even suggested that?' Claire asks, so I type in 'Stephen Hawking's paper on parallel universes' on my phone and give it to her. I can see her scanning various articles.

'He also looks into a theory that Einstein initially developed into time travel and wormholes.' I take the phone back and type in 'Stephen Hawking's theory on time travel' and find an article by Forbes. Claire skims through it - she's surprised by what she is reading.

'I can see where you're coming from Lewis, but it's all theories and speculation,' she says quietly.

A more convincing argument springs to mind, 'How about the Mandela Effect which the world's leading scientists at CERN have been investigating?' For once I seem to know something Claire doesn't. 'They've noticed that some molecules appear and disappear, and they think that maybe, and bear in mind these are the world's most respected scientists, they believe that these particles are disappearing into a parallel universe – things like muons and quarks and dark matter. To be honest, I don't really get it, but the idea supports what I'm suggesting – we're travelling in time or to parallel universes.' I Google CERN and the Mandela Effect and hand my mobile over to Claire again. She takes time to skim through a number of pages and looks as dazed as I have the many times I've tried to get my head around what they are implying.

'Hmm,' Claire seems slightly stunned that my ideas may have some substance. 'But why can only you and Danny do this... this time travelling in your sleep?'

'Perhaps we're not the first to have "travelled" like this.'

'What?'

'Perhaps others have used dream travelling to help themselves with stuff.'

Claire's brow creases, 'Eh?'

'Remember in class the other day we were reading about Leonardo da Vinci and how he was way ahead of his time?' Claire nods. 'Well, suppose he travelled through his dreams to the future and saw helicopters, and so drew the plans for one, but obviously, he didn't really understand what an engine was or how it worked – all he would know is what it looked like.' Claire isn't really convinced, but I think I'm making an impact so continue, 'What about Mary Shelley, you know, the woman who wrote Frankenstein?'

'Yeah, I know who she is,' Claire responds slightly irritated.

'Well, maybe she also went beyond dream leaning and travelled to the future. You know, Frankenstein's monster is brought back to life through the use of electricity – what if Mary Shelley travelled into the future to a hospital where she saw patients being brought to life using electricity, with that thing they use…'

'A defibrillator, you mean?'

'Yeah, that's it. Imagine Mary Shelley saw them using electricity to bring someone back to life and used that idea for her book.' I look at Claire and see she's trying to put all the pieces together.

'You know tribes from all over the world, like some of the Native American Indians, believed their spirits could occupy animals' bodies – so why not a human body, in a different time and place? There are so many things that can't be explained – how did they work out how to do a caesarean section in Roman times? How did the Egyptians, Chinese, the Mayans and Aztecs all get the idea to build pyramids in different parts of the world when there was no means of communication between them? Nobody knows.'

'It's just so…' Claire starts to say something but it pitters out to nothing. I seem to be close, but there's still an element of doubt in Claire's expression.

'Think about all the stories you hear of people saying their friends' personalities have changed. Think about Caligula – you know the mad Roman emperor?' I see Claire nodding, 'He is infamous for being a cruel sadistic dictator, but that was after he woke up following some sort of sleeping sickness,' I nod in the direction of Danny's ward. 'Before that everyone acknowledges that he was a good guy who initiated loads of projects to help your average person. So, he's a good guy one minute, is unconscious for weeks and then wakes up a tyrant. There are probably loads of cases like that, with no explanation, but maybe now we have one. Other dream travellers may have got stuck in the bodies they were borrowing while travelling through their dreams.'

'Lewis, you've got to appreciate how this is quite hard to believe, right?'

'Okay, Claire, explain to me something, how come I can now speak Latin? You know there are loads of accounts of people waking up being able to speak another language fluently.' Claire chews over this for a moment.

'Hold on a minute, you know a few phrases, but you're not fluent in Latin. You've probably picked up a spattering of it from all the films you've seen and the books you've read.' Her response drives me mad.

'What about the fact that I know stuff about the culture, weapons, even the clothes they wear…?'

'Same reason, you and Danny have been reading so much stuff, you've picked up random bits and pieces that you don't even remember reading about.' I pause, take a breath, and try to remain calm.

'Okay, believe what you can see with your own eyes – remember the other day, how Danny's body looked relatively fit? He's been stuck in that bed for days, and yet he seems to be getting more athletic.' Claire frowns as she pictures the scene. When we were alone with Danny in his room on the ward, I pulled back Danny's bed sheet and gestured to Danny's six-pack – I had been trying to buoy her spirits by showing her how healthy he looked. He wasn't like Arnold Schwarzenegger, but you could see he was toned. Claire had been surprised by his physique.

Claire doesn't respond, she's lost in thought, pondering over what I've just suggested. 'A few days ago, if you told me this, I would have called for the men in white coats – now, it's just so…'

I'm relieved – I'm getting somewhere, 'I know it's tough, but please keep an open mind.'

'Hmm, I need a bit of time to process this, I have to be

honest Lewis, it's just so unbelievable. Why can't everyone do it?'

'Well, perhaps it's easier when you are going through a tough time – something happens to the mind. There was an article on the internet – I've spent loads of time trying to work all this out – it referred to a study about dreams which concluded that when you are emotionally stretched, your dreams become more vivid. So maybe there's a correlation between intense emotional circumstances and your ability to first lean your dreams and then travel to different places and times.'

A thought jumps to mind. A few months ago, Claire was talking about a dream she'd had which involved this 'gorgeous hunk'. She puzzled over how a person she'd never known or seen on tv or in real life had appeared in her dream. Had her brain created an image of her perfect man? I thought she might have twigged what Danny and I had been up to and was trying to coax an admission that we'd been travelling, so I feigned a lack of interest. However, it had bugged me, did she know? I also remember feeling pretty narked that her perfect man didn't resemble me in any way.

'Maybe you have travelled, but don't realize it, or remember it.' Claire looks at me dubiously again. 'Remember you asking me how a face you've never seen in your life can appear in your dream?' She looks at me with narrow eyes under knitted brows. 'Perhaps you have met these people, just some other time..., some other place..., as someone else.' Claire stares off into the distance. Another thought strikes me.

'Remember that time on the field trip up north you said you felt a bit weird as the place we went to felt familiar, even though you'd never been there before?' Now she really does look lost in thought.

'Something which doesn't gel - you've talked about how all those famous people have maybe travelled to the future to get ideas to use back in their time, but you and Danny have been going the other way – you've been going to the past, not the future.'

'Yeah, I know, I haven't worked that one out yet. Maybe

that comes with time – remember, we're still amateurs at this. Perhaps I can't recognise futuristic scenes through the windows in the gateway – I don't know.'

Claire is trying to digest everything we've been talking about. She's quiet for a while, breathes out heavily, leans back and looks at me. Then out of nowhere, she smiles, 'You can't really speak Latin, can you?'

'Not that well, just the basics, you know, ordering a pizza, asking for directions to the train station, a few pick-up lines, stuff like that.' Claire laughs – we're friends again - making Claire laugh always cheers me up. My mum appears in the hospital concourse and waves as she approaches. She sees us smiling and that seems to cheer her up, too.

'What are you two smiling about?' I'm about to tell my mum and then realize I can't without referring to dream travelling – I'm stumped.

'Lewis was just telling me a stupid joke - a man goes to see his doctor and says, "Doctor, I think I'm a bit hard of hearing". The doctor asks, "Can you describe the symptoms?" The man says, "Sure. Homer is fat and bald, Marge has blue hair, Bart has spikey hair..."'

My mum laughs. Wow, Claire can think fast on her feet, that's for sure.

We wander through a labyrinth of corridors and stairs, get to the ward and head to Danny's room. The doctor appears from nowhere and says, 'Hi,' but he seems tense. Actually, if he wasn't wearing a white lab coat and a stethoscope, you'd think he was a patient – so gaunt with brown hair that has just started to thin. My mum picks up on his demeanour.

'Is everything okay, Doctor Jeffries?'

'I'm afraid Danny had another one of his episodes, um, his vitals rose rapidly then suddenly dropped below normal levels.' He sees the distress on all our faces, 'But he's stable again.' My mum holds her hand to her mouth. 'Come with me, you'll see he's looking okay.' We follow, but Claire stops.

'I think I'll wait here for you,' she gestures at a sort of waiting area on the ward, 'and give you some time alone with Danny.' My mum and I can't think straight, so we just nod and follow the doctor into Danny's room.

Danny is lying there fast asleep looking peaceful which does ease our worries a little. The nurse is pottering around sorting stuff out, the doctor coughs gently, 'As you can see, he seems fine,' he gestures at the monitors whose rhythmic beeping seems okay, just a little slower. 'We'll give you some time alone with your son,' the doctor says.

'Thanks, Doctor Jeffries. Thanks, Amelie,' my mum says to the nurse.

I hadn't realised Mum knew the nurse, but of course, she probably knows most of the people here – she is a nurse here after all.

'Let me know if there's anything you need, Rachel,' the nurse says to my mum with a slight French accent. She smiles at us both and then follows the doctor out of the room.

Mum pulls up a chair and I sit on the side of the bed. After a few moments just gazing at Danny, my mum takes out one of Danny's favourite books from her handbag – a Roald Dahl story - and starts reading about potions, dreams, and giants. The subject matter unnerves me a little at first, but my mum's soothing voice soon settles me.

The time drifts by and before long it's time for us to leave my brother. Mum kisses his forehead and tucks him in as I look on, and that feeling of hopelessness returns. How am I going to sort this out? I follow my mum out of the room in a trance. Claire stands up abruptly as we walk down the ward, 'Is everything okay?'

'Yes, sorry to keep you waiting.' My mum responds. 'Well, I better get ready for my shift – there's dinner in the fridge, just warm it up in the microwave. Make sure you go to bed early – no late-night films – you need your rest.' My mum looks at me as I nod assent and then kisses both Claire and me on the cheek before heading off to the other side of the hospital where she'll look after other patients – it must be weird working here with a son on a ward a stone's throw away. Once she disappears around the corner, I look at Claire who is looking at me with a very worried expression on her face. She pulls the cuff of my jumper directing me to two chairs nearby.

'What's up?'

'Lewis, I've been doing a bit of research – I've found out a few things...'

'Okay, what?'

'Firstly, you've been calling it dream leaning, but others refer to it as lucid dreaming. This Australian university in Adelaide has been doing research into lucid dreams – they reckon around 70% of people are aware of being in a dream and a few, like you, can control their dreams. But they say you have to be careful, those who have any mental issues might lose the ability to differentiate between dreams and reality. Also…' Claire looks in the direction of Danny's room.

'Go on.'

'Well, according to this doctor's research, you could in theory get "stuck" in your dream. That could be what's happened to Danny,' Claire chews her lower lip. 'But I think you are right, he's "stuck", but in a different time and place,' she shakes her head at the fact she's even expressed such a thought.

'That's great, I mean, I'm so happy you believe me, but what convinced you?' Claire looks uneasy, 'Is there something else?' She looks around, as if scanning for danger, then leans in and whispers hurriedly.

'I found out that various governments have been sort of looking into what you and Danny can do – travelling in time; so they obviously think along the same lines as you and the boffins at CERN. I stopped looking just in case these secret government agencies monitor this type of internet search – perhaps they are trying to find people like you and Danny who have these dream travelling skills.' My relief that Claire believes me, turns to a sense of foreboding. 'This could be really dangerous, Lewis, don't you see?' I shake my head faintly. 'If you are right, do you realize what people, companies, governments, or criminal organisations would do to have the ability to jump ahead and take a peek at what the future holds?' Claire looks around again, she actually looks scared which gets me looking around as well, but I don't know what I'm looking for and face her again.

'What do you mean?'

'You have to keep your dream travelling ability secret – if you don't, you, Danny, and your mum could be in great danger,' I sort of laugh uncomfortably, but stop when I see how earnest Claire is. I lean back in the chair and try to digest what she has just said. Without realizing it, I'm looking up and down the ward trying to identify someone who could be a threat to us. This kind of danger hadn't occurred to me. Claire, who has only just heard of this phenomenon, manages to look at the situation in ways I can't. I'm so out of my depth.

* * * * *

The agent takes a deep breath preparing for the call. Any contact with 'the Boss' was always stressful – if you messed up, there was no mercy, the stories people whispered or alluded to would leave anyone jittery. Breathe in, breathe out, again, slowly. The hand pulls out the encrypted mobile and dials. The phone is answered before the second ring.

'Report' comes the gruff order from the other end of the phone line, no pleasantries.

'Sir, there's a potential candidate at the hospital,' the agent manages to sound calm.

'Describe the candidate,' the voice demands.

'Boy, nine-years old, slim, unconscious, random evidence of activity in his dream state – rapid pulse, high blood pressure, perspiration. Despite having been asleep for a few days, there seems to be no muscle atrophy, in fact, he's looking more toned.'

'Hmm, fits the previous signs of a traveller. Any family?'

'Yes, unfortunately. A mother and a brother. There's a father, but he went missing in Africa on some sort of humanitarian mission for an NGO. They don't know if he's alive or dead.'

'Damn! Ok. We can't remove the boy yet. Keep observing and confirm that he is indeed a traveller.'

'Yes, I-' the ring tone indicates the phone call has ended. A deep breath and a sigh of relief. But that sense of guilt niggles in the back of the agent's mind. The mother and brother seem nice - it's a shame that they might have to be disposed of.

Returning to the ward the agent wonders how many other medical staff at hospitals all over the world have been tempted to defy the Hippocratic oath or its equivalent for money and serve the Syndicate. How many other 'travellers' have been found?

* * * * *

The Boss puts the phone down and looks out at the picture-postcard Alpine view from his study which is at odds with the activity going on in the mansion's forecourt. Movement down there catches his eye; he watches dispassionately as a small body bag is carried out to a car by two men in blue uniform-style overalls. Another traveller dead, the Syndicate will not be happy, but they still have another boy locked up in the lab below and by the sounds of it another possibility in London - that should keep the other members of the board at bay.

He watches as they unceremoniously dump the small body in the boot of the car. They'll have to be more careful next time. He glances at the newspaper article on his desk and winces at their oversight.

Family of Four Killed in Tragic Car Accident

A whole family died in a car accident on a hairpin bend in the French Alps last Saturday. The Dupont family had been on their way to a skiing holiday when their car left the road high up in one of the Alpine passes and tumbled down the mountainside before exploding near the bottom of the valley. Compounding the tragedy, Brigitte, the Dupont's nine-year-old daughter who had previously been reported as missing was among the dead. The police say they are not treating the case as suspicious. Locals have persistently demanded that the local government do something about this treacherous strip of road which has claimed numerous lives.

Source: International Press

The girl had realized that they had already killed her family. That was Brigitte in the body bag – they'd found another girl to put in the car with her parents and sister before sending it plummeting down the valley. Brigitte had been sent to the future to find out some specific information, but she must have looked up her family and found a newspaper report like this one on his desk. Even a young girl like that could work out what had happened – and it wasn't what they had promised her: that she would be reunited with her family once she completed a few missions for the Syndicate and that they would all live in luxury for the rest of their lives.

Brigitte had taken them by surprise. The Boss catches a final view of the body bag before the car boot is closed. She must have been travelling to other destinations and times picking up martial arts skills and other knowledge which she used to carry out her revenge on them when she 'returned': a lab blown to bits and 12 dead – some in the explosion, but some by the girl's own hands before they had riddled her little body with bullets. No, they'll have to be more careful next time. The family will have to go missing rather than die in some sort of accident which will make the news. A traveller must not be able to find out that the Syndicate have murdered their family.

His thoughts wander – it's strange how there's a general consensus that if you travel back in time, you mustn't change events as that would have potentially catastrophic repercussions. Why don't people think more about going to the future to gain valuable information to help steer the present time in a direction that leads to prosperity and influence? Imagine the wealth and power you could gain from knowing what will happen: from the riches you could easily accrue from knowing which lotto numbers would come up, which commodities would become valuable, and the influence you could gain by backing someone whom you knew was going to win a presidential election. The Syndicate would achieve their goals much more quickly with this knowledge.

And who would have thought that riches beyond anyone's imagination and the potential for almost complete world domination could rest on using a little boy or girl who has a particular talent which emerged when they fell asleep?

The Boss looks at the clock, almost midday, time for the board meeting with the other 'Bosses'. Some are faring well in their respective countries, or should he say companies; countries don't actually exist as most people envisage them – nations which run the world – no, companies rule most of the world these days. But they are still based in countries which give that particular nation an impression of power and influence. Okay, some powerful countries or ones with more sophisticated societies fend off the Syndicate's attempts to gain control within their borders, but that would hopefully change when they manage to use the 'travellers' effectively. The 'Bosses' managing those countries are particularly keen on the project. They know that these children might be the key to their survival within the organisation. Nobody is allowed to leave the Syndicate. If you're expelled, it's a death sentence. You are given the choice of committing suicide or dying in an 'accident'.

He is relishing the moment – he was the one who had learnt of these 'travellers'. They could be the answer to their prayers. The Boss pauses as he reflects on that thought, 'answer to their prayers'. If he is successful, they will be Gods in all but name. He is going to save the day and restore the Syndicate to a power which once again rules the world from the shadows.

'The Syndicate' – he shakes his head as he presses a button on his antique desk. There's a faint humming sound as the oak panelling on the far wall draws apart revealing a huge video conferencing screen. The screen is divided into a grid of twelve squares, eleven of which are occupied by men not too dissimilar to himself – more white-haired than grey, but he is pleased to see that he still cuts an elegant figure in his country tweeds. Had they really needed to rebrand – or 'nonbrand' the original centuries-old name of their organisation? He grudgingly acknowledges that it had made sense – don't give an organisation a unique name which is easy to single out and therefore find in seconds on the internet. No, think of a common name which brings up millions of results. Even the most tenacious investigative journalist will struggle to home in on their activities with that much information to sift through.

* * * * *

Danny wakes up in pitch blackness and automatically lurches towards the lamp switch on his right. His hand sweeps through air, but he recoils when his fingertips touch a body wearing coarse fabric. He's not in his bedroom. His touch triggers a slight groan from the person he's woken. Danny screws his eyes tightly shut as his body trembles uncontrollably; he starts breathing rapidly as the panic inside him almost makes him cry out. His little body feels battered and bruised and his mouth and the back of his throat are dry. Where is he? Who is that next to him?

He becomes aware of other sounds coming from the darkness – from all around him, some near, some far - heavy breathing, rasping breaths, a slight wail, weeping - noises everywhere. A shiver runs through him. He bolts up into a sitting position, wraps his arms around his knees, and starts rocking back and forth. He seems to be tangled in a rough fabric. He feels icy cold and his body aches from lying on the hard ground. There is a thin layer of grit or sand on the stone floor which makes it even more uncomfortable. He realizes his eyes are still screwed tightly shut. He dares not move in case he touches another person in the impenetrable blackness – who are they? He wants to scream out for Lewis or his mum.

'Calm down, boy. You're in a holding cell with the rest of the unfortunates.' Danny says nothing – is the person speaking to him?

'Do you understand me?' the man's voice continues. It sounds like an older man's voice. In spite of his fear, he grasps that it doesn't sound particularly threatening, actually, there seems to be a hint of concern in the tone. He feels a hand touch his shoulder, his body jerks back and he hears a little whimper, which he realises came from him. He is too scared to care. His body starts shaking violently.

'Boy, you are safe for the moment, when the guards threw you in here yesterday you were unconscious, so I lay you down here in a corner of the cell and put my cloak around you to keep you warm and try and make the floor a little more comfortable. Try and get some sleep.' You'll need it, the man thinks to himself - we're all going to be sold in the slave market in the morning. Poor kid.

Chapter 4

As I wander to school on another bright morning, I try to figure out why Danny hasn't been able to return to the here and now. This is the first time it's happened, so it's not something I've ever had to think about before. It could be that the host that Danny is using is more powerful than usual and so Danny isn't in control. Or maybe, as Claire mentioned yesterday at the hospital, the university research speculated that a person might lose the ability to differentiate between a dream and reality. So does Danny think that wherever he has ended up is his real home?

I stop in my tracks as another thought occurs to me. Two schoolboys from the year below walk into me and glare at me until they see my expression - they look at the floor and walk briskly off to school. Perhaps those windows, gateways or wormholes, whatever you want to call them, have closed. I've noticed that new destinations appear at the gateway and others disappear – perhaps Danny can't get back because the wormhole home has vanished.

My head is spinning as I walk through the school gates. First things first, look at Danny's diary and find out which window I need to enter in the dream gateway; if it's still there.

I see Claire waiting in the corridor outside our classroom. I walk up next to her and ditch my bag on the floor and turn to her, with my back to Emma, one of the most beautiful girls in the school, but also one of the slyest. Emma and her twin brother Mike seem to have made it their goal in life to make everyone's lives a misery.

'Hey,' I say to Claire who nods hello, 'have you brought

the diary?' She nods again, opening her bag a little to show me Danny's Spider-Man notebook. 'Great.'

'How's this going to help?' Claire asks.

'Danny probably told me about where he's been going to, but to be honest he would go on so much that I would zone out sometimes.' I look at Claire to see if she's judging me – she thinks about it and gives me a look of understanding.

'We both keep a diary of where we go to, so Danny will have written it down in there,' I look pointedly at the book. 'Once we find out where he is, I'll be able to follow him through the same window and bring him back,' this causes Claire's brow to furrow briefly before she nods again. We look again at the Spider-Man notebook which Claire has now pulled out of her bag slightly – it's odd to think that such a childish-looking object could be the solution to our problems.

'Sorry to hear about your brother, Lewis,' I hear a voice and see Claire's eyes narrow as she looks at someone behind me – I turn to see Emma staring right at me with her piercing blue eyes. My heart misses a beat, wow, she's gorgeous, just stood there twirling tresses of her long blond hair in her fingers.

'Oh, um, thanks,' is all I can say.

'He's in a coma, right?' I nod. 'It's such a shame that they can't wake him. It must be terrible for you,' Emma's words bring a picture of Danny in the hospital bed to mind - I don't know how to react. 'You must feel helpless…, oh,' she then reaches out and gives my arm a squeeze, 'take care.' She looks at me, then at Claire, and then she seems to glance down at our bags before turning away and walking towards her brother Mike who is approaching. No wonder people call them the 'Hitler Youth' behind their backs – blond, blue eyed, good-looking. Their only imperfection is their thin sly looking mouths and of course their personalities. Still, I can't help breathing out deeply as I look at Emma – she is stunning.

I turn around to see Claire giving me a look, 'What?'

'Girls use words like you boys use your fists.' Claire looks exasperated at my lack of response. 'Okay, Lewis, how did you feel when Emma asked you about Danny?'

I pause for a minute; how did I feel? I remember my

heart sinking, 'Not great.'
'Bingo!'
'What?'
'Emma knew that asking you about Danny would bring you down. All she was doing was bullying you, she used fake concern to batter you.' I'm not sure I agree with her. 'Remember what I told you before?' I'm not sure which of the many lectures she's given me she's referring to so shake my head. 'If someone starts a sentence with something like, "Shame that you can't..." or is always drawing negative comparisons between you and someone who is doing really well, or in this case always reminding you of the dreadful situation you are in, they are not your friend.' Claire has to pause for breath, 'They are playing with your mind, enjoying making you miserable, bringing you down.'

I suddenly feel so desperately tired, 'Life sucks,' I mutter.

'Hey,' now Claire reaches over and squeezes my arm – this time I know the gesture is genuine. 'Yup, it does sometimes, but we'll get through this, and we've got the diary to help us,' she says brightly. 'Lewis, I don't mean to sound like a know-it-all, but I just don't want to see people hurt you.' She seems to see the despair that I feel and gives my arm another squeeze. 'Sorry. Look, nobody is perfect, even me.' Claire looks at me cross-eyed and with a funny face, I laugh and feel my spirits lift. Mr Morgan turns up with the register, so we all make our way into class, dump bags on desks and get ready for the morning lessons – double physics and then PE - I feel tired again.

* * * * *

Emma walks towards her brother with a smirk on her face, 'What are you so happy about?' Mike asks.

'Oh, just had a quick chat with your favourite person – not!' Mike glares at Lewis. 'Don't worry, he's not feeling great, and I think he'll be feeling even worse later.'

'What are you up to?' Mike asks, grinning.

'Hmm, just a bit of fun and games,' Emma smiles back.

They turn around and follow the rest of the students into class.

*****

I'm sat at a table on my own in the school cafeteria. I sense someone coming towards me and look up to see Claire rushing in my direction. My smile fades as I see her expression – I've never seen her look so fraught.

'It's gone, someone's nicked it from my bag,' she blurts out when she reaches my table.

'What are you on about, what's gone?'

'The diary, it's gone. I definitely had it in physics, so someone must have stolen it when we were in PE, from the changing rooms,' Claire looks around the cafeteria frantically, she looks like she could be sick. I suddenly feel nauseous too as her words sink in. It feels like someone has just punched me really hard in the stomach.

'Are you sure it's gone? Check your bag again.'

'I've checked it a million times, it's gone!' There are tears brimming in her eyes now as she looks down at me. She sits down heavily. 'Lewis, I'm so sorry.'

I've got to stop the stinging in my eyes turning into tears as the implications really hit home – we've lost the only lead to Danny's whereabouts. The world seems to be collapsing all around me. The silence stretches out as I try and pull myself together – I've got to be strong for Danny's sake. After a while I say, 'Look, Claire, it's not your fault – we'll manage without the diary – come to my place after school and we'll find clues in Danny's stuff – something might jog my memory.' Claire doesn't look convinced - even I'm finding it hard to believe my own words. We just sit there, the world going on around us, but we don't seem to be part of it. Just as the lunch break is about to end, we look at each other.

'Ok, I'll come to yours after school.' Claire says. 'Are you coming to class?'

'No, I have to go to the hospital,' I say, not looking at Claire as it's a lie.

I can't face school or anybody at the moment. Claire grabs her bag and heads off to class giving me a wave as she leaves the cafeteria. I wave back, collect my things and head off to the park near the hospital. The park is quiet, thankfully. I sit on the trunk of a fallen tree looking out at nothing. What next?

I head home after visiting my brother at the hospital. While I was at the park, I suddenly had a feeling that Danny might have woken up and all our problems would be over, but there's no change, he's still asleep.

I'm paranoid after what Claire said yesterday; I'm checking to see if anyone is following me, walking home in a zigzag direction trying to lose a tail if there is one. At the hospital, I scrutinised all the staff to see if they looked dodgy. Doctor Jeffries and Amelie the nurse seem genuinely concerned for my brother, so, if there is an undercover agent working for a crooked organisation or government agency, surely it can't be them. However, there are a couple of consultants who have arrived on the scene, and every time I see them discussing something, I can't help but get the impression that they are up to no good.

When they came into Danny's room this afternoon and started asking my mum questions, I couldn't think straight and was silently screaming inside at my mum not to say anything that might arouse their suspicions that Danny is a traveller. She didn't, I don't think, and they left when Doctor Jeffries and Amelie came into the room. If I'm not mistaken, there was some tension there.

Mum is on night shift again, so she told me to get a Thai takeaway for Claire and me. She thinks we're gonna do some homework together. I feel my energy drain out of me at the thought of the impossible task ahead. I turn the corner onto my street and see Claire waiting outside my house.

'Hey', I say, 'How was school?'

'It was fine, but I couldn't really concentrate. I don't know what to say, Lewis – I'm so sorry.' She looks tired – she'll have been beating herself up about it all afternoon.

'It's not your fault, things are always going missing from the gym's changing rooms.' Claire still looks depressed. 'Look, Claire, there's nothing you could have done – it's not like you could have carried the book with you onto the netball court, is it?'

'I suppose not.'

I lift up the takeaway bag, 'Mum's got us dinner – Thai green chicken curry, pad Thai, fish cakes, and your favourite soup, tom yum kung!' Claire's face brightens a little. I get my keys out, unlock the door, take a quick look up and down the street to check again that no one has followed me and then we enter the house. I half expect the house to be trashed like a scene from the movies, but everything is fine, no black-clad agents with guns and torches in their mouths searching the house. We head straight to the kitchen and have a feast which seems to give us a boost.

Claire and I have been talking about random stuff throughout the dinner – I think we've deliberately tried to put off the daunting task by taking our time. But now we head upstairs to the bedroom Danny and I share. I open the door and gesture for Claire to come in and then we stop near the doorway looking around. On one side you have Danny's bed; Mum has made it up so that the Spider-Man quilt is neatly turned over in the top corner revealing his folded pyjamas just below the pillows. The sight causes my eyes to sting again and so I quickly move to my bed where I ditch my school bag and sit down, sinking into the soft mattress. Claire joins me. We both look around at the posters on the walls and then at the bookshelves.

'Where do we start?' she asks.

'I don't know,' I shrug. We look around the room at the Superhero posters on Danny's side and then at some of mine – a Bruce Lee film poster where he's looking on, ready to strike in his kung fu pose, a poster of Shakira, which makes me feel a little embarrassed when I see Claire studying it, and a map of the world. I look at Claire sitting on my bed looking at Shakira who looks down on us seductively and suddenly feel a bit awkward. My cheeks start to burn, they feel like they must be bright red, I quickly glance at Claire's profile as she studies the posters hoping she won't look at me in this state. I look away and study the posters to take my mind off Shakira and Claire.

'Lewis!' She almost shouts out – a weird tone in her

voice.

'What?' I say defensively – I haven't done anything! My mind's all over the place, different thoughts are whirling around in my head.

'It's right there,' I look at Claire who is looking between my Bruce Lee poster and the world map. I'm lost for a moment before I realize she's talking about a clue to help find my brother. 'You and Danny are into your kung fu films, right?'

I try to compose myself, gather my thoughts, and focus on what she's saying, 'Yeah.'

'Well, where does Kung Fu come from?'

I look from Claire to the poster on the wall, 'China.'

'Danny lies in bed every night looking in your direction as he natters away and what does he see all the time?'

I look at Bruce Lee, stand up, and walk to the poster. My finger touches the country that Claire's been talking about – China. It seems obvious when we think about it, Danny loves play fighting kung fu style, and probably dreams of being a kung fu master, so logically, he would have been drawn there.

'Does China ring a bell – did Danny ever talk about it?'

I shake my head, 'No, not that I can remember.' I look at Claire who looks deflated – mirroring my feelings. Then something dawns on her.

'How about Cathay, it's an old word for China?'

That definitely rings a bell, 'Yeah, actually, I think he mentioned Cathay a few times, that's it – Cathay!'

'So what happens now?'

'Tonight, when I go to sleep, I'll make my way to the gateway and find the window that takes me to China.' I can see Claire chewing over what I've just said.

'Remind me how you get to the gateway again?'

'Usually in my dream, I look for a portal, it's normally a door. Once I'm there, as I said before, it's like I'm standing in an open-air gallery in a desert at night. Everywhere I look I can see paintings or windows framed by luminous swirling vapour, but there are no walls – the paintings hover in the starlit sky. Then I examine the different windows, without getting too close or I might get sucked into the wrong place. When I see the destination I want to go to, I head towards it and that's when I go through that nauseating rollercoaster ride.'

'What do you see in these paintings, or windows, whatever you call them?'

'It varies, sometimes it's a close-up of people at home, or walking down a street, anywhere really, other times I'm like a bird looking down on a city or the countryside. To be honest, it's not always easy to work out where the place is, you need to look for clues by studying the people, their clothes, the architecture, or the scenery.'

Claire sighs, 'Wow, that sounds like it could be a bit tricky.' I can't add anything, it will be challenging, I just hope I'm up to it. 'Another thing, when you get to China, how are you going to recognise Danny, he's going to be Chinese, right?'

'I've been thinking - actually worrying about that. I'm hoping that I'll be able to recognise his mannerisms or the look in his eyes – like I recognised him in that situation in the Roman village...' Claire is looking at me dubiously, 'I know, it's not the best plan.' The thought of going to the most populous country in the world, and then going up to people and looking at them to see if they might be Danny sounds impossible and just ludicrous.

'We have to think of a way for you to identify each other when you are in a host – just in case this happens again,' Claire says. She's right. But at the moment I'm just feeling overwhelmed by the job at hand.

* * * * *

Danny wakes up after dozing, opens his eyes, and quails at the darkness which instantly brings to mind his dire situation. He lets out an involuntary groan.

'How are you feeling?'

Danny thinks quickly, should he answer the man? He is wrapped in something which reminds him that the man has tried to help him by giving him his coat, plus there is something gentle in the deep voice – not threatening. 'I'm okay..., thanks.' Danny manages to respond.

'What's your name?' Danny tries to look through the blackness to his left to see the person speaking, but it's hopeless – he may as well be in a cave - it's so dark.

'Danny,' it barely comes out more than a whisper.

'That's an unusual name, where are you from?'

Danny pauses for a moment to try and think of what to say, 'I'm travelling.'

'Where's your family? Where's your father?'

'My father's gone. My mother's at work. Who are you?'

'My name's Barca,' the man replies, looking in the direction of yet another poor soul whose life has been turned upside down. When he first saw the boy being thrown into the cell, he thought it looked like his son, Hamilcar. He went over to check, but instantly realized it wasn't when he rolled him over. But then he felt a sense of responsibility for the small limp body lying there. Nobody took any notice of him as he picked the boy up and returned to the corner of the holding cell. Actually, they were probably fully aware of what was happening but didn't dare question him as he's a big man with the look of someone who can handle himself in a fight. As far as they were concerned, he could do what he liked to the street urchin the guards had just thrown in. So Barca lay the child gently onto his cloak and wrapped it around him to keep him warm. The days in Carthage can be blisteringly hot, but the nights can be cold, sometimes very cold.

Looking in the direction of the boy now, he feels a deep sadness. Another life thrown into the meatgrinder that is slavery. Questions spring to mind: what happened to Danny's father? What work does his mother do that leaves her son wandering the streets at the mercy of predators in all their different forms? How long will it take her to realize that he's gone, probably forever? 'Tanit, please look down kindly on this boy, Danny.'

'Sorry, what did you say?'

'I was just praying to Tanit, hoping that the goddess of fortune will look after you.'

Danny doesn't know what to say. He's never heard of Tanit, but he knows that he needs all the help he can get. 'Thank you. I'll pray to her and ask her to look after you as well.'

Danny dares to look around. There's a little grey area high up in the wall. He guesses it's a window and that dawn must be coming as black has turned to a dark grey. Looking around he can make out the silhouettes of bodies in different states of slumber strewn across the stone floor. There seems to be a slight increase in noise as more of them stir, try to find a comfortable position, and fall back asleep to escape the reality of their surroundings. Danny looks towards Barca's silhouette, he isn't sure, but it looks like he is staring in his direction. He becomes aware of the tangled clothing around his body. 'Thank you for your robe,' and starts to unravel himself from it.

'Keep it for the moment, and try and get some rest, we have a long day ahead of us.'

Danny thinks for a moment, what does Barca mean by that? 'What will happen to us?'

Barca doesn't know what to say. He can almost feel a pair of big, innocent scared eyes looking up towards him. He doesn't have the heart to tell him what awaits him: a whole life of slavery. If he's very lucky, he'll be taken into a nice household where his owners won't beat or abuse him too much. But most boys Danny's age who look fairly healthy end up working in the mines, or on a farm tilling the ground from dawn till dusk or become a ship's slave. In those brutal conditions, he'll be lucky to survive a year. It all came down to Tanit, the goddess of fortune. In a blink of an eye, she can change from a caring mother figure to a heartless crone, seemingly oblivious to people's suffering. Maybe Danny will be bought by a nice family. They'll find out in a few hours when they'll be herded to the slave market. Barca feels his heart breaking. Who is he kidding, he thinks to himself, Tanit has already abandoned Danny. The boy won't last a year.

* * * * *

I wake up and it takes me a moment to try and work out where I am. The warm sun heats my body where I lie in a meadow of tall grasses and colourful wildflowers. When I look at my arms, I see that I have jet black hair and my skin is a lovely colour, like the English breakfast tea my mum drinks after she's added milk. I'm Chinese - I can't see my facial features yet, but I'm relieved to know that I seem to be in the right place. I rise into a sitting position which causes a kaleidoscope of butterflies to dance away from the blossoms surrounding me. I take a moment to take in the scene and become aware of another sound other than the sound of dragonflies bobbing around and the chirping of the invisible cicadas. It's the sound of a sitar or some other exotic stringed instrument. The sound seems to be coming from the trees in front of me. Cautiously, I get to my feet, constantly alert for danger, but I can't help being drawn to the soothing almost dreamlike music – am I in China, or is this a dream? I reach the tree line and continue through the forest. The sound the instrument makes sounds familiar, like something from a film set in ancient China. Somewhere to my left, I can hear water flowing in a nearby stream or river. I reach another glade in the woodland, stop, and quietly take cover behind a tree.

In the middle of the meadow, a white-haired man with a long beard and moustache plucks at a stringed instrument resting on his lap, creating enchanting sounds which seem at one with the surrounding scene. Sat next to him is a girl about my age who is practising her calligraphy with wonderful smooth swirling movements. I feel a sense of optimism as I realise from the clothes they are wearing I really am in China. The sight warms my heart - I don't want the moment to end – I feel a calmness envelop me.

A noise from my right breaks the spell. I hold my breath as I make sure I'm hidden behind the trunk of the tree. Moving slowly, I peer to my right where the noise came from and recoil. There's a ragtag band of soldiers, no, they must be bandits judging by their scruffy appearance, stalking their prey: the girl and the old man. Without thinking I shout a warning. In the blink of an eye, the forest erupts: startled birds explode from the trees while a deer springs into the far treeline, its white tail bobbing out of sight in an instant. The old man is on his feet having taken in the danger. He grabs the girl's hand and flees in the opposite direction leaving all their stuff behind. Meanwhile, the angry bandits are looking in my direction trying to see where the warning came from.

I don't have time to think – I dash from my hiding place and instantly hear the crunching sound of men running through the forest floor – the bandits are after me. Fear gives me speed and I tear through the forest leaping over fallen tree trunks and small brooks, ducking and weaving past branches in my way and when I listen, the sound of pursuit sounds far behind me. I'm breathing hard, I risk a quick look behind me and am immediately flying through the air after my foot trips on a tree root or something. I land heavily and make a racket tumbling in the forest's undergrowth. I'm winded, I strain to get air into my lungs past the pain in my midriff. I can hear the bandits racing towards me, I stagger to my feet, still struggling to breathe and feel dizzy, I think I've knocked my head as I can feel a dampness on my forehead and something trickling down, I touch the area on my head and my fingertips come away red. The noise is getting closer, I lurch away from it – then through the spinning world around me, I see dark figures appear – they slow down, and I think I can see vicious smiles, but everything is distorted by the knock I've had – the whole world is swimming before my eyes.

I stumble backwards away from them and the sound of cruel laughter. The nausea almost makes me sick; I trip over again and quickly, awkwardly get back to my feet. Now I see them, smiling, waving their vicious knives, cleavers, and hatchets at me – taunting me, relishing the fear they can see in my eyes. A look of alarm on their faces makes me turn around to see that I'm on the lip of a cliff edge with nothing but the torrent of a river cascading over a rocky riverbed below me. I lose my balance – wave my arms frantically, but it is too late – I'm falling, arms and legs flailing through the air.

Chapter 5

I meet Claire before school at the café. Again, she's there before me with two chocolate milkshakes on the table in the same quiet corner. I bring her up to speed on my experience the night before. She sits there completely absorbed in the story, most of the time with a look of shock on her face.

'So the last thing you remember about the dream is you falling?' she asks, and I just nod. 'But doesn't that mean your host might have died in the fall?'

'No, if he had died, I wouldn't be here now - I would have died as well, I think.' I'll probably find out tonight – I wonder if he's okay and whether I will end up in his body again.

'Tell me something, how does time work when you travel in your dreams? Is it the same as when you travel abroad where you just change the hour or date, but time passes at the same speed?'

'No, sometimes it does, but other times one night here can be the equivalent of a week or two, maybe more, on the other side. I don't know why.'

Again, Claire chews that over for a bit as she sits back in her chair. 'Lewis, when all this is over you and Danny need to choose safer times and places to travel to,' I nod. I look away as I have a flashback of the conversation I had with my brother which quickly turned into an argument. The same thought had occurred to me and scared me to a point where I told Danny that he couldn't travel anymore because it was too dangerous. He wouldn't listen. I think of the rage I went into and the sight of my brother running away from me and locking himself in the toilet, and feel ashamed. Clare brings me back to the present. 'You'll both have to brush up on your history and geography, so you have a better idea of what you are looking at when you peer through those windows in the gateway.'

'When this is all over, I'm not going to allow Danny to travel anymore – it's just too risky - I can't go through this again.'

Claire looks at me for a bit and then starts shaking her head slightly, 'There's no way you'll be able to stop him travelling, you have to be realistic about this.' Claire and I are quiet for a while, just taking the odd slurp of the milkshakes.

'I can't get my head around the potential this ability brings you.'

'Yeah, it's crazy, right?'

'If I had your skills, I would study under the greatest minds in history, learn from the best – physics under Einstein, philosophy under Plato, or just live in a place and learn the language.'

'Yeah, but you might not have to study under them – you could be them.'

'What?'

'You don't have to be their student; you might end up in these amazing people's bodies – they'd be your host. I think, but can't be certain, that if you reside in a person's body, you pick up all their skills.'

Claire's eyes open wide in wonder, 'I hadn't thought of that.'

'Yeah, it's really mad, eh? We've talked about it before; Danny wanted Jimmy Hendrix as a host so he could get his guitar skills, and I'd be happy with any of the all-time rugby greats – or football legends.

'Then there are all the other possibilities - we were pretty keen on the idea of finding lost treasure – you could go back in time and see exactly where people hid their chests of gold and jewels.' I look at Claire to see if she's as excited by this idea as we were – she's not.

'Yeah, lost treasure, lotto numbers, horse racing, boxing matches…' Claire shakes her head, leans in, and whispers, 'That's why we have to be careful – people would kill for that kind of information.' I feel that chill run through my body again. The café is empty except for the waitress, we should be safe here. But paranoia leads me to start studying the woman in her apron when Claire interrupts, 'Hey, we best go, or we'll be late for school.'

* * * * *

Later that same day the twins are walking down the street towards their favourite café. In front of them, a little old lady fumbles with her bags trying to balance out her groceries, a handbag full to bursting point, and an umbrella. In the process, she drops her purse without realizing it and continues to walk slowly ahead. Mike swoops down and picks up the purse, turns to Emma, 'Shall we?' Emma smiles and nods and the twins walk up to the lady, past her, and enter the café.

'What do you fancy?' Emma asks.

Mike looks into the purse which he carefully keeps out of sight and smiles as he looks up, 'I think we can splash out.'

'Can I help you?' the barista asks while banging out old coffee granules and turning a handle which emits a cloud of steam.

'Two large Frappuccinos with caramel and marshmallows, a slice of carrot cake and,' he looks over at Emma who is pointing at somewhere in the cake counter, 'a slice of double chocolate fudge cake.'

The barista quickly prepares the order and sets it on a tray on the counter, 'Anything else?'

'No.' Mike waits while the barista taps on the till, then hands over money from the purse, takes the change, and walks off without a word.

The barista watches the two walk away, shakes his head, mutters, 'You're welcome,' and turns to the next customer. He glances outside where there's a commotion. People have stopped to help a little old lady who looks distraught while frantically looking through her bags.

The twins settle in a corner of the café while watching

the hubbub outside around the little old lady, look at each other, smile, and breathe out a shared sigh of contentment. Emma pulls out a Spider-Man notebook with the neat and careful handwriting of a young child written on the front of it. Mike looks at it, 'Anything interesting?'

Emma slides the book across the table and says, 'Have a look.' Mike eyes the book with contempt but picks it up. He leafs through the book reading an extract here and there. Frowning he looks up at Emma questioningly, 'This is just a bunch of Danny's dreams – who cares?'

'Look at it more carefully.' Mike does as instructed; after a while both eyebrows slowly arch but then return to their normal position. 'So a nine-year-old boy keeps a dream journal and has the ability to stop having nightmares by "leaning" his dreams – again, who cares?'

'Mike, think about what we know. Lewis and Claire put a lot of value in this book, so there must be something important about this,' she nods at the book. 'They're not stupid and the way they were going on about it seems to suggest that the reason Danny is in a coma might have something to do with his dreams.' Mike looks bored. Exasperated, Emma tries to hook her brother's interest. 'And by "leaning" your dreams it looks like you can *be* whoever you want and *do* whatever you want in your dreams.'

A cold look in his eyes is reflected by his thin smile as the possibilities dawn on Mike, 'That could be fun. So how do you do this?'

'It seems quite simple really from reading Danny's step-by-step guide in the back of his book. You treat your dreams like a film set where you are the director and the main star. You can control everything in the dream by thinking or shouting commands.' Mike is quite happy at the simplicity of it all and at the prospect of unrestrained antics in his dreams. His attention is drawn to the small gathering outside around the now weeping old lady. A policeman is talking into his phone while the barista helps the lady sit down on a chair he has brought out from the café.

'And so how has this got anything to do with Danny in a coma?' Mike asks distractedly.

As she retrieves the book, Emma looks momentarily confused, 'There's some stuff in there towards the end which I don't quite get, things that don't make sense – it's like his dreams have become real, but that can't be right. It must just be that his "dream leaning" ability is more advanced.' Mike has already lost interest and so she puts the book back in her bag, 'As you say, Mike, "Who cares?"'

* * * * *

'So, what will happen to us?' Danny asks again after getting no response from Barca the first time. He can see Barca's face now that dawn has arrived, but for some reason, he seems reluctant to reply. 'Will I be sent to the court for a trial? I'm innocent, I didn't steal anything. I was trying to give the girl her purse back - it had come untied from her belt. And so I picked it up and that's when her sister pointed at me and started screaming "thief", but she knew I didn't steal it as she had also seen the purse fall to the ground. I don't know why she did that. The judge will make her realise what she saw, right?' Danny stops babbling and looks over to Barca again for reassurance.

Barca takes a moment to choose his words carefully. Is it worth sugar-coating the reality of Danny's situation? Would that be a kindness, or would it leave him unprepared and therefore at greater risk? He decides to be frank but sparing with the full implications. 'There won't be a trial.' Danny's head whips around.

'But, I'm innocent, I haven't done any-' the boy's face mirrors the thoughts racing through his mind, the unfairness, the questions, the growing feeling in the back of his mind that this situation isn't going to have a fairy-tale ending.

'Sorry, Danny. There won't be a trial. Trials are for citizens of the city or people of substance. The City Watch officer will have taken a look at the rags you are wearing and meted out his own swift justice after concluding that you are just a street urchin'.

'But, I-'

'It doesn't matter if you are innocent – it's too late.

There's no easy way to say this, but you are to be sold into slavery.' Barca looks into Danny's eyes to see if Danny has understood.

'But Barca-'

'Danny, my first lesson to you is to stop using people's names.' Danny looks up at him confused. 'You are going to be a slave. Slaves are not people, they are goods to be bought and sold and dealt with in any which way the owners wish. From now on you must address men as "master" and women as "ma'am", if you use a person's name they will beat or flog you.' The boy looks incredulous. 'The one thing in your favour is that slaves cost money, and nobody likes to waste it by buying something and then "breaking" it. The more money you are sold for, the better chance you'll have of being kept fairly safe and so will only suffer beatings occasionally, you know, just to keep you in your place.' Danny's aghast expression spurs Barca on to try and soften the blow. 'You are young and fit with an intelligent look about you, if you are lucky, a good household will buy you with the idea of educating you to become a household's clerk's assistant.' Barca can see that Danny is struggling to process all of this – his face blank and staring into nothing. 'And another thing, once you are bought, don't look at your new owners in the eye. Don't speak to them unless they ask you something.' Barca can see Danny's resolve crumbling, but the boy has to be aware of these things, for his own sake.

Danny is struck dumb. For a moment the groans, the desperate whispered prayers, and the occasional sound of sobbing from the other occupants in the cell cease to exist. Danny is stuck here. He is going to become a slave and as such, it sounds like he will be in a real-life nightmare, worked into a state of relentless exhaustion. This thought makes his heart sink further as he remembers Lewis warning him that if he's too tired, he may not be able to steer his dreams and so might not be able to leave his host's body and return home.

His host's body. Guilt engulfs him. His host. Some poor boy was getting on with his life, whatever that might have been when Danny took over his body. And now, due to Danny's actions, the boy, his 'host', is going to be sold into slavery. So even if Danny can leave this place and go home, he'll be leaving some poor kid in a terrible situation. That was another thing Lewis warned him about. Travelling wasn't the same as dream leaning where you could play act and change things for fun because they were basically just dreams. No, travelling was someone else's, your host's, reality. You have to act like a spectator, not interfere with their lives.

Danny feels awful. He studies himself. What kind of boy has his soul occupied? Looking at himself he sees a scrawny dark-haired child dressed in rags. He's barefoot, the soles of his feet hardened by never having any footwear. He has a few scars on his arms and his legs. Whoever this boy is, he's poor and was unlucky before Danny came along. And now it seems Danny has made this child's life even more wretched. Danny's thoughts are interrupted by the sound of footsteps, the jingling of keys, and shouts of command coming from outside the cell.

*****

As I prepare for bed and my mission, I wonder if I'll even be able to get to sleep. I switch off the bedside light and look up at the ceiling. A faint light sneaks through a gap in the curtains from the streetlight allowing me to make out objects in the room – I look over at Danny's empty bed and breathe out heavily. My mind works overtime with everything I need to do. There's no way I'll be able to sleep. I go through the different ways I have used to help me nod off: picturing a pebble dropping into a dark pool and trying to follow the ripples out as far as possible; trying to visualize the colour white; but I settle for counting, not sheep, but my slow deep breaths.

Sounds of activity wake me. Before opening my eyes I try to remember where I am - at home or on my travels? Flashbacks of falling jolt me and drive me to sit up, but soft hands stop me and push me back. I open my eyes and gaze straight into the most beautiful dark eyes I've ever seen. My heart skips a beat as I feel completely entranced by those black pools staring back at me – I could easily lose myself in them. Where am I? I look around from my comfy roll mat and see I'm in a rudimentary bamboo hut with a thatch roof. The outside light penetrates gaps in the walls casting wonderful patterns and capturing dust motes mid-float.

Her smile seems to emit more light in the dark hut. A warmth spreads throughout my body and I feel that if I were to stay here forever, that would be just fine with me. I can't help myself from smiling back at her.

She's saying something which I can't catch, I can never understand the local language immediately after travelling. Words are hard to discern, in the same way as when you dive into a swimming pool – sounds are distorted and then slowly become clear as you surface. 'Grandpa, grandpa! he's awake!'

A wooden door creaks on its hinges and a voice comes from the silhouette standing in the doorway. 'Good, good.' He walks towards me and nimbly sits down next to my straw-filled roll mat. 'You see, Han, never underestimate people,' he says to his granddaughter. The two exchange a glance which raises a smile on both faces. The grandfather has an amazing face which I could just study for ages. It looks like a walnut – in a nice way: wizened with white hair on the head and forming a long white beard and moustaches; eyes that glow like car lights in a dark tunnel; and skin which also resembles a walnut in colour. Photographers would do star jumps to capture the striking features of this face – I know I would buy a copy.

Another voice hails from outside and is invited in. The door opens and a huge jolly portly Chinese man enters, exchanges greetings, and comes to sit cross-legged by Grandpa. 'Ah, he looks better, much better than the sack of clothing I found on the riverbank.' Grandpa and Han laugh quietly.

'Nor should you overestimate people,' Grandpa says to me. What does he mean? Who is he talking about? He seems to talk in riddles. I think I might still be a bit sick. My thoughts jump around – I wonder how old he is. 'How are you feeling?'

'I'm fine thank you, what happened? Where am I?'

The three of them look at each other before Grandpa considers something and then begins, 'My granddaughter and I were enjoying a time of tranquillity through art and music in the meadow when you, young man, probably saved our lives.' Memories of bandits creeping through the wood preparing to ambush Grandpa and Han appear in my mind. 'There were probably too many of them for me-' I laugh thinking the old man is being funny, suggesting that he could defeat a whole band of thugs, but he raises an eyebrow questioning my reaction, and the other two's foreheads furrow while they study me more closely. Thankfully Grandpa continues, 'We were able to run back and lose them in the wood, especially as most of them were set on hunting down the person who had ruined their plans,' he looks at me intently. Han and the big man's expressions exude open wonder and gratitude. 'Buddha be thanked, you managed to escape them but at a cost. Yuekong, here, found you washed up on the riverbank, you were lucky, you seemed to have dropped into deep water, and then somehow not drowned. Someone is looking after you I think,' Grandpa again looks at me with those merry eyes, tinged with curiosity.

'He was very lucky indeed, I almost got stuck in the mud trying to lift him out of the river. I would have looked an idiot rooted to the riverbed with him flung over my shoulder,' Yuekong says with a smile which is shared by the other two.

'Now then, my turn to ask you a few questions. Who are you, and where are you from? While you were unconscious you were talking in a language I have never heard before.' I take a moment to think how to answer without giving away that I'm a traveller through time.

'First of all, thank you, thanks for looking after me,' I look over at Yuekong, 'and for saving me from slipping back into the river and drowning.' Yuekong gives me a big grin and mutters something like it was nothing. 'My name's Lewis,' obviously they have never heard that name before, and try to repeat it, unsuccessfully, so I repeat it, 'Lewis, Le-wis, Lu-wis.' Eventually, they sort of get it. I have to think quickly, what do I tell them about where I am from? 'I'm from the west, I was travelling with my brother when we became separated a long way from here. So now I am searching for him. The journey has been long and taken me to many strange places.' Talking of Danny chokes me a bit, and the strain is evidently etched on my face.

'Rest, Lu-wis. You have been through much. Let your body recover its "Chi". You can stay here as long as you like, maybe you can help us with our crops.'

'What is your name? You've told me that this giant is Yuekong, and this is your granddaughter Han, but who are you?'

Grandpa smiles and says, 'My name is Tianyuan.' The three of them seem to wait for a reaction, but they don't get one as I have never heard that name before.

'Thank you, Tianyuan.'

There's a pause, I've done something which has left them even more curious about me, but I don't know what.

'Rest Lu-wis, we'll leave you in the capable hands of Han,' I smile at the prospect of being able to spend time with her. My thoughts are read by Tianyaun, who smiles and mutters, 'One step at a time, young man.' Yuekong puts his fist into the earth floor, locks his arm, and then heaves his huge weight up from his previous sitting position. Grandpa springs up with such energy he looks like he could continue up through the thatch roof if he wanted to.

The big man turns to Grandpa as they walk outside, 'Did you hear about General Qi Jiguang?' The words seem to bring a heaviness to the air in the hut.

'What's happened?' Grandpa looks back at Han and me and continues towards the door, pulling at the big man's sleeve, guiding him out of the hut.

I just hear the big man say, 'He lost a battle against the pirates,' before they step outside and out of earshot.

'What are they talking about?' I ask still looking at their retreating backs before the wooden door creaks shut behind them.

'The wokou pirates,' Han responds, the tone of the words transmitting a sense of despair and fear.

'Who are they?' Han's gaze locks onto me, questions seem to flood her mind.

'You don't know of the wokou pirates?' I shake my head, never heard of them before. 'You are a strange one, Lu-wis, with a strange name and language. You have never heard of the wokou pirates – a scourge that has been plaguing our country for centuries. And you didn't react when Grandpa told you his name.' I'm clueless. Usually, my mind merges with my host's so that I speak the language and am aware of customs and events in my current location. But my host isn't familiar with this place or with the name Tianyuan and so nor am I. My ignorance is obvious. 'My grandfather is a well know Shaolin master – people fear his name.'

'But if he's a Shaolin monk, how is it that he has a full head of hair, a beard, isn't wearing an orange robe, and has a granddaughter?'

Han's eyes narrow and again she studies me intently, 'You have heard of the new rules that some Buddhist orders want to introduce. Many don't agree, including my grandfather. They honour their monastery through deeds and piety. They only wear orange and shave their heads when they go on a pilgrimage or prepare for war, but otherwise, they can live life like everyone else. At least for the time being, anyway.'

'Are you saying that your grandfather is like Bruce Lee?' I regret it as soon as I say it.

'Who is this Bruce Lee? I know of a Weng Lee from the Heinan monastery, a martial artist of great repute, but not of this Bruce Lee. Which order does he belong to?'

'I can't remember exactly.' I need to change the subject quickly to avoid too much scrutiny of my slip-up, 'Who are these wokou pirates?'

'The wokou pirates are basically just criminal gangs made up of all nationalities, Japanese, Korean, Mongolian, Chinese, and even white devils.'

'White devils?'

'Yes, people from the West whose skin is white. They have blue eyes, sometimes green or brown. Their hair can be brown or even the colour of gold thread.' I quickly glance at my body - of course, I'm not white - my host is Chinese.

'They have no honour and have become more brazen. The pirate clans sometimes work together – that means they have thousands of men and fleets of ships to raid and pillage wherever they wish. Rumour has it that they intend to capture our capital city. The brigands you saved us from were probably a band of wokou pirates who are raiding further and further inland.'

'Yuekong mentioned Qi Jiguang, is he leading the fight against them?'

'Yes, we call General Qi Jiguang the God of War. It is bad news if he has suffered a defeat, the people already despair, and see him as our only hope. But as grandfather says, we shouldn't listen to rumour and gossip, but find out the facts before reacting to news.'

I'm starting to feel a mix of emotions. The news of the God of War fighting and maybe losing a battle against the pirates seems to have little bearing on my purpose – to find Danny. However, I'm enjoying being here with Han. Now I feel guilty because I'm allowing myself to lose track of my goal because I'm drawn to this lovely girl.

'You need to rest, I'll come back later to check on you.' With that Han gets up, collects the small bowl of water and cloth, and leaves the hut casting a quick glance down at me before the door creaks shut. I lay back looking up at the thatch roof, a confusion of thoughts rolling through my mind. What do I do? Where do I go next? Should I stay here and hope that Danny is in the vicinity? Is destiny guiding us together or apart?

Chapter 6

I'm waiting for Claire and my mum in the hospital concourse when the two consultants, who I've seen wandering around on Danny's ward, see me sitting there and head over.

'Hello, it's Lewis, isn't it?' the dark-haired one asks. I nod. 'I'm Doctor Davies, and this is Doctor McCormack. As you may know, we've been sent here by the government to look into how we can improve the system. We're also drawing on our years of experience to help out with any, umm, challenging cases.' I study them now; they don't really look old enough to have 'years of experience'. They are both of average height and build, but where Doctor McCormack is hairy – dark beard and hair, the bespectacled Doctor Davies is hairless – no hair at all on his head or face. 'How is your brother doing today?'

'I haven't been up yet; I'm just waiting for my mum. I think if there was any change, they would have contacted us.'

'Yes, that's right – a case of no news is good news,' Doctor Davies says, and Doctor McCormack mutters something in agreement. 'Has anything like this ever happened to Danny before or to anyone else in your family?' They both seem to be studying me intently which causes alarm bells to ring in the back of my mind. I pretend to think about the question carefully.

'No, never. Nothing like this has ever happened, that I know of anyway.' They nod at my answer, but both seem to be checking my expression for any hint of a lie. Just then Claire sidles up, thank God, so the doctors nod hello and thank me, wishing Danny a speedy recovery then walk off to the café.

'What did they want? Claire asks sitting down and peering after them.

'They just asked me about Danny and if anything like this has happened to him before or anyone else in the family.' Claire frowns as she studies them a bit more closely before looking back at me.

'Do you think they might be a bit dodgy?'

'I don't know, but I'm not sure if I trust them – are we being paranoid?' I ask.

'No, not at all - better to be paranoid than dead.' I look at Claire and once again try to work out how I've managed to get all of us into this mess.

'Anyway, how did you get on last night, did you manage to travel back to China? Were you okay after the fall?' I nod to all her questions then tell her about Tianyuan, Han, and the Wokou pirates. She digests what I've said and then asks, 'Do you think they might be able to help you find Danny?'

'I don't know. I'm not sure how to explain my situation to them, or even if I should.' I look to see if I can see Mum, I can't, but I do see the two doctors - they seem to be talking about us. I can almost feel them struggling not to look in our direction – strange.

'What's the girl Han like?' Claire asks. I look at her but then look back at the doctors who glance over in our direction before quickly turning away.

'That's weird, I'm sure those doctors are watching us.' Just then, I see Doctor Jeffries walking through the concourse, he spots me and changes direction to come over to us. The other two doctors see him, collect their things and walk away without looking back.

'Hello Lewis,' Doctor Jeffries says as he walks up to our table. He nods a greeting at Claire. 'How are you both?'

'Fine thanks doctor, and you?'

'Very well, thank you.' he smiles, and continues, 'You're here to see Danny?'

'Yes, I'm just waiting for Mum.'

'Well, I can tell you that his condition hasn't changed, but at least we haven't had any of those peculiar episodes –

no rapid heart rate or rise in blood pressure, so that's good.'

'Thanks.' A question leaps to my mind, 'Excuse me, doctor, who are those consultants who are also looking after Danny?'

Doctor Jeffries's face seems to cloud for a millisecond, but then he smiles, 'Oh, they're here looking into how to improve the system - streamlining the system more like. But I'm Danny's doctor, so make sure you ask me or tell me anything related to your brother, okay?' He looks intently at me for confirmation.

'Yes, sure, Doctor Jeffries.' There's something unnerving about his manner, too. Just then my mum turns up.

She says a quick hello to Doctor Jeffries who reiterates that Danny is stable and then Mum turns to us, 'Shall we go up?' Claire and I both nod. We say goodbye to the doctor, grab our things and head to Danny's ward.

* * * * *

The door to Danny's jail cell flies open, the darkness vanishes in a blinding light as the guards bawl at the occupants to come out. The inmates stand quietly and move forward a couple of paces at a time as the adults are manacled to a long chain. Danny and the other children are roped together by their left wrists, but the rope is coarse and soon starts rubbing painfully, especially when the guards yank it.

The soon-to-be slaves are drawn forward one by one to have buckets of water thrown over them while one of the guards uses a coarse brush to wipe away any filth from their bodies. Even though Danny is expecting the splash of water, it still takes his breath away, and then he feels the sting of the brush all over him. Shivering and miserable, Danny moves on a few steps and the child behind him goes through the same process.

Thank God Barca had taken pity on him and looked after him – keeping the dodgy-looking men and women away with a hard stare or a few intimidating words. As the jailers roughly push and whip the desperate and bedraggled prisoners out into the jail's courtyard, Barca stands near Danny trying to whisper words of hope and encouragement. But then they are separated as first the adults and then the children are led through the jail's big heavy wooden doors out onto the street.

Danny is struck by the lack of compassion in the crowds who contemptuously look down on the passing line of human misery. He can't face it anymore and so looks at the ground like all the other prisoners. Images flash through his mind: his capture, the night in the cell, and now fearful visions of what awaits him at the end of this march through the streets of Carthage. At best, he might become a household slave with a compassionate master – that will be like winning the lottery. Possible, but unlikely. From the whispered conversations he overheard in the jail the worst outcome will be if he is sent to the mines – a life expectancy of just a few weeks, possibly months if he is lucky - is that lucky? he asks himself. He might end up on a farm or on a boat where he'll work as a ship's boy until he's big enough to pull an oar. By the sound of it, life on a ship isn't much better than the mines - if he doesn't die of exhaustion or disease, he'll be whipped to death at the oars. And that's provided he isn't rammed by a Roman warship which involved sinking to the bottom of the sea chained to the oar deck with everyone around you screaming and going literally crazy.

Earlier, while they were waiting for the jailers to empty all the cells, Barca had sensed that the conversations going on around them were scaring Danny, so he talked to the boy about the events going on in the world outside. Carthage and Rome continue to fight for domination of the Mediterranean region. Originally Carthage ruled the seas, but a few years ago, the Romans copied the Carthaginians' ship design and then enhanced it by introducing a thing called a corvus: a wide ramp with a kind of sharp beak on its underside which when dropped hooked the bridge to an enemy ship. This allowed the Roman soldiers to deploy and attack in formation – stabbing at the enemy from behind a shield wall – a tactic which is effectively winning them an empire.

At the market, the slaves are divided into separate

wooden enclosures. He is thrust with the other children into a holding pen guarded by thugs with the soulless eyes of dead fish. The pens are instantly surrounded by crowds of shoppers, looking at them and sometimes asking the guard to haul one of the slaves over to be inspected like someone would examine a horse: roughly opening their mouths to check their teeth, their posture, hair, skin, and prodding their bodies to check muscle tone.

Barca told him to try and stand straight, with shoulders back, chest out, and to keep a subservient but confident look about him – he didn't know what subservient meant and was too embarrassed to ask. He tries to shake off the cowed look that so many of the others have adopted and stares around hoping to catch the eye of a kindly-looking buyer. Danny doesn't seem to be attracting any attention, let alone the wealthy couples looking for house slaves - his best bet according to Barca.

Looking around he can't see any couples. Then, he sees them – a man and woman in fine clothes surrounded by four huge men with studded wooden clubs clearing a path through the crowd so that the couple can take a closer look at the 'goods' on sale. They've looked at the men and the women and are now walking toward the children's pen. Danny stands straighter, sticks his chest out, and keeps his shoulders back. He makes sure he doesn't look at them in the eyes, but looks at an imaginary spot in the distance, just above eye level, as Barca suggested. There are other buyers milling around, but even though they look like hard men, they steer clear of the couple's bodyguards.

Danny has to fight the urge to look at the couple directly and beg them to buy him. He keeps his cool and continues to look straight ahead.

'How about that one?' he hears a female voice.

'Nah, too skinny, she looks like she'll be dead by the time we get her home.'

'What about that one?'

'The tall boy with the long hair - looks healthy.'

Danny risks a quick glance to see who they are talking about. A quick look reveals that they are appraising a boy a few feet away – they are about the same height, so Danny stands a little taller on his toes.

'Look my dear, we are only buying one slave, another guard maybe, but I don't really think we need another one. So it's either a girl to help in the kitchens or a general house boy, we're not leaving here with a gang of them, just one.' There's a pause and then, 'Don't look at me like that, we agreed that before we came. You always buy more than you need.'

'Okay, okay. How about that one, the boy standing on his toes?'

Danny's heart stops. They must be talking about him. He can sense the couple staring at him, so he breathes in, thrusting out his scrawny chest. He tries to appear calm and collected but is sure they must be able to see that his knees are shaking.

'I'm not sure, he looks a bit odd, is he breathing in?' There's a pause. 'Guard, bring that one closer.' A guard yanks on the rope at Danny's wrist almost tumbling him to the ground. He's pulled up to the wooden fence which divides the slaves from the buyers. Suddenly Danny feels a firm hand grip his jaw and then fingers forcing his mouth open.

'Teeth seem okay, no sign of disease.' Then the hands pass over his arms and shoulders painfully kneading the flesh. 'Not a lot of muscle, but not too bad. Looks a bit ragged, but healthy. Might scrub up okay. What do you think dear?'

'Check his hair for lice.'

Danny winces as his head is grabbed and his hair pulled apart so that they can inspect his scalp for nits. 'No lice by the looks of it.'

Their attention has drawn the auctioneer over. 'Ah, you have a good eye for quality, sir, ma'am. This boy is new, arrived last night.'

'Where is he from? Why was he enslaved?' the woman asks.

The auctioneer makes a big fuss of looking at his manifest, 'From the streets, he was picked up by the City Watch last night. He isn't branded so he wasn't a slave before, but due to the laws of the city, as you know, any undesirables can be sold as slaves.'

There's a moment's silence, 'How about that one over there?' The woman asks and so the couple move further along the fence to another boy, taller and stronger looking than Danny.

'Another good choice, sir...' Danny doesn't hear what the auctioneer says after that, his spirits drop - he berates himself for not looking good enough. But maybe they are just checking all the slaves, before deciding. He supposes it's just like anyone who goes shopping – they'll shop around looking for the best value for their money. He might still be in with a chance.

'He's got lice!' he hears the man shout angrily at the auctioneer. Danny would usually feel pity for the other boy, but instead, he feels his spirits lift, then he feels guilty, then he realizes there's no room for sympathy in this situation – it could mean the difference between life and death.

Danny becomes aware that someone is looking at him, he glances up and quails at the sight of a man staring directly at him with his one eye - the other eye is hidden behind a patch, which in turn hides the central part of a scar which runs from the man's forehead to his jaw. The pirate-like resemblance doesn't stop there. He's wearing a waistcoat over a blouse and loose baggy trousers held up by a sash wrapped around his waist. As he moves, sunlight reflects off the curved sword at his waist on his left and a vicious-looking dagger on his right. The man turns to the two men flanking him in similar pirate garb and says, 'He'll do.'

Both men respond with an 'aye'; the one on the leader's left leers at Danny in a way that makes his skin crawl. The man's belly bulges from beneath a waistcoat, the dark taught skin looks ready to burst. His sweaty face is slightly hidden by long matted dark hair. Danny gulps, he hopes the couple will bid for him, otherwise... he looks at the three men walking over to the auctioneer's platform. He tries to keep calm; he reassures himself that they can't be pirates otherwise the City Guard would have caught them and executed them or sold them into slavery as well. They must be sailors of some kind judging by their appearance. He hopes the couple will buy him, then looks over at the sailors – please God, make the couple buy him.

Chapter 7

The base of my back aches from spending two weeks working on the farm ploughing the fields and sowing seed for the crops which are the lifeblood of the community.

One of the curious things about travelling is the way time changes speed – two weeks here can be just one night back home. The thought of the time which has passed leaves me riddled with guilt, worry, and a sense of failure – I'm nowhere near finding Danny. Tianyuan agreed to write notices for the announcement boards and poles in the centre of all the neighbouring villages and towns as well as the outlying monasteries. It asks for anyone called Danny to come to Tianyuan's village. The memory of that conversation adds to my feeling of uselessness – he asked me for a description of Danny which of course I couldn't give – I don't know what his host looks like. I'm not sure my excuse of not wanting dodgy characters looking out for my brother was very convincing – Tianyuan just stared at me for a moment – studying me.

I press my fist against my lower spine to massage the tight muscles and look up to see Han and Tianyuan walking towards me smiling. They both have cloth bundles tied to their staffs which rest on their shoulders and must contain food judging by the mouth-watering aromas on the light breeze. Tianyuan is also carrying the musical instrument they were playing in the meadow when I first saw them – called a guqin, and Han is cooling herself with her fan.

Every morning since I recovered, Tianyuan has been teaching me some kung fu techniques with staff as well as kicks and punches. They all have great names: Leaping Tiger;

White Snake Shoots Venom; Unicorn Plays with Water; and my favourite, Golden Dragon Embraces Moon which I've learnt to change swiftly into the lethal Dragon's Kiss – a frighteningly simple deadly move that Tianyuan seemed keen for me to learn, but only on condition that I never tell anyone about it.

Another condition for him teaching me kung fu is that I become a novice monk under his tutelage – I don't mind as the Buddhist way of life is really interesting. He is constantly talking about Chi - your life energy or life force, and Zen - the peace of mind and the state of being relaxed rather than angry and stressed. He keeps telling me how everything is connected and how we need to be as observant about the things we can't see or hear as the ones we can. To be quite honest, he loses me - I'm not sure how I can be observant of the things I can't see. When I ask him, he just chuckles and tells me I'll understand soon enough – a response which I'm starting to find very irritating - which I guess means I haven't reached a good state of Zen. This is even more infuriating as Tianyuan says that to be a true kung fu master you must be Zen or your emotions will hinder your fighting ability. But I'm going to persevere, I have to be able to control that rage that explodes out of me.

I now know that Tianyuan carries the staff not to help him walk or for support but as a weapon. His is made of white oak which is deceptively heavy and as strong as iron. I've got bruises all over my body bearing witness to how fast Tianyuan can wield it. He moves it so fast it's hard to see, in fact, most of the time I only know he's swung his staff after the event when I feel a light tap at different points on my body. It seems I'll never be able to reach anywhere near his skill levels, but Tianyuan assures me that I will with time and practice.

Another lesson I've learnt is to never underestimate your opposition. If you saw Tianyuan walking down the street seemingly being supported by his staff, you might be inclined to offer him help, not knowing that he's probably one of the most fearsome warriors on the planet. He says this is also an asset – he quotes Sun Tzu, the renowned military strategist who wrote The Art of War, 'Intelligence, observation, and cunning are as important as fighting ability.' If a person sees you as a weak adversary, he or she is in for a shock when you 'ti tā de pigu' which means 'kick his ass' – he seems to find this phrase very amusing.

Walking alongside Tianyuan with a spring in her step is Han. She is full of surprises. I still haven't forgiven her for the other day…

'You must show my grandfather more respect, the respect that is expected by him and all who know of his reputation,' she told me seriously.

'How do I do that?'

'Well, firstly you must address him using superlatives such as "the most magnificent" followed by grand or noble creatures, such as a dragon, owl, and so on.'

'What? So I should say something like "Oh magnificent tiger?"'

Han looked down and nodded solemnly, 'Yes, Lu-wis, exactly. I can see that you will get accustomed to our practices very quickly.' I felt pretty chuffed with her compliment. 'But remember that you must use a different address each time - to repeat the same address is considered poor form.'

Blimey! I'd thought. I made a list of terms of address, so I could use them the next time I saw Tianyuan. The following day Tianyuan and Han approached me while I was working in the fields. I both welcomed and dreaded the sight - a rest from the back-breaking toil turning the soil was welcome, but the prospect of inadvertently disrespecting Tianyuan by not addressing him correctly was stressing me out.

'How is the work going, Lu-wis?' he'd asked.

'It's getting there, and my body seems to be getting stronger by the day,' I paused before adding, 'Oh magnificent tiger.'

Tianyuan's head whipped around, 'Pardon, what did you say?'

'I, umm, it's getting there, and my body seems stronger,' my voice went up an octave before I added, 'Oh glorious panda,' he looked at me with consternation, Han looked at the ground, and then she turned away. I thought she was embarrassed by the hash I was making of it.

'Lu-wis, what's got into you? I think you have been in the sun too long.' Then Han burst out laughing which drew both our attention. Tianyuan looked back and forth between Han and me, 'Han, have you been up to your silly games again?'

'No, Grandfather, oh wisest of yaks,' she then crumpled to the ground holding her belly crying with laughter.

Tianyuan then turned to me. He had a glint in his eye and was evidently trying to keep a straight face, 'Lu-wis, be careful with this one.'

Looking at her now you would think that she was the epitome of a young Chinese schoolgirl: smiles, energy, with long black hair swirling through the air mirroring the swish of her long cotton robe, but don't be deceived by her slender frame. Evidently, her grandfather has been teaching her kung fu since she could walk. I've sparred with her and feel ashamed to have to admit that I'm nowhere near her level. I don't get a kick or punch anywhere near her before she seems to dance away and come back using her svelte body like a whip generating enough power to knock me to the ground every time. I love her face, but not when she's grinning down at me lying in the dust after she's 'ti wǒ de pigu'. And she's deceptively strong - I've seen her wield that heavy staff as if it were as light as a feather.

I see her smiling at me now as they both get closer – her eyes are twinkling – I wonder if she's up to more mischief... She's cooling herself with her fan which sends a shiver down my spine – that thing is scary. It's cream-coloured with a classic Chinese landscape painted on it - rocky outcrops on either side of a meandering river, apparently of a place called Guilin. I hadn't realized that the ribs supporting the paper of the fan are edged with razor-sharp blades. I was trying to pull at a vine hanging from a tree so I could use it as a rope to bundle some firewood when Han walked up, leapt in the air, and with a swirl of her fan the vine was surgically cut in two; the vine was tougher than rope.

'Hello Lu-wis, how's the sowing of the seed going?'

'Fine thank you, Grandfather Teacher.' I have since learnt that 'Grandfather Teacher' is the correct form of address for Tianyuan. He told me to call him by his name, but Han told me it would be more respectful to address him as others in the village did – the teacher of all their martial arts teachers so therefore 'Grandfather Teacher'. He smiles at the respect I show him and surveys my work and then the countryside around where we stand on a beautiful spring day.

'You're doing well, but I wouldn't sow the seeds too close together, they'll compete for the same nutrients.' I look down at the lines of seed I've sown in the field and my heart sinks. I'll have to start again. 'No,' as if he reads my thoughts, 'you don't have to change what you have done, just approach it differently in the future.' Is he still talking about the seeds? I never know. 'Anyway, it's too beautiful to spend all day working, we're off to have a picnic.' Great, that is music to my ears. I quickly pick up my tools, hide them among the roots of a tree marking the corner of Tianyuan's plot and collect my hat, yak-skin water bottle, and the white oak staff Tianyuan gave me last week. Once I'm ready we start to walk towards the forest.

'Where are we going?'

'There's a meadow near the waterfall that's showing off its spring flowers,' Han smiles at me. But I've stopped in my tracks – the only meadow I can remember is the one where we almost got killed by the pirates.

'Not the one you're thinking of Lu-wis, this is a different one, on the other side of the river, hidden from any marauding bandits,' Tianyuan reassures me. We walk along the riverbank to the lovely sound of babbling water and dragonflies competing with crickets to provide a musical soundtrack to this gorgeous day. As we walk Tianyuan tests Han on the flowers and plants we pass, asking their names and what they can be used for. The flora not only provide a splash of colour, but all seem to have different healing properties: the red wolfberry which can be eaten fresh or dried and helps boost your immune system; the lilac viola blossom which is a remedy for snake bites and infections; the fragrant yellow honeysuckle which soothes a sore throat and can cure flu or cold; the white, yellow or pink magnolia flower which clears congestion; and so many more my head starts to spin.

My thoughts drift as Tianyuan continues to quiz Han. One thing I can't get my head around is the fact that people used to live with the constant threat of life-changing danger. I've read loads of books on world history, but until I came here, it's hard to describe the reality that at any time, whether you're asleep in your bed, having your dinner, or looking for firewood or whatever, you may be attacked, killed, or sold into slavery. I'm just surprised everyone here doesn't walk around twitching and jumping out of their skin at every unexpected noise. Life here can seem to be considered cheap, but actually, it's not: there's an acceptance of their 'lot' and a gratefulness for every day that passes without a shocking incident. The general populace seem inured to news that such and such was killed, raped, or sold, and the horrifying thing is that it wasn't a rare occurrence, but ever-present.

To give them some sort of chance against the pirates, the elders of the local villages had gathered and determined that they needed to be able to at least defend themselves, and if necessary, fight back. It didn't take them long to deduce that they had the perfect person to train them - Tianyuan. Han told me that her grandfather saw it as an honour to help those in need and happily complied, donating his payment to help construct the defensive wall around their village. First, he taught the most promising students from all the surrounding villages to become teachers themselves. Yuekong, the man who found me unconscious on the riverbank, was one of those people who showed promise and so he and the other chosen soon taught their own village folk martial arts skills using an array of weapons or just their fists and feet.

Having Tianyuan's undivided attention as my own personal Shaolin kung fu teacher is a massive privilege. I don't think I'm usually the best student, but if the subject interests me, then I'm a quick learner. Of course, who knows how these skills will help me in my search for Danny; but they could, and so this is an added incentive which has resulted in me giving that bit extra every second of every lesson I have with

Grandfather Teacher.

As we walk along the riverside with Han answering correctly every question Grandfather Teacher fires at her I feel a wonderful sense of well-being – my senses seem more acute. I can smell the wonderful fragrance given off by the flowers, the birdsong adds to nature's harmony, and the colours seem more vivid than usual. As the land rises we follow a path away from the river through a forest where bluebells carpet the floor in a wonderful lilac and I imagine that I can smell garlic, then spot the plants' little white flowers. The sun dapples the forest floor creating an even more enchanting scene, it really is turning into an unexpectedly lovely day.

The forest thins and then we step into a wild meadow. We follow Tianyuan to a spot he deems suitable, in the centre about a hundred meters away from the forest edge and on a little rise. Han unties the cloth bundles to reveal a feast: rice cakes, chicken legs and wings in a spicy glaze, some bams – bread buns with a variety of fillings, and honey cakes. Tianyuan brings out a clay bottle of wine from the folds of his robe and cleans his long reed pipe while Han and I spread out the picnic. The food is making my mouth water, but I wait for Tianyuan to start as etiquette demands. He reaches over and grabs a chicken leg, which is like a starting gun being let off, Han and I grab one thing, savour it, and then another, the pace only slowing once we have sated our appetites.

There are just crumbs and bare bones left when Tianyuan pours us a cup of wine each and lights up his pipe. Han takes a sip of the fragrant wine with the cool delicate flavour of honey and flowers and then puts her cup to one side and starts plucking at the guqin on her lap. I wasn't sure what to make of this unusual stringed instrument initially, but it seems to suit the time and place and now I love it. I lie back on the soft grass and doze.

I sense it before I hear Tianyuan ask Han to stop. The birds have stopped singing and there's an unnatural stillness to the forest. Grandfather Teacher scans all around the treeline, his eyes almost disappear into the creases of his face. Han and I also search for any movement. A shout shatters the silence and slowly figures emerge from all around the forest edge, we are surrounded. Fear grips me as I recognise the rabble walking slowly towards us. I grab my staff as I leap to my feet and adopt a defensive stance. Han tucks her fan behind her shoulder, concealing it in her robe, and picks up her staff to face the enemy coming from the other side. I glance back at Tianyuan and am almost unmanned by the sight before me. He's getting to his feet like an old man. I'm not sure if he's acting or not.

The nearest pirates are now only 25 meters away, I look around and my courage fades as I count at least 50 of them. They are close enough for me to discern the sly looks on their faces. They slowly draw their swords, cleavers, and axes, limbering up by swinging their weapons in all directions.

'What do we do?' I mutter under my breath glancing back to see that Tianyuan has only just gotten to his feet and seems more reliant on his staff for support than usual. He surveys the scene – looking around like a hunched myopic old man.

Chapter 8

Possessed Minister Sentenced to Death

The Texan minister Matthew Bryant was found guilty of five counts of murder in a court in Fort Lauderdale on Monday. The town community of Bethesda are still reeling from the events that saw their minister of twenty-two years open fire on them during a Sunday morning service. The congregation managed to overcome the 'possessed' minister only after he stopped to reload his revolver.

Matthew Bryant claims he was possessed by the devil and has asked to be executed. The townsfolk of Bethesda have asked for clemency as prior to the event the minister had been a pillar of the community, which has led to some speculating that he was indeed possessed.

Source: The Texan Telegraph, December 17th, 1857

Doctor Death Dies in Custody

Doctor Mwelbe who spent a week on a rampage of violence and murder has died in his jail cell of injuries he sustained during his arrest in the town of Kwable, in Central Africa. The previously highly regarded physician suddenly turned into a demon according to staff and patients at the local hospital; he stole a panga from a gardener and used the 45-cm-blade to terrorise the nearby villages and countryside for over a week before his arrest. Nobody has been able to understand what happened and no explanation was given by the doctor who seemed to be rendered mute by the shocking trail of misery he had caused. Some have suggested Juju spirits might be responsible.

Source: The Central African Chronicle, August 4th, 1963

'I'm surprised you occupied a man's body,' Mike says to Emma as they sit at the breakfast island in their home's kitchen recounting their exploits from the night before.

'Not as surprised as I was to wake up in a man's body!' They chuckle at the bizarreness of these new experiences. 'It's also weird that last night was the equivalent of around a week in Africa for you whereas I was only in the States for a day.'

'Yeah, as you say, the speed that time passes seems to depend on which wormholes you go through and when you go through them,' Mike shakes his head slightly, 'Yeah, really mad.' He looks over at his sister, it always amazes him how alike they are – if she cut her hair and wore his clothes, she could easily pass as him.

'We have to do the next one together – I saw a gateway to Germany; it must have been during the war because there were swastikas and German soldiers everywhere. That could be a lot of fun,' her eyes gleam with the prospect.

'Yeah, okay,' Mike nods but isn't enthusiastic. Africa was so much fun.

* * * * *

Selling human livestock is a slow process. They started with the men first. Some were bought individually; others were sold in groups. Barca was in one of those groups bought by a wealthy merchant with a small army of guards to herd them away. Danny's friend managed a quick nod and a weak attempt at an encouraging smile before being moved out of the slave market while their new owner poured a small purse of gold coins into the avaricious hands of the auctioneer.

One of the slaves tried to escape as he was unshackled and marched up to the timber platform where the buyers could bid for the 'lots'. He didn't get far, and to Danny's horror, a nearby guard bludgeoned him to the ground and would have continued beating him had the auctioneer not intervened, berating the guard for damaging his goods. The incident hardly registered with the crowd who started chatting amongst themselves while the unconscious body was dragged away by the ankles, the exposed parts of his body and face getting scraped by the abrasive sandy ground. And then the next slave was marched up, having seen what had just happened he was shaking uncontrollably, which affected the bidding and so the auctioneer cast the guard another look of disdain. The guard just shrugged and walked away.

Then the women were sold. They too were sold individually or in groups. Danny was surprised to see individual women bidding for the groups. Each of them had at least one huge guard armed with a club, a staff, or a whip. The buyers entered a frenzy of bids for one group of particularly attractive women, each buyer glaring at the other female bidders until evidently, only one buyer had enough to outbid the others. She almost looked comical with the excessive make-up plastered on her face, and gaudy gold jewellery jingling from ears, nose and wrists - until you looked at her eyes which were as devoid of compassion as the merciless guards. The wails and tears streaming down the faces of the newly enslaved women deepened Danny's sense of despair.

The sun was overhead by the time the children were brought up to the auction platform, adding to the oppressive atmosphere - sweat stung the eyes, and the skin seemed to feel every grain of sand while the mouth became increasingly dry. One by one the boys were taken up and their virtues extolled to the onlooking masses. Some of the crowd didn't seem to be buying, just there for the show.

And now it's almost Danny's turn, one more boy in front of him and then it will be him displayed on the platform. He quickly scans the crowd to see if he can spot the couple, only to spot the three sailors staring at him. Danny searches harder and with almost a gasp of relief spots the couple a bit further on from the men. He holds his breath hoping they won't buy the boy in front of him. He finds himself judging the boy on the platform, is he as strong as Danny? Does he look as healthy? He does, and not only that, he's also taller and carries a bit more muscle. But the boy is sold to another person who quickly pays and leaves pulling the child by the rope which he has repositioned around the boy's neck.

'Lot 56, a fine young healthy boy, new to the slave markets.' Danny is pulled by the rope out of the pen and pushed up the wooden steps to the platform. The sun shines directly into his eyes, so he squints and turns his face away from the glare. He feels the auctioneer's hands on him, roughly raising his arms, prodding his chest and back, and opening his mouth – the crowd just stare, seemingly unaware of the humiliation Danny is going through. 'As you can see, no sign of disease, quite the contrary, a fine specimen that will be of use in any household,' at this point, the auctioneer can't resist looking at the couple, Danny also glances swiftly in their direction. 'Who will give me four shekels?' Danny scans the crowd as intently as the auctioneer.

The tension is unbearable, this moment, these mere seconds will determine whether he'll be worked to death or live. His heart leaps as the couple look at each other, the woman nods and so her husband makes a bid. 'I have four, anyone give me five?' The bid by the sailors almost makes Danny's knees give way. The auctioneer can't hide his delight, having two parties keen on one lot is perfect – more coins for his purse. Danny looks over at the couple, the man nods at the auctioneer who then looks at the sailors. Back and forth, back and forth.

'Do I have 12 shekels?' Danny looks at the couple. They pause, the husband looks at his wife and shakes his head. 'Who will give me 12 shekels?' Silence. People look around to see if the couple or any new bidder will pay an exorbitant amount for the boy. The silence creeps on, 'Going once, going twice…' Danny stares imploringly at the couple, tears well up in his eyes. They look at each other one more time and again, the husband shakes his head. 'Sold to the sailors for 11 shekels,' and with the thwack of a small wooden mallet on the platform's wooden rail, Danny belongs to the sailors.

The transaction happens quickly, the leader pours silver coins into the auctioneer's greedy palms while the sweaty leering sailor with the big belly moves the rope roughly from Danny's wrist to around his neck.

They start walking briskly through the streets of Carthage; Danny struggles to keep up so has to break into a jog every few paces otherwise the rope pulls and rubs the skin. As they pace through the parting throngs of people in the streets they chat. Danny can barely follow the conversation - he trips and with a strangled yelp falls to the ground halting the sailors in their tracks. Coughing and instinctively trying to loosen the rope around his neck Danny's eyes water with the pain; in between gasping breaths, he glances up at the three. The leader glares at the creepy man.

'For Tanit's sake, Karalis, at least try and keep this one alive until we get to the ship!'

'Yes, Captain,' Karalis responds in a non-committal way which seems to enrage the leader.

'I'm serious Karalis, I may as well just throw 11 shekels into the sea – it would save me time and effort. If I have to throw another dead boy into the sea, you'll be paying for the next slave – see how careful you'll be then.'

Karalis can't maintain eye contact with his captain and looks at the ground. The conversation about Danny seems to draw the captain's attention to the boy. 'What's your name, boy?'

Danny looks up, the sun is behind the captain and blinding, causing him to shield his eyes with his fist, which replicates the way sailors 'knuckle' the forehead to show respect, 'Danny, sir.'

'You don't have to salute me, boy,' the three men laugh. 'You seem intelligent and a boy with spirit. The way you stood to attention, shoulders back, chest out, looking straight ahead – just like a little guardsman, drew our attention in the slave market. We need a ship's boy with spirit and someone who can take orders like a soldier.' The captain stoops down to look at Danny in the face with his one eye. 'Do as I say, and you'll be all right.'

'Yes, sir,' Danny manages. The talk of soldiers and the three men's scrutiny of him, makes Danny instinctively stand to attention, again.

'Well done,' the captain seems happy. 'The man holding you by the rope is Karalis, he's the drum master, he keeps all the slaves at the oars under control and rowing in rhythm. This is Salicar,' Danny looks at the tall and swarthy man standing to the captain's left, every movement sends ripples of muscle tensing under his skin. He nods and seems to smile, but Danny can't be sure – is there a hint of kindness in his eyes? 'He's the boatswain, which means he's in charge of the equipment and the ship's crew – he keeps everything ship-shape as it were. And I'm Captain Gisgo.

'Right, we need to get back to the ship so we can sail on the next tide.' Captain Gisgo turns on his heel and they start walking quickly through the streets again.

'It'll be good to get away from these crowds and the smell of a city,' Salicar says to no one in particular. He has a strong deep voice, Danny hopes he will be his boss on the ship and not the drum master, Karalis, who looks at him in a funny way.

'Yes, cities are only good for a few days to rest and replenish our supplies, and then back to sea, clean air and masters of our own destiny,' Captain Gisgo acknowledges.

'Will I have time to brand the boy, Captain?' Karalis's question stops them in their tracks again. The Captain turns puce with anger and stands close up, getting in Karalis's face.

'What did I just say? I told you to take better care of our ship's boys. Don't you remember the last time you branded a boy? You almost killed him.' Karalis looks ready to argue. Captain Gisgo moves his hand to the hilt of his dagger as he eyes his drum master, daring him to respond. Danny looks quickly from one to the other, gulping at the vision of Karalis taking a red-hot branding iron out of a fire and approaching him with a sly grin on his face.

'Yes, Captain, as you say, Captain,' Karalis looks down at his feet.

Captain Gisgo stares at him a moment longer, then

looks at Danny, 'Salicar, take charge of the boy. We won't bother branding him. It's a waste of time anyway, where is he going to run to when we're at sea.' Salicar takes the rope from Karalis's tight grip and as if to make a point, takes it off Danny's neck and returns it securely, but not tightly, to Danny's wrist. Then they are on the move again.

Danny hasn't seen this part of Carthage before; it gives him an indication of how vast the city is. They pass gardens, mansions, and amphitheatres on their way to the turquoise sea which is visible at the end of the huge avenue they now stride down. The honey-coloured sandstone walls of the magnificent buildings on the boulevard create an aesthetic backdrop for the green of the shrubbery which produce a beautiful display of red, purple, blue and yellow flowers. The palm trees which flank each side of the avenue stand swaying gently in the breeze like guards on parade.

Then suddenly the avenue slopes down and they march through an arch in a huge wall guarded by a troop of soldiers checking the passes of those entering the city. They walk out from the cool shade of the arch and before them are two enormous harbours. There are so many ships that their masts create the impression of a forest swaying and floating on the water. The nearest harbour has around 200 hundred war ships evidenced by the troops marching around and the array of military uniforms present. The harbour in the distance has the same number of ships but is filled by merchant shipping judging by the goods and civilians crowding the piers. Captain Gisgo leads them to the military harbour.

As they round a curve along the pier wall they come to an abrupt halt. All three sailors stand and inspect one of the biggest ships in the harbour which appears to have just finished loading on the last sacks and amphorae of supplies. It's a quinquereme, one of the most feared ships that sail the Mediterranean Sea; it can reach a ramming speed of 13 knots powered by the 300 slaves on the oar deck. The remaining crew of 120 live on the 45-meter-long main deck. Captain Gisgo and his lieutenants scrutinise the rigging, how things are being stowed away, how the ship sits in the water, and then seem to exhale together with a look of satisfaction.

Danny fails to feel the same enthusiasm – by the sound of it, ship's boys don't last long on this boat, especially with predators like Karalis after you. The ship was one of the biggest in the harbour, but Danny wonders if it is big enough to offer enough places to hide.

* * * * *

'There may be too many of them. Han, my dearest, you must not let them take you alive, understand?'

'Yes, Grandfather.' Han is remarkably cool which just makes me feel weak and cowardly. The three of us face outwards, each with a 120-degree arc to defend. Han and Tianyuan have walked out without me noticing, evidently giving us a bit more room to manoeuvre.

'Grandfather Teacher, maybe we can fight a way through one side so that Han can escape into the woods,' the words come out of my mouth before I realize I've thought them.

Tianyuan turns his head to look at me and smiles, his kind eyes seem to look deep into my soul. 'Lu-wis, you are a good man, this band might look stupid, but they're not. See how they've left a screen of men at the fringes of the forest, just for that eventuality. No, we fight, kill, and keep killing. Remember to keep moving, follow the example of the dragonfly, move like it, confuse your opponents - don't let them predict where your body will be so they can wield the killing stroke.'

The pirates stop around 15 paces away, their leader walks forward a couple more steps and halts, sneering at us. 'Ah, so we've found our little butterflies at last. This time you won't be flying away. And you,' he turns pointing directly at me with his sword, 'We have something special in store for you for spoiling our fun the last time.' I try to face him like a man but feel weak as a kitten.

'Remember Zen,' I hear Tianyuan say from behind me. He's facing his enemy, but continues quietly, 'Clear your mind of emotion and focus everything on the present and the enemies around you.' I grip my staff in front of me, my palms feel sweaty, so I move my fingers slightly to get a better hold of it.

I concentrate on what is before me. Tianyuan is right, most of them are not stupid. Most of them haven't bunched up around us, they've left space between them so they can manoeuvre and wield their weapons without injuring their gang members. They have formed loose concentric circles around us. The air is thick with tension, just waiting for the spark that will ignite a fight to the death. The pirates closer to me seem impatient, held back on an imaginary leash, but they also seem half-crazed in their eagerness to fight, to prove themselves to their peers. That's good, they might be careless. I study the expressions on the ones in the next surrounding circle, they are something to worry about, calm - unruffled by the prospect of violence that will take place in the next few seconds. I need to get to them quickly. The outer circle has sunk into a spectator mode, assured that they will not have to take any part in the action. Give them a bucket of popcorn and a soda and they could be watching Cinderella at the cinema.

I shouldn't have smiled; it provokes two pirates who lunge at me with the tips of their swords. I dance through the air between the blades and whirl my staff left then right catching the men with the ends of the heavy staff on the back of their heads, there's a sound like two coconuts being hit and they are down and out. There are noises and flashes of movement all around me, but in my mind I picture just those opponents surrounding me, forming a sort of radar in my mind of their positions and picking up little snapshots of the enemy. The one behind me seems jittery, he's surprised by how easily I downed two of his mates. I hear a swish and stab back with my staff without looking around and feel the reassuring contact as the end of my staff hits soft flesh, then hear a thud as the body hits the ground, but in the same moment I've sprung diagonally towards another opponent and smashed my staff upwards into his face – a mist of red lingers in the air - the only sign that he was once standing there. Move, strike, move strike, strike, move, move, strike.

For some reason there's a pause, both sides back off

panting, surveying the scene and reassessing the situation. Wily old Tianyuan duped his opponents into thinking of him as a frail old man, now there must be six men on the floor who will never think that again. Han's opponents thought they were dealing with a defenceless little maiden; but there are four bodies around her, one of them has her staff stuck somehow in his body, two of them have terrible open wounds pouring blood onto the meadow - she must have drawn that fan. I caught a glimpse of Han during the fight, she was leaping around as if gravity didn't exist anymore, her opponents seemed clumsy as they slashed at thin air. I look around me and see three still down and two crawling away from the action. My spirits lift, that's at least fifteen of the enemy out of the fight, if we can keep this up then maybe we have a chance.

My legs start to tremble as the adrenalin kick fades, I curse myself - I don't want to let the enemy see me shaking. Tianyuan always emphasises that when a fight actually starts, you mustn't show weakness or tiredness, this can have as much of a debilitating effect on the enemy as a blow to the head. Everyone will be exhausted, but if they look at you and you seem fresh, ready for more, their fatigue is magnified. I look around, just with my eyes, not moving my head. Their leader strides into my line of sight, fuming.

'Useless fools!' he skips towards one of his injured men who is trying to get up on all fours and kicks him viciously in the chest, there's a groan and the man slumps back flat on the ground. 'You let an old man, a girl, and a boy beat you!' I can see spittle flying from his mouth, his face red and swollen with rage. Then he stops and takes a few slow deep breaths as he looks at us one by one. 'Who are you, old man?' There's no answer. I knew there wouldn't be. Another lesson Tianyuan taught me was not to engage in conversation during a fight, don't give the enemy anything. Don't be distracted. Keep focussed on the danger around you.

The silence draws out as their leader just stares at Tianyuan, I control my breathing, not wanting to look breathless. But I am. Now the fighting has stopped I can feel the bruises and a stinging pain in my back. There's a wet feeling there too and I feel suddenly exhausted. There's a smell of iron, or is that a taste of it? I don't know if that is coming from the blood of the fallen or from me. I just want to lie down and sleep. I think I might be dying. Who will save Danny? I should have let Claire join me in the search. At least then she could take over and my brother would have a chance. The thoughts make me feel even weaker, but I still manage to hold my posture and follow all of Tianyuan's teachings. If I die, I want to take their leader with me. I try to control my anger - maintain my Zen. But I feel feeble, I'm sure the shaking in my hands and knees must be visible.

'I'm not wasting any more time with this,' the leader says as he makes a gesture with his hand above his head. I see movement as the pirates from the inner circle move back, retreating backwards not taking their eyes off us, and the ones from the middle circle move in. They are all notching arrows to their bows, studying us as they walk forward to replace our previous opponents. At 10 paces out they stop and wait for the command, pulling slightly on their bows, but not sighting them on us yet, just keeping them drawn, pointing at around 45 degrees towards the ground in front of them. They are too far for me to reach before I get shot down in a hail of arrows. This is it then, the end. I'm surprised that I can accept my death with such little emotion, just sadness that I wasn't able to get Danny back. I look at Han and my sadness deepens – it would have been nice to spend more time with her.

'On my command shoot the old man and the boy, leave the girl - she's our reward.' The leader looks at Tianyuan, hoping to relish in some sort of expression of dismay or any kind of reaction to his words, but again he is disappointed which fuels his anger further. Fortunately, he wasn't looking at me, a surge of rage reinvigorates me, but I take slow deep breaths to calm myself so I can think straight. I know I have one chance at killing him before the archers kill me. I can use the heavy staff as a spear and hit the point on the body that Tianyuan taught me to hit, the lethal Dragon's Kiss. I adopt a sort of Golden Dragon Embraces Moon stance, but in a way which makes it look like I'm defeated, with sloped shoulders, staff held loosely in my right hand, appearing like I'm about to drop it on the floor, but I've turned my palm outwards ready to launch it at him like a spear.

He raises his arm, ready to signal the command 'fire' when I feel the ground vibrate. Then everyone starts to feel it, looking at each other questioningly. A Horn is blown and then the vibration turns into a deep rumble, horses burst out from the forest galloping towards us from all directions. The outer ring of pirates look like mannequins - static - they are run down, speared through or slashed with long cavalry sabres. The second ring turn to face the threat. I've gleaned from novels that foot soldiers don't have a chance against cavalry if they are isolated – they need to form up as a group in a shield wall bristling with spears, and now I see why. The powerful horses are racing down on them, solid muscle hurtling directly at them. Before the pirates can work out which way to dive, they are trampled under the horses' hooves or literally cut in half by the rider who has the advantage of height, speed, and the phenomenal power generated by a galloping horse.

The pirates are stunned by the sight of the calvary reaping their comrades like a farmer harvesting wheat, and so I take my chance, I move from the Golden Dragon Embraces Moon to a spear throw stance and hurl the staff at the leader who turns just in time to face me when the staff thumps into his body right where I aimed. Even though there was not much speed in the staff, the weight compensates, achieves its purpose. There's a look of surprise on the leader's face as he looks at me before dropping to the floor dead.

In a few more moments the cavalry have annihilated the pirates - bodies lie strewn across the meadow. The cavalry leader reins in in front of Tianyuan as his men form a defensive circle around us. 'Chan, take your section out and make sure there aren't any more of them lurking in the forest. Remember your orders, no prisoners.' With that, a man barks some orders and a wing of cavalry peels away from the others, breaking into two patrols as they ride off into the forest.

'Xi, attend to our wounded, Wen, make sure there are no enemy survivors.' Riders dash here and there obeying the commands. Then the cavalry officer turns to us, 'Do I have the honour of addressing Grandfather Teacher Tianyuan?'

Tianyuan walks forward a step and stops, 'You do, and who do I have to thank for the timely rescue?'

The cavalry officer leaps down nimbly from his horse and carries out the traditional salute, right fist punched into open palm which then enfolds the fist while making a slight bow. 'My name is Captain Sun Qi of the God of War, General Qi Jiguang's forces, commanded to rid our land of the pirate scourge. We have been sent by the God of War to find you and deliver a message.' With that, Sun Qi reaches into his robe and pulls out a bronze cylinder, kneels down on one knee in front of Tianyuan, and presents it in both hands briskly, arms extended, while facing the ground.

Grandfather Teacher takes the bronze cylinder and extracts a roll of paper tied by a ribbon and sealed with a dab of red wax. After examining the wax seal, Tianyuan breaks it and unties the ribbon unrolling the scroll. Typically, there's no emotion as he studies the message. 'How did you find us?'

'We rode into your village where they told us you'd headed off in this direction for a picnic. Our scouts spotted some of the pirates sneaking through the woods seemingly setting up an ambush. I decided to ambush the ambushers, our duty is two-fold, to find you, but primarily to eradicate our homeland of these bandits.'

'Once again, thank you, Captain Sun Qi, we would be dead by now if it weren't for you and your men.'

'I am very happy to be of service, Grandfather Teacher. May I ask for a response to my commander's invitation?'

'It's quite a request, I hope you won't mind me deliberating over it for a short time with my family. I will have an answer for you by tonight.' Captain Sun Qi just nods his assent then looks at the dead pirate leader at his feet, and then at me.

'A good move, young man, maybe you can accompany Grandfather Teacher if he accepts the mission,' I nod but don't understand what's happening.

The sky seems to swim, I feel really weak. I can feel that cold wetness on my back again. I feel the area with my fingers, it is wet and feels swollen and hard. When I look at my hand it is red with blood, 'I think I need some cobwebs,' then everything goes black.

Chapter 9

'There seems to be trouble in the ranks of the Hitler Youth,' I say looking over towards Emma who strides ahead of Mike her face set, her thin lips barely visible. We dump our bags at the end of the corridor outside our class and lean against the wall.

'How did it go last night?' Claire asks quietly.

I let out a long sigh, 'No luck. I'm not sure I'll be able to recognise Danny – he could be anywhere!' I don't tell her that I think I was wounded in a fight with the pirates, I don't want to stress her out. My host must be alive, otherwise, I would have died as well. I'll find out how badly I was injured tonight.

'But don't the wormholes send you to the same sort of region?'

'Yeah, I think so, but can't be certain.'

'I've thought of a way to help us identify each other when we are on our travels – that is when I manage to do it. I'm not sure I'm even lucid in my dreams yet… Anyway, we use a badge or pin like the beautiful butterfly brooches that Amelie the nurse wears – but not so expensive. What do you think of a dragonfly pendant? We could use a code word as well to be doubly sure,' Claire says looking at me for acknowledgement that it's a good idea.

'Sounds good,' I say but am distracted by a nagging feeling that I've been searching in the wrong place. 'Claire, it's been weeks now, and no sign of Danny. If he were in any of the villages, towns, or monasteries, he would have seen one of Tianyuan's notices asking him to report to him. I'm not sure he's even in China.'

She looks troubled, 'Maybe we should have another look in your room?'

'Yeah, I think we need to – I've got rugby training tonight, so how about tomorrow night?' She nods.

'It's weird, I just can't picture you as a monk,' she says shaking her head as she studies me. Just then our form teacher Mr Morgan turns up.

'Good morning, Lewis, Claire,' we both return the greeting. 'Lewis, this must be a difficult time for you, remember what I said, if you need any help, please do ask,' I nod thanks. 'Emma,' Mr Morgan looks beyond the corner of the corridor where we're stood. I peek around the corner and see Emma – she couldn't look more guilty; has she been eavesdropping? 'Make sure you and your brother aren't late again.'

Emma holds her school bag to her chest and scuttles away saying, 'Yes, Mr Morgan.' The teacher wanders off to the staff room, while Claire and I just look at each other.

'Was she listening to us?' Claire asks.

'I'm not sure. But I suppose even if she was, she wouldn't understand what we were talking about, so what can she do?' Claire shrugs and then we decide to go into the classroom early.

* * * * *

Emma grabs the strap on Mike's backpack pulling him away from a couple of his friends. 'Oh, so you're talking to me now, are you?' He says accusingly.

'Well, it's your fault, I told you I wanted us to travel together to the same place – why didn't you just choose the German window when you were in the gateway?'

'I've told you – I made a mistake – I couldn't work out which one it was.'

Emma looks exasperated, but her face clears as she considers what she's just heard Lewis and Claire talking about. 'You despise Lewis, right?'

'Yeah,' Mike's face darkens. 'I don't see what Claire sees in him.' Mike briefly looks very vulnerable. Emma studies her brother briefly, his demeanour confirms to her how deep his feelings for Claire are.

'Well, what if we managed to get rid of Lewis while he's travelling in his dreams?'

Mike's ears prick up, 'How?'

'He's been going to China, looking for Danny. We've got to go through the Chinese gateway and find a monk wearing a dragonfly pendant - that'll be Lewis.'

'But I thought Danny was in Carthage.'

'Yes, but we're the only ones who know that since we chucked Danny's diary in the bin. Anyway, Lewis thinks Danny is in China for whatever reason. So all we have to do is go there – together,' Emma looks at her brother sternly, 'kill Lewis, and then there's no way anyone can link us to the murder – just like the others.' Mike's expression brightens. 'No Lewis, therefore, no Danny, and poor old Claire will be all alone, and might need someone to comfort her,' she pauses to see if her brother has worked out who that person might be. 'But we have to do it together, right?'

Mike nods and smiles, 'Excellent.' They turn and walk back to their classroom for registration – an extra spring in their steps.

* * * * *

They all walk from the harbour up the gangplank and onto the deck of the ship they've been scrutinizing. A shout of, 'Captain on deck!' brings the hustle and bustle aboard to a sudden halt. Captain Gisgo takes a moment to survey the scene, checking the deck is clear, the rigging in order, sails furled correctly, and cargo being stowed securely before bellowing, 'Carry on!' which causes everyone to spring back into action. The sailors seem to be swarming in a haphazard manner all over the deck and up the rigging or tossing bundles along lines of men just missing others darting to and fro.

A snapping sound above draws Danny's attention – colourful pennants which adorn the top of the two masts are being whipped in the wind. Lanyards slap against the ship's masts, and the rigging creaks and groans as the ropes take the strain and release it providing a kind of music which Danny finds surprisingly comforting.

The sound of bare feet running on the deck shifts Danny's attention to the sailors. They are a motley crew, mostly a dark brown colour with a few that must have come from other parts of Africa – huge black men with bald heads. All are tattooed, barefoot, and wearing loose cotton pastel-coloured blouses tied with pieces of cloth at the waist which hang down over baggy long shorts. 'We'll sail on the next tide,' Captain Gisgo breaks Danny's examination of his new surroundings. He turns to his boatswain, 'Salicar, make sure those merchants haven't cheated us,' he hands over a parchment, then looks at Danny, 'Get the boy to help you.'

'Yes, sir,' Salicar nods then scans the manifest quickly looking at the two columns - inventory and quantity. 'Okay,' then looks down at the new ship's boy, 'what did you say your name was?'

'Danny, sir.'

Salicar crouches down so that he can show Danny the manifest. 'Look at these markings, I need you to count all the sacks with those shapes on them.'

'You mean the ones marked "barley?"' Danny asks reading the line of the parchment the boatswain is pointing at. Salicar and Captain Gisgo's heads whip around to look more closely at Danny, eyes narrowing.

'You can read?' Salicar asks.

'Yes, sir,' Danny responds and sees the expression of doubt on their faces and so reads various items on the manifest, 'barrels of water, sacks of oats, amphorae of wine, pots of dates-'

'Hahaha! Captain, you certainly got value for money – the ship's boy can read – excellent,' Salicar is clearly overjoyed – his tedious task of checking the manifest has just become a lot easier. The Captain actually smiles when he looks down at Danny. Whether it's because he's impressed with Danny's skills or just the fact that he got a better deal than he'd realized at the slave market is hard to discern.

'Can you count as well?' the boatswain asks.

Danny frowns as he studies the horizontal and vertical

lines in the column marked total. 'What do the lines mean?'

'Each horizontal line equals one, and each vertical line equals 10 of something,' Salicar responds. The boatswain looks down with bated breath, daring to hope that this slave can count as well as read.

Danny looks at the column for amphorae of wine and sees three vertical lines and eight horizontal lines, 'Um, that means there should be thirty-eight jars of wine,' he looks up hoping he's got it right, eager to please Salicar and the Captain.

Salicar checks the manifest and beams, 'That's right, Danny, well done.' He then turns with a proud expression on his face which Captain Gisgo receives with a smile and then claps the boatswain on his back.

'This is good news indeed – and a good omen for our voyage, carry on.' The Captain turns and heads to his cabin, but stops midstride, 'But remember that he needs to help Karalis on the oar deck, the oarsmen will need watering after they row us out of the harbour.' Danny's spirits plummet as he glances fearfully at the sweaty drum master who is berating two sailors, cuffing their heads.

The morning flies by as Danny checks the cargo roped to the deck's side rail or stowed in the front and back compartments below deck which the sailors call the fore and aft holds. Once the manifest is found to be in order, Captain Gisgo orders the ship to set sail at steerage speed, which actually didn't involve the sails, but the oarsmen, who row out at a slow drum beat of two knots per hour. Danny is then ordered down to the oar deck along with four other sailors to water the slaves powering the ship. The hatchway is just in front of the captain who steers the rudder, his eyes fixed on the waterways ahead barking commands to the crew and the drum master. Danny follows the sailors down the ladder into the oppressive atmosphere of the deck below; there's an awful smell in the sweaty environment below decks which is only lit by shafts of light pouring through the hatchway and grills which run along the whole length of the ship's main deck. Slaves had to be kept healthy, so the shipbuilders had been instructed to allow as much ventilation and light to reach the oarsmen as possible, but it still didn't stop it from being a living hell for those chained to the oar deck.

There are three tiers of benches: on the bottom tier, one man manoeuvres his oar to the rhythm beat out by the drum master. Behind him and on a bench slightly higher two men work a bigger oar. And behind them and a little higher again are two more men doing the same. Danny calculates that there were 90 oars on each side and so 300 hundred men concentrating on raising and pulling the oars in an oval-shaped movement. Danny is frozen in awe at the sight of 300 heavily muscled men lathered in sweat pulling the oars in time to the drumbeat, but then a fear of Karalis takes his mind off the oarsmen. He stands there holding his bucket along with the other sailors waiting for the order to water the slaves.

Danny hears Captain Gisgo order the sails to be unfurled which means the oarsmen can ship their oars. Karalis barks at him to ladle water to each man in his section which is in the aft of the ship where Karalis sits next to his drum. He quickly runs from slave to slave ladling out water to each man not daring to catch their eye. Danny finishes his section and then turns to the ladder which leads to the main deck. He steps back in horror as shafts of light illuminate the biggest man he has ever seen chained to the deck on the opposite side of the ladder to where Karalis sits. The huge man seems very ill – sweating profusely and delirious. He lies flat, manacles and leg irons fixing him to the deck for all to see – as if on public display. Danny can see that the leg iron on one ankle has caused an infection where the swelling caused by the puss seems ready to burst. Danny approaches slowly, raises the man's huge head with difficulty but manages to pour some water slowly into the man's mouth.

Pain shoots through the back of his head as his body is flung to the floor. Stars swim in front of his eyes as he tries dizzily to rise to a crouch, he looks up to see a furious Karalis looming over him. 'Not him, he doesn't get any food or water. If you don't row, then you don't get fed.' The drum master then faces the 300 slaves who glower back at him silently. 'Let this man, Titus, be a lesson to you all. It doesn't matter how big you are, if you cross me, you die.' He stares down at the banks of oarsmen with contempt before ordering Danny and the other water carriers back up to the main deck.

After three days at sea with a favourable southerly wind allowing the ship to sail north Danny starts to have time to actually think while he goes about his duties. He helps Salicar monitor the supplies, helps the ship's cook with the meals which usually involves stirring the contents of a big cauldron in a bricked-up area on the aft deck, and waters the slaves. The whole time, he can't get the image out of his mind of the giant on the oar deck slowly dying of infection. Danny stirs the stew and decides he has to do something. When no one is looking he soaks a clean rag in some vinegar and tucks it into his tunic. Then he ladles some stew in a scrap of cloth which had been used to seal one of the jars and is usually just thrown overboard.

Danny quickly scans the deck and when he is sure the coast is clear he clambers down the ladder to the oar deck. He can feel the 300 rowers, chained to their benches through their leg irons, all quietly watching him, shafts of light from the grills forming patterns on their sweaty muscular bodies. He gulps before turning to look at the man Karalis had called Titus, who lies there muttering in his delirium.

He checks up the hatchway to the main deck to make sure no one is watching and creeps towards Titus. He kneels down and studies the infection on Titus's left ankle. Gently, he lifts the leg iron away from the wound and then carefully squeezes the puss which explodes and causes Danny to reel back in horror. He feels a bit sick but squeezes again hoping to see bright blood replace the puss and clear fluid dribbling out of the wound. He frowns as he sees something in there. He leans in to take a closer look and sees that a shard of metal from the leg iron has broken off and buried itself into Titus's ankle. Danny looks at Titus, before carefully extracting the metal splinter which causes bright red blood to pour out of the cut. He pulls out the vinegar-soaked cloth from his tunic and cleans the wound then wraps the ankle in a cloth he'd sterilised in hot water and then dried in the sun.

After tying the bandage off, hiding it discreetly under

the leg iron so nobody will see what he has done, he feeds Titus the stew he wrapped in the cloth and then gives Titus as much water as he dares. Danny collects the splinter and the cloths, stows them in his tunic, and creeps up the ladder not daring to look down the deck at the 300 men who have been watching the scene in silence.

A few days later, Danny is startled when Titus's eyes open and look straight into his. Titus studies Danny for a moment and then says, 'Thank you,' in Latin. Danny's spirits soar, but he jumps out of his skin when he hears someone roar behind him - a blow to the back of his head drives him headfirst into the deck.

'What are you doing? I ordered you not to help this man.' Karalis stands threateningly over Danny freeing his whip from his belt. The whip cracks in the air as he flicks his wrist with an evil gleam in his eyes. 'I'll teach you,' and raises his hand back as Danny cowers in the corner with nowhere to run.

'Stop!' he hears someone shout. Captain Gisgo and Salicar have clambered down the ladder and are surveying the scene. 'What's going on?' the Captain demands.

'The ship's boy has been feeding this slave against my orders, so he must be punished.' Captain Gisgo looks at Karalis, then at Titus and Danny, and then back at his drum master.

'Has your sick mind clouded your judgment? These slaves power our ship – we need them, especially in battle to ram our enemies – which they can't do if they are delirious with disease and hunger!' Captain Gisgo looks ready to murder Karalis but takes a deep breath. 'Salicar, I need you as boatswain to keep an eye on our cargo and supplies and that includes these slaves. If you see them poorly treated, then report to me.' Salicar nods as the Captain turns back to Karalis and gets into his face, 'No more warnings,' Karalis looks away. 'You,' the Captain says looking at Danny, 'finish watering the oarsmen and then report to Salicar,' he then turns and goes up to the main deck followed by Salicar. Karalis eyes Danny with a hate that almost makes his eyes glint in the dim light of the oar deck, before he too turns and climbs up the ladder.

Danny grabs a bucket and goes from man to man ladling out water. He can feel the sting from Karalis's slap on the back of his head and a bruise emerging on his chin where he hit the deck. Older bruises on his body remind him not to look at anyone directly or speak unless spoken to. Danny feels alone and close to utter despair as he makes his way down the gangway.

'Why does this boy help us?' he hears a man ask in Latin – a language Danny learnt on his many trips to Rome. The memories of those happier times with Lewis highlight the pain and the miserableness of his current situation causing tears to well up in his eyes as he goes about his duty.

'The boy has a good heart. He's saved Titus from death,' another man answers to murmurs of agreement from those around him. The man, who Danny has deduced is called Magnus, is their leader. At the mention of Titus, Danny looks over at the giant who is looking back at him, studying him. Danny averts his eyes and carries on with his duty. Magnus notices this, 'Boy, do you speak Latin?'

'Yes, sir,' Danny responds, risking a quick look at Magnus whose muscled body is lit up by shafts of light coming through the grill above him which adds to the aura of command he exudes.

'So you speak Latin among other skills. Where did you learn to heal?' Magnus continues.

'My father was a doctor, sir.' Thoughts of his father add to Danny's misery, and he cuffs his own eyes to clear away the tears building up.

'What's your name?' he asks.

'Danny, sir.'

'Look at me, Danny. You do realize that you could have lost a hand for stealing food to help Titus?' Danny looks up at Magnus and nods and is surprised to see, through his blurry vision due to the tears in his eyes, that the man is looking at him with respect. 'My name is Magnus, I'm the Primus Pilus, the senior centurion, of the First Legion, the most feared legion in the Roman empire. These,' he waves his arm gesturing at his fellow men, 'are what's left of the Prima cohort's 800 men – the rest died as we fought a defensive action to allow our legions to escape onto our ships.' He turns to look at all the men on the oar deck who look back silently but with pride in their eyes. 'These are the finest 300 men you'll ever have the honour to meet.' Danny can see the men seem to grow in stature at these words. 'You saved Titus, thank you,' Magnus extends an arm out which Danny looks at, he then looks up at Magnus, puts the bucket down, and goes to shake his hand. Magnus grasps Danny's forearm in the traditional Roman soldier's way. Danny instinctively clutches Marcus's huge forearm and holds it. Magnus sees that the small boy is at the end of his tether and draws him in, hugging him gently. This act of compassion causes Danny to finally break down, he sobs uncontrollably in the Centurion's arms – Magnus offers words of comfort as he gently holds the boy.

'Brothers!' All the oarsmen face their leader. 'I propose welcoming a true fighter to our brotherhood. He has risked his life to save one of our own, knowing the danger he has put himself in. Who will second me in nominating Danny as a new member to our ranks.' There's a roar as all the oarsmen second Magnus's nomination.

Danny looks around bewildered, unsure of the moment's implications. 'Danny,' Magnus looks at him man to man, 'You are now part of the 1st century of the First Legion, Rome's most revered soldiers. Welcome brother!' To cheers from all around, Magnus once again clutches Danny's forearm generating a surge of energy that tingles through his body.

The noise of someone scrambling down the ladder draws everyone's attention. There's a tense silence as Salicar, worried by the commotion below and aware that Danny was on the oar deck, raced down the ladder followed by a few armed sailors. The group freeze on the gangway as they survey the strange spectacle. 'Danny,' Salicar finds his voice, 'You're needed on deck.'

After a gentle squeeze from Marcus, Danny releases his grip on Magnus's forearm, turns, and walks down the central gangway between the banks of oars. As he passes the oarsmen, he hears a constant stream of 'Welcome brother', some reach out and ruffle his hair or tap him gently on the back. At the ladder leading to the main deck the giant, Titus, extends a shovel-sized hand and manages to give Danny's shoulder a gentle squeeze, and a nod.

Chapter 10

'Report,' the voice orders. Once again, the phone has been picked up by the second ring.

'The boy has been unconscious for three weeks now. No muscle atrophy, in fact, he may have put on muscle; there have been frequent periods of high heart rate and blood pressure which may indicate physical activity.'

'Okay, we've waited long enough. Today's Tuesday, let me think – yeah, we'll do the extraction on the weekend, fewer hospital staff to ask questions and plenty of visitors to hide among – instructions will follow. Make sure you are on duty.'

'Yes, sir,' the agent responds but 'the Boss' has already rung off. Looking at the family in the ward's corridor outside Danny's room the agent crushes any feelings of regret or guilt. Failing to serve the Syndicate in any way was not an option.

* * * * *

Danny wakes up and takes a moment to work out where he is, then realizes that he's lying on sacks of grain in the store area of the hold below the foredeck. He moves slightly which causes the grain in the coarse sacking to shift to accommodate his form. Looking up, he sees light streaming through the gaps in the planking above his head. He feels surprisingly good: they've completed their two-week patrol along the African coast and are now moored back in Carthage's military harbour. He's gotten used to his duties, but still feels a little embarrassed by the friendliness of the legionaries on the oar deck – his new 'brothers in arms'; the thought brings a smile to his face. On top of that, he's managed to find a place to sleep – hidden away from some of the strange members of the crew and their leery looks. Every evening he checks nobody is watching before he sneaks down here and snuggles up with the cat on the hessian sacks and is usually asleep within a heartbeat out of sheer exhaustion. He doesn't particularly like cats, but this cat kept the rats away during his sleep and seems to like snuggling up to Danny, so it's become a temporary partnership between animal and boy in a hostile environment.

Things really do appear to be improving, Danny reflects. He smiles at the response he got the other day from a play on words his Dad had used on a family holiday on the coast. Danny had been looking over the front of the ship, the bow, and was mesmerised by the dolphins racing alongside – it was an amazing sight. He became aware of Salicar standing beside him and immediately started to rush off and find a job to do before he got scolded. However, Salicar told him to relax, they were on their way home and so the mood of the ship was upbeat at the prospect of returning to their families or the bars in Carthage. Salicar followed Danny's gaze, 'Beautiful, aren't they?'

'Yes,' Danny nodded, returning to the guard rail, watching the dolphins racing each other. 'Aren't they afraid we'll catch them?'

Salicar laughed, 'Don't worry about that. Firstly, nobody is skilled enough to hook one of them – they are too clever, and secondly, it would be considered bad luck to do so.'

This added to Danny's enjoyment of the scene. The dolphins made a trilling sound, 'It sounds like they are laughing at us.'

'Aye, they probably are – taunting us for our lack of speed.'

'So are they doing it on porpoise?' Danny looked up shyly at Salicar to see if he had caught the pun. Salicar paused, then quickly examined Danny's mischievous expression, and barked out a laugh momentarily causing the crew to pause in their work.

'You're a clever one, "on Porpoise", I'll have to tell the Captain that one.' He continued to chuckle for a while. There was a companionable silence as they watched the dolphins swim off into the sunset.

Danny smiles at the memory and shifts a little on his makeshift bed of grain sacks. The sound of hammering on deck interrupts his thoughts, nails are being driven into wood causing a staccato effect. Danny stretches his arms and legs in all sorts of directions, a morning routine that he thinks the cat has copied – or maybe he's copied the cat. Captain Gisgo barks an order which is immediately followed by the sound of running feet slapping on the deck. This seems to be the cat's cue to start its daily rat-catching duties. It springs up and starts moving silently among the sacks and other supplies, occasionally stopping and hunching up while peering into all the dark recesses. Danny realises that he'd better show his face, or he'll get a slap or the whip of someone's belt. He peers carefully through the hatchway up to the main deck, and when nobody seems to be looking his way, scampers up and tries to blend in among all the activity.

'Where have you been?' he hears the Captain and turns to see him red in the face with anger. The moment's feeling of well-being a minute ago evaporates instantly. 'Go and help Salicar,' with that the Captain cuffs Danny on the head propelling the boy towards the boatswain who has another manifest in his hands and is standing by piles of cargo.

Salicar looks at Danny and glances at the Captain. 'Don't get on the wrong side of him today – he's in a foul mood. We've had new orders,' he points toward all the hammering in the aft section of the main deck where sailors are building two temporary cabins. 'As we are the most experienced crew, we've been given the privilege of escorting the new governor of Palermo to Sicily. We'll be the flagship of a fleet taking him, his family, and a load of his entourage to their new posts on the island. The Captain's livid – having to erect two cabins to accommodate the governor and his two daughters messes with the Captain's feel for the ship – it throws the trim out and can affect its manoeuvrability. On top of that, as a governor, his social rank means Captain Gisgo is theoretically no longer in charge of the ship.' Danny peers across at the Captain who is scolding two sailors who have apparently not secured some of the stores correctly. 'Anyway, Danny, help me check this manifest – we sail on the afternoon tide.'

At midday the crew parade on deck in their new white uniforms; the sailors' usual motley array of clothing has been stowed away – the crew of a flagship need to look the part. The men line up in ranks for the governor's inspection. Danny stands to attention looking ahead at an imaginary point on the horizon. The Governor looks him up and down and moves on to the next sailor. Another person's silhouette indicates someone else is inspecting him. Curiosity gets the better of Danny and he risks a look at the person and almost takes a step back. The sister who caused all his misery stands there looking down at him with a frown which turns to a smile when she notices all the bruises and cuts all over his body. Jezebel moves on and then another surprise in the form of Dido stands in front of him. Both their eyes widen in shock - there's an awkward moment before a look of concern etches itself on Dido's face, 'Are you okay?'

Danny takes a moment to find his voice, 'Yes, thank you, ma'am,' He looks at the lovely Dido who looks back at him warmly.

'Call me Dido. I'm so sorry my sister caused you so much pain. Listen, I'll try and arrange it so that you are given the duty of looking after me so we can have a chance to talk.' Dido pauses, 'As long as that is okay with you?'

'Yes, ma'am, I mean,' he whispers, 'Dido,' and smiles back at the lovely girl before him. After the crew are dismissed, everyone prepares to cast off - Danny can't stop smiling.

The voyage to Sicilian waters has taken ten days due to the lumbering cargo ships the fleet is escorting. Danny has enjoyed every moment – the Governor was more than happy to have someone entertain his youngest daughter and so keep her out of his hair. They have become firm friends –

better than he'd fantasised about, but maybe with more cuts and bruises than he'd imagined.

Danny was able to tell Dido stories which had never been heard in that time and place. Even though some were slightly childish, they were new and so he noticed that even some of the sailors would find tasks to do near to where the two children were sat. Danny kept his audience spellbound with his retelling of any kind of story, from fairy tales to film storylines – from Snow White and the Seven Dwarfs to the plot for Star Wars. He smiles to himself when he recalls the sailors repeating the stories, often all mixed up, to groups of eager listeners in the evenings. One night the crew got quite animated debating who would win in a fight between Darth Vader and Prince Charming – some thought Darth Vader would win as he had a lightning sword, but others felt Prince Charming must be the greatest warrior as he had won the heart of a princess and was clever enough to beat the witch's magic. The counterargument was that Darth Vader must also have magical powers to be able to sail ships to the stars. The argument got quite heated until Captain Gisgo shouted at them to shut up. Danny can't wait to tell Lewis about that, he's sure his brother will find it hilarious. He has to stop himself from thinking about Lewis and his mother and whether or not he will ever see them again; he doesn't want Dido see him cry.

Fortunately, Jezebel seems to hate her sister as much as she hates Danny, so they've been spared her company. She really is a 'nasty piece of work' as his Dad would say; again Danny stops thinking of his Dad – it's too upsetting.

He can see Dido and her sister standing with their father at the bow's guard rail, listening to the Captain. 'It's too dangerous for a fleet to enter that fog bank, we'll have to go around it which may add a day to our voyage.'

'Why?' Jezebel asks, she has hated every minute of the voyage and is desperate to get ashore.

'In some fog banks you can't see your hand in front of your face, let alone the other ships or rocks,' the Captain answers patiently.

Their discussion is suddenly cut short as the prows of three ships burst out of the fog wall on a direct course for their convoy. The Captain shouts, 'Identify!' up at the sailor in the crow's nest.

'Roman,' comes the reply.

'Battle stations!' roars the Captain and at once the ship bursts into life with the 180 oars suddenly shooting out and sweeping into the sea leaving trails of water which catch the sunlight. The beauty of that spectacle is at odds with the preparations for battle: sailors distributing swords and small round shields; archers standing at the bottom of the rigging ready to clamber up and pour death onto the enemy; shields held at the bow to defend against enemy missiles; and the governor's daughters retreating to their cabins in the rear with their guards forming a defensive wall - the drum beat seems to mimic the quickening heartbeat of all on board. Danny thinks he can hear the sound of horns. They aren't coming from their fleet – is he imagining the sound? He looks at the Roman ships – he's learnt that the wind whipped away noise at sea – are they signalling someone? The Carthaginians have the benefit of the wind behind their sails and now the oars bite into the water causing the ships to leap forward – Danny instinctively grips some rigging as the surge forward forms a bow wave that almost reaches the main deck.

The Captain smiles in delight as he surveys the convoy's fighting ships manoeuvring themselves to ram the three smaller Roman ships, 'Watch and learn, sir, you're about to see how superior our sailing skills are to the Romans' – the reason why we dominate these waters.'

'What are those plank-like things in the centre of their decks?' The governor asks. A grim look steals away the Captain's hubris, 'They're called the corvi – wide ramps the Romans use to board our ships. They have a beak-like structure at the end which hooks into an enemy's deck allowing the Romans to board in their formations. But we are the better seamen - have no fear, they can't use those ramps if we ram them midships.' The Romans seem to be desperately trying to turn in the wind, but it leaves the length of their ships exposed to the rapidly approaching Carthaginian rams. 'Ramming speed!' the Captain bellows as the drumming increases to 80 beats per minute, Danny grips the rigging even more tightly as the distance between the ships is quickly eaten up, 'Brace for contact!' barks the Captain. A second later, bodies fly to the deck as their ship skewers their prey midships. In an instant, the armed Carthaginian sailors pour onto the enemy's main deck, joined by the crew of another ship which has rammed it from a different angle. Their sense of elation is obvious – relishing an easy victory over their hated enemy.

Then there are shouts of alarm as the bronze rams of more ships punch holes in the fog bank to rapidly reveal a fleet of Roman quinqueremes. The Captain shrieks orders to disengage from the floundering Roman ship, whose crew have been joined by the oarsmen. Romans powered their ships using freedmen, not slaves. These loincloth-clad men appear from a hatchway pouring on deck to join the Roman Marines in trying to repel the Carthaginian boarders in a fight for their lives. Their ship's timbers and rigging groan in her final death throws, but she seems reluctant to give up the fight; the Carthaginians can't disengage their ships' rams from her punctured hull as the Roman fleet draws closer at incredible speed.

* * * * *

I seem to be experiencing déjà vu. I'm lying in the same hut I woke up in a few weeks ago with Han looking down at me, a look of concern on her face.

'Lu-wis, it's good to see you back with us,' she smiles. 'How do you feel?'

It's a good question. I feel exhausted and there's something tight wrapped around my waist up to my chest. There's an itchy feeling in my back on my right side, when I move it feels like there's a tightness in the affected area which could rip or tear if I move. 'I feel fine thanks, Han, how are you?'

'You are not a good liar, Lu-wis, but I am fine, thank

you for asking.'

'What happened?'

'One of the pirates must have caught you in the back during the fight. Don't worry, I've made sure there's no foreign matter in the wound and cleaned it with hot water and herbs. You need to rest. The wound will knit together nicely after Grandfather Teacher's excellent needlework.'

'Thanks, Han.'

'Who taught you about the use of cobwebs for stemming the flow of blood?'

'My father taught me. He's descended from a famous family of physicians in his country.'

'Very impressive, I would like to meet your father one day,' Han smiles at me, and I feel there's a deeper meaning to those words.

For some reason, I feel tears pricking my eyes. I don't know if it's relief at seeing Han is okay, hearing that I'm not dead, the impact of the wound, thoughts of my missing Dad, or trying to come to terms with the fact that I've killed a man, more than one, a thought that adds nausea to the mix. My mind is flooded with these different thoughts which makes me feel suddenly emotional. I'm not going to cry in front of Han.

'You've been through a lot, Lu-wis,' she gives my arm a gentle squeeze and looks at me with those enchanting eyes, 'You must rest, my dear.' Those words make my heart lurch, she touches my cheek gently, then stands up and walks out of the hut giving a quick backward glance – déjà vu.

Chapter 11

When I wake up, I realize that I've not moved at all – I've had the sleep of the not-quite-dead. There's a lot of noise going on outside – horses whinnying, men shouting orders, numerous conversations, and the occasional bark of laughter. I guess the cavalry have swamped every free space in the village. I raise myself on my elbows and look towards the door which opens and then Han appears and approaches with a bowl of broth.

'Hey Lu-wis, you look much better. Here, have some of this.' With that, she starts spooning soup into my mouth. It's the best soup I've ever tasted, I haven't got a clue what it is, but who cares.

'What's happening? it sounds like there's an army on the move outside.'

'Grandfather has accepted the God of War's summons.' I obviously don't understand what Han is talking about, so she explains, 'He has asked Grandfather to train an army of civilians in martial arts in preparation for a big battle.'

I take a moment to digest this information. Last night, back in London I wasn't sure what to do – if Danny might not be in China, was there any point in coming back here? I look at Han and realize why I did. 'Are you going?'

Han stops serving me soup and looks at the hut's floor, a look of frustration on her face. 'No, I am not invited. Even though I can beat any one of them in kung fu, my place is here apparently.'

This is a dilemma. Deep down I know that if Claire and I find out tomorrow night in London that Danny is in a different time and place, then this might be the last opportunity I have to spend time with Han. But say Claire and I work out that Danny is actually here in China, then since he hasn't responded to any of the notices in the local villages and towns, he must be in a nearby region. Grandfather Teacher and the cavalry commander are heading to a place where the local citizens are converging in order to learn kung fu and beat the pirates – if Danny is here that's where he'll be heading, I reckon... maybe. So if I go with them, find Danny, and beat the pirates, I can come back here and hang out with Han as much as I like.

Han seems to read my thoughts, 'You don't have to join them, you are wounded, you should stay here and recuperate.'

The door opens and Tianyuan walks in. He sits nimbly beside me and Han, studies the colour of my eyes, then opens my mouth, examines my tongue and smells my breath, and sniffs around my bandaged torso. He then takes my pulse with the fingers of one hand and gauges my temperature with the other. 'It's good to see you looking better, your strength is flooding back, your Chi almost restored.' I remember he taught me how to maintain my Chi - eat healthily, exercise, have positive thoughts, meditate, sleep, and so on. But also, that the opposite of those good practices depletes your life energy – poor diet, idleness, negative thoughts, toxic company, insomnia, and illness or injury.

'Has Han informed you of what is happening?'

'Yes,' Tianyuan's presence has helped me make my decision, 'When do we leave, Grandfather Teacher?' The reaction of my two carers couldn't be more different, Tianyuan smiles, proud of my eagerness, but Han's face drops.

'Excuse me, Grandfather, I must attend to some things,' with that Han stands and strides out of the hut. Tianyuan follows her movement and takes a moment or two to contemplate something. He then studies me, there's a look of concern on that walnut face.

'Hmm.' I wait for Tianyuan to expand, but the silence continues. 'How do you feel about the fight we had in the meadow?' I've learnt that when Grandfather Teacher asks me a question, my expression tells him as much as the words I use, so I adopt a poker face and contemplate my response.

'To be honest, Grandfather Teacher, I have mixed feelings. I am happy that we survived and that we fought well and would have kept on fighting honourably to the end. But...,' I shake my head slightly.

'Take a moment to consider your thoughts.'

A conversation with my dad comes to mind. He loved quotes. I remember one which he used to say all the time, especially when I would ask him why he needed to go on those humanitarian missions. 'My father used to quote a famous man from my homeland, John Donne, "Any man's death diminishes me, for I am involved in mankind". My father used to repeat this often so that it's etched on my mind, he saved lives, but I killed at least one man in that battle. I feel confused - virtuous, guilty, strong, sick, elated, ashamed.'

Tianyuan looks sad as he contemplates my thoughts. 'Those are wise words. Life is precious, and battle is terrible. It is important to consider the consequences of your actions. We can't always be sure that we are fighting for the right side, but in this case, there is no doubt. Don't think of the pirates you killed, but of the lives you've saved by ridding the world of those savages.'

My course of action is clear. Not only will I keep searching for Danny, but I will also do what is needed to help Tianyuan and the people of this village who have taken me in and treated me as one of their own, without any questions or desire for reward. 'As I say, when do we leave?'

After two weeks in the saddle, my bum feels normal again and I'm starting to feel a little more upbeat; Han had been hard to gauge when we said our farewells, quiet and distracted. I despair at the thought that I might never see her again, so I try not to think about it – I'm surprised by how much it has affected me.

Initially, I had bruises all over my nether regions from riding. and when I dismounted, I could barely walk, a sight which caused great amusement among the cavalrymen. But now I seem to have developed a toughness, stamina, and new muscles so that I relish the prospect of getting in the saddle and the journey ahead. China is a beautiful and diverse country. We've travelled in a south-easterly direction through plains and mountains, urban and rural areas, crossing rivers, through never-ending forests, followed paths or made our own when necessary.

The local people who see the dust kicked up by our column of horses usually flee at first. You can feel their eyes on you as you ride. If they recognise the banners of the Imperial Guard, they'll emerge from their hiding places and do whatever they can with their meagre resources to accommodate us. After a day in the saddle the simplest bowl of rice with tofu, or whatever, tastes wonderful.

My comrades in arms are a cheerful good-natured group who have welcomed me into their brotherhood. It is probably helped by the fact that in their eyes I'm a student of Grandfather Teacher whose reputation demands respect. They saw what we had achieved against overwhelming numbers in the meadow, even if we wouldn't have lasted much longer, we had done the seemingly impossible. Every morning and evening we practice martial arts, an order from Tianyuan which nobody questions however tired. Grandfather Teacher uses me as his assistant instructor which helps me enormously; I've found that when I try to teach a move, my own skills improve. Also, I've developed a deeper understanding of how different movements work well together or could be defended against and then the actions required to launch a counterattack. In return, the cavalrymen have taught me a range of soldiering skills such as scouting, field craft, and tips on how to ride a horse leisurely or in an attack.

The sun has started its descent and so I'm thinking it must be almost time for lunch when we come around a hillside and halt. Below us stretching out across some fields in a bend of the meandering river is a vast camp. Canvas tents are arranged neatly in lines which form a grid square with the biggest and most elaborate tents in the centre.

A wooden palisade is being erected with guard towers every fifty meters which involves a huge amount of labour.

The wooden stakes forming the five-meter-high wall are being buried on the inside of a trench whose earth is being used to form a steep slope up to the palisade. Any attackers will have to navigate a ditch filled with sharp stakes and then climb up a steep slope to reach the wooden palisade wall which they will then have to use ladders to scale - all while being shot at by the heavily armed defenders.

All around the camp there's other activity going on: formations of troops carrying out drills, pairs of soldiers practising with a variety of weapons, and cavalry spearing or shooting arrows at targets while at the gallop. Meanwhile, blacksmiths, carpenters, cooks, and other tradesmen are busy plying their trade.

'Impressive,' Tianyuan remarks.

'Thank you, Grandfather Teacher,' Captain Sun Qi responds.

* * * * *

Wokou Pirates Rampage through Region

Communities are being warned that the brazen wokou pirates are pillaging further and further inland. Town and village elders are commanded to organise guards on a 24-hour watch system so that the local people can be forewarned of any threat. The Government assures the nation that they are preparing to eradicate this scourge from China. General Qi Jiguang, the God of War, is organizing a force that will annihilate all the bands of pirates which have been a curse on our lands. A recent raid in Nan Hai wiped out the community in a particularly savage attack where those who were not enslaved were murdered.

Anyone with any information about the movements and numbers of the pirates should inform their local government officials.

Source: Translated from a Chinese notice posted on bulletin boards throughout coastal China in 1553.

Summer is definitely on its way, so I've started wearing T-shirts again. When I brush my hair, I notice my arms are pretty muscly, the tautness in my forearm, triceps and biceps push healthy-looking veins to the surface. I've noticed a few of the boys at school checking out my physique and some girls looking at me with a strange look in their eyes – the training I'm doing with Tianyuan is really paying off.

Claire and I head over to the Chinese takeaway near my house – it's Friday night and Mum is on night duty, so she's given us some money for a weekend treat. I have a craving for something spicy like Szechuan chicken or some kung pao beef. While we're waiting to be served, I can hear the staff nattering away in Chinese. It's our turn to order, so I ask Claire what she fancies and then order the food... in Chinese. The guy's jaw drops, and I see a couple of the girls rushing around behind the counter stop in their tracks. Then they break into a babble of Chinese firing questions at me which I answer and then realize that the whole waiting room has gone completely still, everyone including Claire is looking at me with a mix of consternation and wonder; I'm feeling pretty good about myself. Claire leans in and whispers, 'Well done on keeping a low profile – I mean, you're fluent in Chinese without ever taking a Chinese lesson – that wouldn't look odd to anyone looking for someone with your particular travelling skills, eh?' I'm brought down to earth with a bump.

Claire tries to placate me after telling me off. 'How are they getting along with the pronunciation of your name?'

'I'm getting used to it. Lu means road and wis can mean route to wisdom, so my name means road to wisdom, something like that. But don't you start calling me Lu-wis or I'll ask them,' I nod at the takeaway staff, 'to add something special to your meal,' she laughs and as Tianyuan would say, harmony is restored.

Claire and I are in my bedroom sitting on the floor cross-legged with all of Danny's books spread on the carpet between us. We've been here for ages literally going through every book, cover to cover to find any clue as to where Danny is. I've resigned myself to the fact that he's not in China. But then a niggle of doubt re-emerges, maybe he is there? I really don't know.

'Sorry, this is all my fault – I deduced that Danny was in China,' Claire says looking tired and miserable.

'Hey, it's not your fault at all – don't even think that. What you said made sense. I've been thinking about it and I'm sure I remember Danny using the old word for China: Cathay – it really really rings a bell.' We sit there deflated looking at the pile of books almost accusingly – they've let us down by not revealing Danny's whereabouts. I rest my back against the side of my bed and look up at the ceiling, racking my brain for some sort of clue.

'Have we missed anything?' Claire asks giving a cursory look around the room.

'No, I don't think so.' I look randomly around. Nothing.

'What's that?'

I follow the direction of Claire's hand and see a big heavy book on the floor below Danny's bed almost hidden by the edge of his Spider-Man quilt. For whatever reason, over the last few weeks I've avoided looking at Danny's neat and tidy bed. We both scamper across the floor and peer at the book. I pull it out and see it's my dad's old Encyclopaedia of Ancient History. My heart skips a beat, 'Oh my God! Dad gave this to Danny because he seemed fascinated with it, always getting it off the shelf in the lounge and studying each page carefully – we'd all think it hilarious; he was only about five at the time.'

We study the pictures of the seven ancient wonders on the book's cover for a moment. I want to open it but I'm afraid it will just be another false hope, so I just stare at it. I can feel Claire looking at me.

'Open it, Lewis. But be careful, hold it by the spine and let it fall open – I saw it in a film once, the book opened to the page where the last person looked.' I glance at Claire, nod, and then carefully hold the spine of the heavy book in the palm of my hand and let the covers fall away from each other. And there it is.

We both slowly breathe out and study the page.

There's a painted illustration of an ancient city with honey-coloured stone buildings, palm trees, and a turquoise sea in the background. In the foreground there are people wearing loose robes, ladies wearing veils and gold jewellery, and soldiers in bronze breastplates over white tunics, armed with spears and swords. Carthage. Not Cathay. I've wasted all this time searching for Danny in the wrong place. I get up and fall onto my bed, close my eyes, and try not to think about the huge mistake I've made. The possibly vital time I may have lost. What a fool.

'Are you okay?'

I look up at Claire who is standing looking down at me, her face radiating concern. 'What have I done? It might be too late.'

'You don't know that, Lewis,' she says passionately, 'but we do know that Danny is still alive because he's there in hospital. And now we know where he is, so tonight, you can go there and find him.'

She's right. I get up and look at the book again – I need to memorise the images so I can recognise Carthage in one of the windows at the gateway. The people have skin the colour of my wooden bookcase, wear robes and some have cloth wrapped around their heads in a sort of turban. Although the city appears to be located where the desert meets the sea, there is some greenery. Okay, I can do this, even though I feel completely exhausted. Looking up at Claire I see she is too.

'You're right, I'll go there tonight.' Claire doesn't respond for a moment, just looks at me sitting on the side of my bed and nods.

'I have to go, it's late and I'm knackered.' She picks up her stuff and then notices all the books on the floor.

'Don't worry about that, I'll put them away.' Claire fails to hide a look of relief. I walk her down the stairs to the front door, we're both too tired to talk, and our minds are racing in all sorts of directions. 'Claire, thanks for your help.'

She shakes her head a little, 'Good luck, and be careful, Lewis.' She reaches out and grips my hand, 'Please be careful,' she repeats and looks like she wants to say something more but stops herself. We look at each other for a moment before she releases my hand, turns on her heel, and walks away without looking back.

I'm tidying up the books in my room in a sort of trance as I try to deal with a clash of loyalties. There's no doubt that Danny is my first priority, but I can't help feeling that I'm letting Tianyuan and Han down. I know my presence there won't make any difference as my host has all the same abilities as me. The host can do anything I can do. Whichever way I justify it to myself, I still feel a sense of guilt – I'm not actually there in person as it were. But maybe if I find Danny and bring him home, I can still make it to China to fight the pirates in the final battle. Yes, that's what I'll do.

I've cleaned my teeth and am lying here in bed trying to stop my mind from racing or I won't be able to sleep; I need to focus on images of Carthage. My eyelids are feeling heavy, I yawn...

I can see the images of different places through the windows of swirling blue vapour within the starlight. Something is wrong. I fight off a growing feeling of dread and start going through the images again, scrutinising each one more carefully. But it's no good, I can't see Carthage anywhere - has the gateway closed? Please God, no! I can feel myself starting to panic - hold on, what's that? I see some men dressed in similar clothing and with similar features to Carthaginians. I walk closer to the window to have a closer look and realise it isn't Carthage - the window zooms out to reveal mountains and forests, but it's too late, the wormhole is pulling me, drawing me in.

* * * * *

Danny watches one of the oncoming Roman ships break away from their fleet and steer a course directly for his ship. The Romans' oars move in an almost hypnotic synchronicity in and out of the water. Captain Gisgo is screaming down the hatchway into the oar deck to reverse oars and disengage, but their earlier prey is snagged onto their ship's ram. A crash and sense of flying through the air announces the arrival of the Roman ship. Danny winces at the rope burn on his hand where he failed to keep a grip on the rigging in the collision. He looks quickly around the deck. Images of the archers flying to their deaths from the masts merge with those of men thrown to the deck, some will never stand again.

The Roman ship has reversed oars and has skilfully come alongside. Danny hears someone shouting, 'Release' in Latin and a shower of javelins rain down on them. Most of the lethal iron-tipped spears are aimed at the stern where the officers are stood around the rudder; sailors fall to the deck impaled, including Captain Gisgo who leaves this world with a look of surprise fixed on his face. Again, another order in Latin, 'Release the corvus'. Danny hears a groaning sound and then sees a huge platform with a vicious-looking spike at the end crash down from the Roman ship onto his ship. A sailor's cry is abruptly cut short by the crushing impact of the huge gangplank which is now pinned by its 'beak' to their ship. Roman Marines immediately storm onto the Carthaginian deck and form an impenetrable shield wall; vicious short swords, the Roman gladius, glint silver in the sun as they shoot in and out from behind their shields to kill the enemy.

Danny hears the Roman centurion calling 'Advance' every few seconds whereupon the Marines use their shields to batter their way one pace forward into the Carthaginians. As Danny zooms in on the Roman leader he sees the centurion looking nervously over his shoulder. Danny follows his gaze and sees the reason for the centurion's alarm - two Carthaginian battleships are towing a cumbersome troop carrier, its deck crammed with hundreds of soldiers ready to join the fray, towards the raft of ships now surrounding Danny. In a desperate bid to save their flagship and the fleet's honour, the Carthaginian ships' shrewd captains skillfully row their ship on either side of the troop carrier in a way that will send her alongside Danny's beleaguered vessel.

However, three Roman quinqueremes have spotted the new threat and set a course to ram the advancing Carthaginians. One of the Carthaginian captains loses his nerve and cuts his tow rope only to be skewered midships. The Roman ship reverses its oars pulling out its ram and the frantic activity on the stricken ship suddenly disappears as it sinks like a stone to the seabed. The remaining battleship captain holds his nerve and manages to direct the troop carrier's bow alongside Danny's ship. There's a thud and a roar as scores of Carthaginian soldiers leap aboard. Danny looks around quickly and surveys utter chaos. The Romans are retreating towards their gangplank, but the Carthaginian soldiers on the troop carrier start to panic as they see two Roman ships bearing down on them. Screams and shouting can't shift the bottleneck of soldiers trying to disembark over their ship's bow and then another two thumping crashes in quick succession heralds the arrival of the Romans.

Although around two hundred troops have managed to join the battle there are hundreds still on board the rapidly sinking Carthaginian troop ship. Panic spreads like fire as soldiers stab and slash at each other on the ship's bow to get away; others cut off their armour and leap into the sea; some seem dumbstruck – standing there dazed watching the nightmare unfold.

Danny is mesmerised by the seascape around him. The Carthaginians didn't have time to furl their sails making their ships easy targets for the Roman fire arrows. Looking around the fleet, Danny spots at least 12 on fire whose crews abandon their ships by just leaping off – most sinking straight to the bottom as in their desperation to flee this nightmare they have forgotten to take off their armour. Others swim in all directions – some to safety others into the path of crushing ships' bows belonging to both sides. Danny's ears pick up the stretching and snapping sound of rigging along with the splintering of planking in the hull and decks. The enemy ship snagged onto their ram is putting an enormous strain on the hull of their ship – the tar which seals the planking keeping the ship watertight is being forced apart. He's heard the sailors talking about how at a critical point when a ship has taken on too much water and suffered too much damage, a boat could sink to the bottom of the sea in seconds; sucking all the crew with it in a bubbly whirlpool that even the best swimmer can't escape – nobody can swim in foam.

An image of his Roman friends on the oar deck flashes

in his mind. He knows that his ship is going to sink as soon as the ships forming this huge raft manage to disengage – he has to save his 'brothers' chained to the deck of this doomed vessel.

A quick scan reveals that the white uniforms of the Carthaginians now massively outnumber the Romans in their red tunics who are pushed towards the bow of the ship away from their gangplank which has been raised to stop the Carthaginians boarding the Roman quinquereme. Danny sidesteps around the fighting on deck where some Roman soldiers have become separated from their cohort and now fight back-to-back against the odds. He sees an opening towards the oar deck hatchway and sprints forward sliding the last few paces towards the ladder which will take him below decks.

Salicar looms over Danny holding a shield in the air to defend them both from Roman arrows and javelins. 'Boy, get to safety, hide in the hold until all this is over, quick!' Danny nods and then looks on in horror as Salicar's expression turns from concern to agonised confusion as a spearhead appears in the centre of his chest, blood spreads quickly in a perverse resemblance of a rose blooming in fast time, its stamen the spearhead. He doesn't have time to grieve for one of the few men who's shown some kindness towards him – he clambers down the ladder to the oar deck.

Karalis has been knocked unconscious by the ramming and so Danny darts forward, unties the keys from the drum master's belt, then picks up the first padlock on the starboard side. The padlock connects the long chain, which runs through links nailed into the oar deck and the leg irons on the oarsmens' ankles, to a heavy ringbolt at the foot of the ladder. He fumbles with the keys in his free hand and drops them but manages to grab them before they fall through a gap in the planks into the rising seawater in the hull below. Danny takes a breath before trying again. Trembling, he inserts the key into the padlock and twists, but nothing happens. He wiggles the key around in the lock and tries again. Nothing. He pulls that key out and tries the other one. It slides in and a clicking sound unclasps the padlock. He releases the chain which immediately rattles away as the oarsmen pull it through their leg iron links. Danny leaps up and goes to the port side where he uses the first key to do the same.

Magnus races to the front of the 300 men, looks back and bellows, 'First Legion! grab the short oars and any other weapons you find on deck!' Titus has spotted Karalis regaining consciousness and looms over him. The drum master quails at the sight. Magnus grabs Danny, 'You don't want to see this.' He takes one last look at his men and with a roar leads them up the ladder into the fray.

The freed oarsmen form ranks on deck – the first and second use the short oars and javelins which litter the deck to punch, bludgeon, and skewer the enemy from a safe distance. The ranks behind arm themselves with whichever weapons they can scavenge from the dead and wounded. Three years of rowing has maintained their physical strength, but the constant brutality and random cruelty of their captors has caused a rage to simmer away which they now vent in a viciousness that would make a veteran wince. The freed slaves form a second front catching the more numerous but less well-trained Carthaginians between a hammer and anvil – they are the hammer; and the anvil are the rock-solid lines of their saviours – the Roman marines and legionnaires. They have regrouped and created an impenetrable deadly wall of shields between which their razor-sharp gladiuses continue their grisly work. The Carthaginian forces are crushed together in the middle of the deck and so are unable to manoeuvre; some leap overboard preferring a death by drowning to being cut to shreds by the approaching terror.

Smaller battles are still being fought at the stern and bow of the ship. Danny ducks and dives trying to avoid the blades whipping out in all directions as men fight desperately for their lives. He slips on a pool of blood, gets back to a crouch, and sees Dido and her sister cowering behind their father and their loyal slave who brandish swords in the direction of a handful of Roman marines who have encircled them. Without thinking Danny shouts, 'No!' and runs full sprint towards them. As he gets nearer he shouts, 'No!' again, but this time in Latin.

The Roman soldiers pause and look around only to see a Carthaginian boy running at them. They laugh, 'Think you can handle the boy, Silus?' The one they are taunting scowls and faces Danny, while the others turn back to Dido and her family. Danny stumbles as he realises he is running straight onto the point of Silus's sword. He tries to get to his feet but is kicked backwards by the Roman who now raises his sword for the killing blow. Danny is paralysed for an instant too long. The sword comes sweeping down.

Chapter 12

I wake up on cold ground in an alleyway between wooden shacks. I've learnt to stay still and take in my surroundings before moving after arriving at a new destination, but it's dark so I'm struggling to get a sense of where I am. From one end of the alleyway, I can hear people speaking quietly, so I walk the other way but come to a steep slope marking the edge of what must be a village halfway up a hill. I have no choice but to turn around and walk towards the noise. There's a lot of activity in the centre of the village as around forty men rope bundles of goods together, their breaths forming little plumes of vapour which adds to the crisp feel of dawn. In the distance, the sky is lightening where the sun is about to reveal itself from behind some far-off snow-capped mountains.

    I assume I'm part of this party and join three guys who are helping to heave packs onto each other's backs. The men study me suspiciously before looking at each other, then shrug and seem to be relieved to be able to unload some of their burden onto the newcomer. They take off some of their own supplies and rope them to my back and then shuffle slowly to an open area that serves as a gathering point. Someone at the front of the human baggage train shouts, 'Ready?' My host translates the word automatically in my mind. This seems to suggest that I am from these parts, so even though I'm loaded up like a donkey, I feel a sense of reassurance.

    We start up the path that follows a gorge, I have a quick look down and see foamy white water cascading down the rocky riverbed. The climb steepens and I start to feel it in my thighs and my lungs as I gasp for breath.

'We should get paid for this,' grumbles one of the two men walking side by side in front of me.

'You know the score, we provide the assassins with provisions, and in return, they offer us their protection.'

'Their protection! Yeah, right, tell that to Hassan.'

'Hassan was an idiot – you can't provoke the Imam, nobody in their right mind would antagonise the man in charge of the assassin's castle.'

I try to digest what I've just heard. I've played the games and seen the film - I'm on my way to one of the most feared places in the 13th century.

'Imam is a strange title for the chief of a bunch of trained killers… doesn't seem right.'

'It's been the traditional title for the leader of Alamut Castle for over a hundred years now.' The speaker stumbles on some loose rock on the path and looks back angrily at the guilty pebbles and in the process sees me trudging along behind them, listening to their conversation. In a hushed voice, he continues, 'Anyway, keep your mouth shut or you'll end up like Hassan.' The other man looks at him and in response to some sort of hidden signal looks back directly at me. His bland expression turns to one of fear in an instant, then he looks ahead quickly, and they both continue trudging forward in silence.

The sun breaches the horizon casting long shadows revealing our destination - a mountain which actually looks like a huge boulder nestled on the valley's side. Studying the hill I realize how easy it would be to defend. The boulder shape of the hill makes it impossible to climb and the narrow path that rises precariously around the edge wouldn't allow more than one person at a time to file along it. Just looking up at it makes me feel tired and so I look down at the path and try not to think about it; I just concentrate on plodding forward putting one foot in front of the other without turning an ankle on the scree-covered trail.

After a couple of hours, we file along the precarious path which curves into the hillside with a walled gateway ahead of us. Any attacker would be exposed for around 200 meters before they reached the wall. I hear someone spit above and behind me and see an archer covering the path from a vantage point 10 meters up – it really is an incredibly easy place to defend. We pass through the gateway one at a time and soon crest the top - revealing the mountain fortress. Crenellated walls surround the numerous buildings within. Armed guards stand around silently watching us. They wear pastel-coloured cloths wrapped around their heads and around their mouths, so only their inscrutable dark eyes can be seen studying us as we unburden ourselves of our packs. A captain of the guard examines the contents and sends members of our party off to different stone structures all over the fort. I approach gripping my pack in front of my thighs by the coarse rope handles which make me walk awkwardly.

'You're not from the village!' he scowls at me. I gape at him and then look around desperately as faces turn towards me, eyes narrow as their hands go to the hilts of their daggers.

'Seize him!' before the leader finishes his command two of the well-trained guards pin my arms behind my back. I'm so stunned I can't form any words of protest.

'Follow me, we'll take him to the Imam. A bit of a distraction might cheer him up,' he says the last part under his breath. He walks off and the guards push me along roughly behind him. We enter a modest stone building but then stand at the top of some stairs which descend down a tunnel hewn into the mountain. I stop causing the guards to bump into my back.

'Sir, I was only trying to help the porters with their packs.'

'Save it for the Imam,' the captain of the guard says before starting down the stairs into the gloom. Torches flicker and fizzle in iron sconces along the rough rock walls; stairs seem to meander down, then level off, turn here and there, and down again. We pass little cell-like rooms whose inhabitants sit quietly meditating or just silently watching us walking past - assassins or prisoners? I can't tell. A scream rips through the air – it's as if the cry of excruciating pain is trying to escape the confines of the passageway. I now truly understand the phrase 'blood-curdling scream' – the hair on the back of my head stands on end and my blood seems to freeze in my veins. When the captain of the guard sees the terror in my eyes, a sly grin spreads across his face, 'That was the castle's shaman – I don't think he'll be healing anyone again.' I feel clammy and woozy. My knees buckle, so the guards lift me to my feet and push me forward. I think I'm getting delirious, I'm being led towards the screaming, but the sound seems to be less piercing and seems further away.

My mind races. My dad always said that people survived in life and death situations by keeping a cool head, so I keep reciting 'Keep a cool head' again and again in my mind like a mantra which surprisingly works. I quickly try to piece together what I know. Their leader is torturing his shaman or doctor to death. He must have failed him somehow. Blimey, what do I know that might help me? A thought springs to mind but seems too much of a long shot. Another scream pierces the air - I realize I have no choice. I try to speak, but all that comes out is a croak. I try again, 'What is wrong with your leader?'

The captain of the guard looks over his shoulder at me suspiciously, 'Why do you want to know?'

'I,' my mouth is dry, I'm about to take a huge gamble – 'I'm a trainee shaman.' The guards both halt as their commander stops to face me. All three of them scrutinise my face trying to detect a lie.

'You are a shaman?' One of the guards scoffs.

'No, I am an apprentice shaman.'

'If you're lying, you'll regret it big time.'

What have I done? Was I brash in suggesting that I am a shaman? What do I know? But I reason, if it gives me time, it's more than I had a moment ago. With time I have at least got a chance – I can pretend to make up some potion – stress it needs time to be ready and then fall asleep and then travel back to London, leaving this nightmare place behind. Hold on... I can't do that – I can't leave my host here; I'll have to think of a way to escape.

The guards push me forward, but we have to stop to let a couple of guards pass who are carrying a limp bloody body – I conclude it's the shaman and my knees almost give way again when I realize that he's dead. The chamber that he was just brought out of is at the end of the tunnel – one way in, one way out. The heavy iron-studded wooden door stands open allowing the faintest light from the room to illuminate the entrance.

'Sire, we have captured an infiltrator posing as a village porter who says he was just trying to help the villagers with their packs. He claims to be a shaman,' the guard commander calls out from where we stand, outside the chamber. There's no sound. Even the guards seem terrified as we wait to hear from the Imam.

Time seems to stretch – I'm not sure, but I think I can hear a conversation going on inside. Then silence. 'Enter.' The captain of the guard grabs my tunic and then pushes me roughly inside so that I stumble to the ground in the centre of the room.

'By your leave, sire,' there's a pause and maybe an acknowledgement or something as the guard commander closes the heavy door.

The room must be big as the light from the oil lamps in each corner barely reaches the whole wall. The flickering flames make the roughly hewn walls look like they are alive and writhing adding to the already malevolent feel of the place. The smell from the oil lamps isn't nice, but it seems to mask a smell I can't quite place – oh no, it smells like barbeque - it's the smell of scorched human flesh. My head spins with the realization and I feel like I'm about to pass out. 'Keep focused' I tell myself. I try to concentrate on something, anything. The oil lamps, a source of light and warmth. A dark pungent ribbon of smoke seems to be pouring upwards from the lamp and disappears into the blackness above. I'm shaking like a leaf, there are beads of sweat forming on my brow, even though the room is icy cold.

A candle on a stand on the far side lights up a wall hanging which seems to be made of cloth. It's not a picture, just lots of what appears to be writing, all lines and curls, but too far for me to make out, only that it is indeed writing. A chill races down my spine as I remember that I'm not alone.

'Interesting,' the word seems to be carried by a cold

breeze from above and behind me. My mind conjures up images of some sort of supernatural being, rendering me literally scared stiff. I know that even my tried-and-tested kung fu skills are no match for a demon from hell. Light footsteps come closer to me.

'Turn around.' Trembling, I obey the command and see an otherworldly figure standing halfway between light and darkness looking down at me. I remember that I thought I'd heard a conversation and look for the other person in the room, but there is no one else. I look at the face studying me and the last warmth in my body seems to vanish leaving me cold to the bone. He takes a pace closer to me so that I can see his face more clearly - long dark hair matted to leathery creased skin, beady eyes above a crooked nose with lips that can barely be seen – evil incarnate.

'Who are you?' the dark eyes look deep into my own.

My voice catches in my throat, 'Sire, my name is Lewis. As the guards mentioned, I was just trying to help the villagers carry the packs, and it's true - I'm an apprentice shaman.' He doesn't take his eyes off me, but when I mention shaman, he automatically feels the side of his jaw. My mind races. I might be able to help here. I used to be fascinated by a really old book my dad had: Y Methygion Myddfai, which translated from Welsh means The Physicians of Myddfai. It was handed down to my dad from his ancestors who came from a village in West Wales and was what had inspired him to become a doctor. The book had wonderful illustrations of plants and flowers annotated with beautiful cursive writing in a language that I couldn't read, but my dad could. We tried some of the remedies, including some for toothache and abscesses in the gum - amazingly they worked.

Was it clove or oregano oil for toothache? One was for toothache and I think the other was for abscesses. But which one?

'Sire, is the pain from the tooth or the gum?' He is taken aback. His eyes narrow on mine - a fleeting look of uncertainty passes his face. He probably doesn't realize he touched his jaw when I mentioned the word shaman. I've got his attention now as he must think I really must have a physician's skills. I have to think quickly. Clove oil springs to mind, yes, that's it! It's used to numb the pain from toothache and oregano oil is used for an abscess. But I have to pretend to make some sort of elaborate potion to give me the time to work out an escape plan.

The silence in the room is deafening. I can almost see him trying to work out how I know where his ailment is, and he can't. 'My pain stems from the gum, which is tender and swollen.'

'Sire, if you will allow me to examine the area,' I stand up straight. Having been in a crouch on the balls of my feet, my legs are stiff, but I try and mask the discomfort. I look into his mouth and try not to wince at his foul breath. The gum is swollen and red rather than a healthy pink. 'Sire, I need to go to the kitchens to get the ingredients for a cure.' He studies me and then calls for a guard to escort me there.

Under the watchful eye of the guard, I mix one portion of olive oil to four portions of dried oregano into a glass beaker, it should be 1 – 1 but I haven't got the time to let it infuse slowly over weeks. I boil a pot of water and carefully place the beaker in the bubbling water to heat for 5 – 10 long uncomfortable minutes with the guard suspiciously watching my every move. I'm relieved to smell a vaguely familiar herby aroma and see that the oil has turned yellowish-brown. There are some vials on a shelf, so I grab an empty one and notice that one of the others is filled with a brown syrupy substance; I uncork it and smell cloves – perfect. I sterilise the empty one and fill it with the oregano oil and indicate to the guard that I'm ready.

We march to the Imam's chambers where he sits in his throne-like chair. 'Sire, if you will lean back so I can administer the treatment.' He looks at me again and then beckons his guards with a slight movement of the head. I apply the clove oil to numb the area and then the oregano oil for the abscess. The guards stand on either side of me with their daggers gripped halfway out of their scabbards ready to cut me down if I make a false move. The Imam frowns, then looks at me. 'The pain is easing,' he says seemingly pleasantly surprised. Even the guards let out a sigh of relief, but not as big as mine.

The moment is broken by rapid knocking on the door. The Imam barks, 'Enter,' and a guard appears panting and informs the Imam between gulps for air that the armourer has injured himself and is bleeding profusely. The Imam leads the way. We pass cloaked assassins who look down out of respect for the Imam, but then stare at me directly – an unfathomable look in their eyes. A guard opens the heavy door to the armoury which reveals a horrific array of weapons, some of which look like they belong in a butcher's shop.

I see the armourer clutching his forearm with blood-soaked fingers. He is one of the few men who is bareheaded allowing me to gauge his age as somewhere in his late fifties or early sixties judging by his long white hair and weather-beaten face. He looks at me suspiciously but doesn't say anything when I examine the injury as I'm with the Imam. The blood is not pulsing, thank goodness - it's not an artery, but a vein. I ask the guard to get some ice or snow, he looks for confirmation from the Imam who nods and then rushes off. There's a leather strap on the table so I grab it and use it as a tourniquet on the armourer's upper arm. I grab some cobwebs from the ceiling, heedless of the spiders which scramble away into the dark recesses of the armoury and mix in a little soot from the fireplace. Then after washing away the blood and ensuring there are no foreign bodies in the gash in the forearm, I pack in the webs and soot. The blood stops immediately. The guard returns with some ice which I put in a cloth and hold against the wound for a few minutes. Then I dry the forearm and wrap a strip of cloth tightly around the wounded area and tie it off. I tell the armourer that he needs to loosen the tourniquet half a turn every 15 minutes or so.

The whole time I've been treating the armourer I've been plotting my escape. If the Imam trusts me then he might allow me to leave the castle at night whereupon I can run as far away from this place as possible before finding somewhere to sleep and then travel back home leaving my host in safety. I pause for breath and look at the Imam hoping for some sign of approval but am disappointed. 'You will finish your shaman training here,' he tells me before turning to the guard, 'once he has finished treating the armourer, take him to the shaman's quarters.' I try not to let my dismay show.

'Yes, sire,' the guard answers standing to attention. The Imam returns his gaze to me.

'I leave all the shaman's belongings to you; these include all his scrolls on medicine – study them well because you are going to replace him as the assassins' new shaman. Don't disappoint me, or...' He doesn't bother to finish the sentence, just looks at me to make sure I understand the unspoken threat, then turns and strides out of the room.

The guard takes up his position outside the armoury's door while the armourer looks at his arm trying to move it this way and that, opening and closing his hand into a fist.

I glance at the vicious weapons mounted on racks and can't believe what I'm seeing – it's like something out of a horror movie. The armourer misinterprets my study of the weapons as some sort of macabre interest. 'Ah, so you like what you see, let me show you,' he goes through the merits of each weapon which makes me feel sick. However, one piece of kit grabs my attention – it's a leather harness which you wear across your shoulder blades with a peacock's tail-feather spread of throwing knives tucked into leather sleeves. There are wrist straps that have the same purpose, concealing knives which are easy to access and throw at your enemy. Tianyuan's monks could do with a bit of kit like this against the pirates.

I'm worried. Two weeks have passed and I'm still here – I haven't been allowed to leave the castle and so haven't been able to implement my escape plan. Another thing that's been nagging at me is the fact that I froze when confronted by someone with the Imam's reputation. If that happens when I fight the pirates, I'll be cut down in the blink of an eye. I console myself with the fact that in my confused state of mind, I thought I was facing some kind of demon rather than a man of flesh and blood.

Surprisingly I'm enjoying a relatively easy time. My lodgings consist of two rooms – a bed chamber, and a study with a laboratory in the corner. The previous shaman was a meticulous man – I expected to see some sort of mad chaotic room with bubbling beakers and scrolls everywhere, but that wasn't the case – everything is organised. This has made it easy for me to study and cross-reference his notes.

During the day I've been working with the armourer, Bijan, helping him maintain the weapons. He must have been an exceptional fighter in his time. Not many assassins live to old age or get positions at the castle. His experience and skills must have been worth holding on to. We pass the time with him teaching me how to use the different weapons. There's a little training area in a corner of the armoury which is used to check the balance and strength of repaired weapons. Bijan has been impressed by how quickly I pick up his weapons training which allows him to teach me extra tips in their use. He doesn't realize that all I seem to have been doing lately is martial arts with Tianyuan and more recently our cavalry escort. Grandfather Teacher's lessons have trained me to adapt his fighting techniques so that I can use them with most weapons.

'That's enough for today, Lewis, go and get some food and sleep,' Bijan says to me. He then pats me on the back, 'Good work, very good work.' He smiles and then gives me a playful push towards the armoury door, 'Now go!'

'Thanks, Bijan, see you tomorrow,' I take one long last look at him and walk out past the guard who nods at me then head off to my chambers. There's a tray of food steaming under a cloth waiting for me. I remove the cloth to reveal a clay pot of abgoosht and fresh flatbreads. The aroma is mouth-watering. I add a sprinkling of herbs to the lamb stew and pound all the ingredients together into a paste which I then try to savour by not wolfing it down too quickly. When I get back to London, I'll have to find a Persian restaurant so I can take Claire there and see what she thinks of this dish which has become one of my favourite meals.

I've realized something – life here as an apprentice shaman isn't bad at all – I can leave knowing that my host will enjoy a comfortable quality of life. I lie down, close my eyes, and concentrate on clearing my mind of any thoughts.

Chapter 13

'Lewis! Lewis!' Claire bursts into my bedroom, breathless from running.

'What-'

'Danny is awake, he's woken up! He's back!'

My jaw drops, I can't believe it. Before I know it, I'm at the hospital in Danny's room where he is sat smiling on puffed-up pillows, eating ice cream. All the staff are full of smiles standing around his bed – there's almost a party feel in the air. Tears of joy and relief sting my eyes, I rush towards him and give him a bear hug. Then, as if by some sort of magic trick, the staff vanish, and I'm sat with Claire on Danny's hospital bed listening to him describe his adventures. He's been through a lot, but I can't keep up with his story; I think I'm so emotional I can't concentrate. The questions fire back and forth, and eventually, I explain that I have been looking for him in China and am in the middle of preparing for a great battle that will turn the tide against the pirates.

'I want to help,' Danny says.

'No, Danny, you need to stay in the here and now for a while at least.' I see Danny's face drop and don't want to spoil the joy of the moment, 'But once you have rested you can come with me. Claire and I have worked out a way to identify each other. We wear dragonfly pendants and have a codeword.' I have a vague memory of Claire and me talking of dragonfly pendants or pins, but it's out before I think about it. I explain that one of us states that we've seen a dragonfly, and the other then asks about the colours - we verify who we are by saying gold and turquoise.

'Are they that colour in China?' Danny asks.

'Yes, they can be. Then we double-check with a secret handshake.' I show Danny the handshake and he loves it. Claire, Danny, and I relish the moment, and then we're back at the house. Mum tucks Danny in bed, she looks younger, her smile lightening up the room.

'Good night, Danny,' Mum kisses him on the forehead, and then I get the same. Mum looks back fondly as she switches off the main light and closes the bedroom door behind her.

I'm about to switch off the bedside light when I see Danny looking at me, snug as a bug in a rug with his Spider-Man quilt right up to his chin, in his bed, safe and sound.

'Are you going to fight the pirates tonight?' he asks.

'I don't know, Danny.'

'Can I come with you?'

I pause to think through my response, I don't want to bring Danny down on such a wonderful day. The relief of seeing him just a few feet away generates powerful protective feelings, 'You can come with me, but not today.' I see the disappointment on his face, 'You need to rest. Once you have, you can come with me, and I'll introduce you to Tianyuan. He'll teach you some wicked kung fu moves, you'll be my ninja brother.' His face beams at the prospect.

I go to turn off the light, and pause, 'Danny, I'm serious, don't come with me tonight, okay?' He turns away from the light, rolling himself up in his quilt so I can just see the back of his head and a scrunched-up Spider-Man leaping through the air at his back. 'Danny, promise.'

'I promise,' but I'm not convinced. It takes a while for me to nod off as I'm worried that Danny will try travelling in his dreams again.

I'm on patrol with my section in the forests near our base. One of the other elite recruits who I think is called Jie is at point, leading the way. We're in single file formation, each one of us with an arrow notched in our bow. The bows follow the direction that we scan - left, right, up in the trees, and also behind; the enemy has been known to create a little den, right on a path so that they have a point-blank shot at our backs as we walk past. I turn all the way around to check if there are any such hides but it's clear - I nod at the guy behind me who acknowledges quickly before continuing to scan the banks. I look down the path, 15 of us, and a corporal who I think I recognise as one of our training team bringing up the rear. The line of soldiers looks good, spacing appropriate, no sound, armed and ready, scanning left, right, up in the trees, and occasionally behind - excellent.

  I look ahead to see that Jie has come to a halt. I raise my fist in the air, the signal to go to ground. The file of men behind me instantly move to either side of the track, crouching behind bushes or tree trunks, silently scanning out into the forest, and every now and then looking forward, eager to find out what has caused us to stop. Jie is looking dumbfounded at a tree that has fallen right across the path. I hear someone coming up behind, a quick glance reveals it's the corporal who is moving, bent double, quietly to the front, scanning as he comes to check what the problem is. He sees the tree and frowns, starts to move quicker. Jie is about to step over the tree with the wrong foot. Yesterday we were taught to step over any obstacle, tree, brook, whatever, leading with your weakest side. So, if you are right-handed, you step over with your left foot. It means that you can cover 180 degrees in front with a weapon. If you don't, your arc of fire is limited, and you are off balance if an enemy attacks from your blind side.

  'Jie!' both the corporal and I whisper loudly in alarm. He's off balance and so turns awkwardly to see what we want, I hear the thrumming of bow strings followed almost instantly by a rapid tattoo of thumps - Jie's back suddenly resembles a huge pin cushion, arrows everywhere. The power of the arrows drives him to the ground, he's dead before he hits the floor. The silence is torn apart by howls and screams as the forest seems to come alive. There are arrows flying down and pirates running at us with swords and axes catching the sun as they whirl them above their heads.

  The thought that they've messed up occurs to me fleetingly - they should have just picked us off from their hiding places as we were vulnerable at the bottom of this gully. But their eagerness to fight has already cost them. A few are peppered with arrows before they reach us. There's chaos as we fling down our bows and draw swords, finding a foe to fight.

A samurai pirate appears in front of me. The sunlight dappling the forest floor casts a strange pattern across his polished red armour. His mask, a laughing demon with flared nostrils and empty eye sockets momentarily stuns me. He laughs maniacally as we circle each other. I'll have to be careful that I don't catch my sword in the branches when I swing it, or trip over any loose branches or roots on the forest floor. The fear seems to have sapped all my strength as if a gust of wind could blow me over. The samurai continues to circle waiting for his moment to strike me down. We've been taught that your enemies' eyes can give them away, a change in focus indicating they are about to strike, but I can't see his eyes, just black eye sockets. A sword flashes down from above, I just manage to leap out of the way, but he's winged me, there's a stinging pain along my right arm. The pain energises me, I feel the strength returning and leap towards him sliding down on the forest floor, so I skid below his horizontal sword swing. I bring up my sword and punch it through his abdomen, a killing stroke. The sword drops from his hands as he slumps to the floor.

There's no time to study my victim, there's fighting all around me. Groans, grunts, the sound of metal ringing off metal, heavy breathing, and men gasping for lungfuls of air between sword strikes and slashes. I dance around helping my comrades until eventually the two remaining pirates are killed.

I take a moment to catch my breath, leaning on my sword as I look around at a scene of utter carnage. I rush forward to check on our corporal, he's bleeding from a cut across his chest that has torn through his leather armour. But the armour stopped the sword from going deep, saving his life - even though there's blood everywhere, he'll be okay. I clean the wound by flushing it out with lots of water from my canteen then I tear away his blouse and unroll his cloak from his pack. I wrap the material tightly around his chest and back to stem the blood loss. He nods his thanks.

'Take command, Lu-wis. Tend to our wounded, make sure all the pirates are really dead, and put sentries out, just in case there are more of them in the woods.' I nod and rush off delegating people to carry out the corporal's orders. We've lost three men dead, four wounded. I'm surprised, we should have been annihilated and would have been had the pirates just picked us off from their ambush positions.

A conversation catches my attention.

'I don't understand what he's saying, it sounds like the language of the white devils.' My head whips around to look at two of my oppos who are talking over the samurai I fought. When I get there, I can see that the samurai is bleeding out and mumbling incoherently, he doesn't have long. I check to make sure my guys have removed any weapons and then kneel down to hear what the samurai is saying. He's repeating something again and again.

I kneel in closer and feel a chill run throughout my body as I recognise the language. He's speaking English. I freeze for a moment, not wanting to hear the words. But I know I must, so I lean closer, the words barely a whisper now.

'I saw a beautiful dragonfly. I saw a beautiful dragonfly.'

My throat is dry, I lean forward and whisper, 'What colour was it?' The samurai's body stiffens, his hand blindly feels out till it clutches my shoulder. Pulling me even closer.

'Gold and turquoise.'

'Danny?'

'Lewis?' the last word the samurai says before dying. A sob comes from nowhere. This can't be happening. This isn't happening. I cradle the samurai in my arms - my dear brother, Danny, and then scream at the sky before my body is racked with grief.

* * * * *

Claire is enjoying walking through the park with the sun on her face. The sound of a toddler laughing while being chased by the father near the park's playground brings a smile to her face. Her grandmother always advised her to try and enjoy the little things in life, saying that they were sustenance for the soul; being able to enjoy them helped you to get through those unavoidable dark days. The peal of the toddler's laughter brings to mind other sounds which raise her spirits: the sound of early morning frost crunching underfoot on the lawn in the back garden; the crackling of ice when Gran poured her homemade lemonade into her glass – Claire isn't sure if adding slices of lemon to shop-bought lemonade constituted 'homemade' but let that one pass; and the sound of the blackbird's morning chorus – such a simple sound from a simple, but beautiful bird. As if on cue she sees a blackbird which starts singing as if on stage.

Suddenly, the peaceful scene is torn apart by the fierce barking of a dog. Without looking, Claire knows it will be one of those muzzled dogs that always seem to strain at their leashes as if desperate to tear into something with their enormous salivating jaws. The hair on the back of Claire's neck stands on end as she quickly scans the park to identify where the danger is coming from. Ah, she might have guessed, there's the devil dog being held taught on its leash by the 'Hitler Youth' - Emma and Mike. You can see that they are relishing the effect of the terrifying menace they hold in their grasp. They say that the owners sometimes look like their dogs, but Claire didn't think it stopped there - she believed a dog would imitate its owner's character – and in this case, her assumptions seem to be proven right.

Claire feels a sense of relief that the twins haven't seen her, they seem focused on another target hidden from her by some trees. She hears sounds of despair coming from the direction Emma and Mike are heading. The sound is muffled and then Claire realizes why - there's a young boy tied to a tree with a gag in his mouth, looking at the approaching dog wide-eyed in terror. Claire's heart lurches as she realizes that the boy is Danny – but how? He is in a bed on a ward in the hospital.

An awareness starts to dawn in Claire's mind. She can almost hear her own voice saying that this isn't real. She swiftly looks around the park and starts to notice that details are wrong, features are all mixed up – there's a pagoda that doesn't belong – and if she isn't mistaken, the park is surrounded by wobbly skyscrapers which were definitely not here last week... 'Stop!' she hears herself shout. The park scene carries on, nobody takes any notice of her. Is this a dream? She looks at the notice by the ice cream van - she's sure it was advertising a 99-ice-cream cone for two dollars a moment ago, but now it has an advert for the new James Bond film. That's one of the signs of being in a dream, what are the others? She looks at her watch – it's not hers – instead of her nice plain light-blue watch face, she can see Mickey Mouse pointing at the numbers with oversized gloves. Claire realises she is definitely in a dream – maybe this is her chance to lean her dreams, something she hasn't managed yet.

She remembers Lewis's instructions on how to direct her dream. 'Right, Emma and Mike,' the twins look at her awaiting her command, 'You don't belong here, go,' they vanish along with their dog. 'Danny, don't be afraid, go back to your bed, Lewis and I are going to help you,' the gag and rope tying him to the tree fall to the ground, he turns to Claire and smiles, waves, and then disappears. Claire lets out a deep breath, she feels relieved. Then she hears Lewis approaching.

'Thanks, Claire, you saved Danny from them – I'm gonna teach those twins a lesson one day,' Lewis gazes off into the distance with a savage expression that scares Claire.

'Don't say that Lewis, they're not worth it.' Although it was her saying the words, Claire is like a spectator – she can see Lewis and herself in the park, facing each other with a palpable sense of emotion between them. All of a sudden, Lewis turns to her, reaches out slowly, and gently caresses Claire's cheek. There is a look of affection in their eyes as they draw closer for a kiss...

Claire wakes up with a start. She's breathing rapidly. Both her hands grip the duvet as she looks around the room. She pinches herself which stings, she's definitely awake. What did that dream mean? Does it imply that she has feelings for Lewis? That can't be right, they are friends – any romantic feelings between them would be weird.

Another thought occurs to her - had she directed her dream? Or was that just a dream about her directing her dream? Had she stopped having a nightmare and turned it into something nicer? Had she wanted to kiss Lewis or was that just a dream playing with her mind? As her breathing returns to normal she lies back in bed and looks up at the ceiling. Right, Claire analyses the situation, she was lucid in her dream – that's great, it's a start. If she can advance to travelling in her dreams, she can help Lewis search for Danny. Does she tell Lewis about her dream? Maybe just parts of it…

Chapter 14

I wake up feeling awful, but why? Images of being on patrol with my section flash through my mind… and then I see Danny dying in my arms - my guts churn and my chest feels like something's been ripped out - I have to face the fact that I have killed my brother. Surely, no one can feel more wretched – I wouldn't admit it to anyone, but I just want to die, I don't think I can live with myself. My mum answers the phone, she makes a strange sound and now she's rushing up the stairs, oh no – I dread to see her grief-stricken face when she opens the door. The door flies open and Mum stands there with a look which doesn't fit with how I'm feeling. Looking at Mum I feel baffled – I haven't seen her look so happy in ages.

'Danny is awake! Danny is awake!' my mum is actually jumping with joy running in circles around the room, kissing me on the forehead, checking Danny's bed, and kissing me on the forehead again. I don't get it, this feels a bit like déjà vu, but instead of Claire bringing me the good news it's Mum. What's going on? I've just seen Danny die by my own hand. I can't work out what's real and what's not. I pinch myself and feel the pain, it was just a dream! Thank God!

* * * * *

Magnus surveys the mopping-up operation going on all around him. A quick movement catches his eye – it's Danny sprinting towards a group of Carthaginian civilians encircled by Roman soldiers. A sudden look of horror on his centurion's face draws Titus's attention to where Danny has just slipped in a pool of blood on the deck in front of a Roman marine's sword. Titus moves faster than anyone would believe possible for a man of his size – he can see Danny trying to stand up only to be kicked back to the deck. The soldier raises his sword for a killing stroke aimed at Danny's head. The boy has no time to react as the sword comes sweeping down. Titus leaps the last few yards reaching out with his sword which manages to turn the soldier's blade, but there's still enough power in the Marine's strike for it to club Danny's head. The boy lies motionless on the deck.

Two men roar, 'Halt!' simultaneously. Magnus looks around quickly to see who else gave the command and sees a Roman legate regarding him from across the deck where all activity has stopped. They nod at each other before getting on with restoring order.

Suddenly the ship slopes down at the bow and lists to the starboard side, seawater rising rapidly. Magnus yells, 'Abandon ship!' which is echoed by others around the deck, and then they herd everyone onto the corvus which allows the men to rapidly withdraw onto the seaworthy Roman quinquereme roped alongside. Titus carefully picks up Danny's limp body and joins the other evacuees hailing 'First Legion!' so the uniformed Romans know that the loin-clothed clad men are friend, not foe. As soon as the last person steps aboard, the gangplank rises at the same time as the oars are reversed which quickly propels the ship away from the doomed vessels.

A wrenching sound draws everyone's attention to the sinking ships. The snapping and splintering sound of beams and planks reaches a crescendo before the first Roman ship to be rammed in the battle pulls Danny's ship below the surface with it - in seconds, foam, bubbles and some flotsam are the only indicators that two ships were there a moment ago. Then all is quiet.

Danny can hear someone asking, 'Brother, are you okay?' but his head is swimming and a sudden nauseous feeling forces him onto his side where he is sick. Hands support him and rub his back. It takes a while for his vision to focus on the huge head of Titus who looks over him with a look of concern stamped on his slab-of-granite face.

'Is he ok?' Danny hears Magnus's voice and sees his face appear behind Titus's left shoulder looking equally worried.

'I'm ok... thanks.' Danny tries to stand but the world swims around and he wretches again before Titus lays him on some folded sail along the ship's side rail.

'Take it easy, little brother,' Magnus says, and adds, 'you saved us.' The Centurion then looks over at Dido and her family who are under guard and being spoken to by a Roman officer in splendid uniform, 'And them. We all owe you our lives.'

'Primus Pilus Magnus?' a voice enquires. The three of them turn to see a Roman officer looking at Magnus waiting for a reply. Magnus stands to attention, forearm slapping across his chest in salute, 'Yes, sir. Primus Pilus Magnus and the remnants of the first cohort of the First Legion reporting for duty.' All around the deck, the freed Roman oarsmen jump to attention slamming their forearms across their chests.

'At ease gentlemen. I'm Legate Cato of the Second Legion. Your reputation precedes you, Primus, you saved the legions in that retreat on Sicily. General Scipio will be both relieved and pleased to see you when we get back to Ostia – he's there preparing an army to beat the Carthaginians once and for all.'

'Thank you, sir,' Magnus responds.

'No, thank you and your men. We were in a bad place till you arrived – you lot saved the day, especially when their reinforcements arrived.'

'Actually, sir, it's our youngest member of the First Legion that saved the day.' Legate Cato looks at Magnus uncomprehendingly. 'I mean this lad here, Danny. He unchained us from the oar deck on the ship that just sank. Without him...' he left the words unsaid.

The legate looks down at Danny who tries to stand to attention but gets dizzy again and falls to his knees supporting himself on outstretched arms against the deck.

'Easy, soldier. You rest there. I'll get my medicus to look you over. Centurion!' he barks. A grizzled veteran flanked by two men instantly appears before the legate. 'Get our hero down to Lucius, make sure he gets the best treatment.'

'Yes, sir!' the centurion barks in response and nods to the soldiers on either side of him. They move towards Danny, but Titus's giant form bars their way as he scoops Danny up in his arms and indicates to the centurion to lead the way.

The legate watches the men take Danny to the doctor, 'The boy is Carthaginian, is he not?'

'He was enslaved in Carthage, but we're not exactly sure where he is from – he doesn't seem to be able to remember.'

'Don't worry, Primus Pilus, my medico will look after him. He'll get the reward he deserves back in Rome. I'll make sure my men take good care of him.'

'I don't think you need to worry about the care side of things, sir, Titus won't let anyone lay a finger on that boy.'

'Gods, I wouldn't like to see anyone try – then again maybe I would,' he turns to Magnus giving him a mischievous smile. 'Right, Primus, come to my cabin and you can fill me in on what's been happening to you and your men over the last few years.'

Danny wakes up feeling much better. He stretches, savouring the feeling of lying on a feather mattress with clean sheets enveloping him in a lovely warm cocoon. He looks up to see Titus leaning over him, holding his hand in his shovel-sized paws with a gentleness that seems incongruous with the Herculean figure before him.

'How are you feeling, brother?' Titus's face breaks into a smile that would send most people running for the hills.

'I feel great, thanks, Titus. Can I get up now and do a bit of exploring?'

Titus laughs, 'No, not yet, soon, but not yet.' The giant sees the look of disappointment on Danny's face and continues, 'The medicus has said you must rest until we are sure that blow to your head hasn't caused any long-term damage. You were knocked out cold – we thought we may have lost you,' Titus's face looks strained for a moment.

'What happened?' Danny asks.

'I'll tell you what happened,' a voice comes from the cabin's door, 'you saved our lives, that's what happened,' Magnus appears grinning as he joins Titus at his bedside. 'The legate has nominated you for an award for your bravery and for saving the day. When we get to Rome you will live a very comfortable life - the legate also announced that he intends to adopt you.' A cloud passes over Magnus's face, 'I would have adopted you myself, but it sounds like me and the boys will soon be needed back at the frontline, finishing off the Carthaginians for good.' Danny can't hide his sadness at the news that he wouldn't be able to stay with his new-found family. The two Romans notice his downcast expression, 'Don't worry, we'll be in Rome for a few months providing intelligence while we recuperate. The men, Titus, and I will show you the sights of Rome – the most magnificent city in the world.' Danny beams with joy at the prospect and both men laugh. 'Rest, Danny, you'll need all your strength for all the fun and games we're going to have when we get home.'

For the first time in weeks, he was happy and able to relax. Magnus and Titus turn once more to wave goodnight before closing the cabin door behind them. Danny stretches out and feels energy tingle throughout his body, a wonderful feeling of happiness, expectation, and relief. He gets himself comfortable and watches the lamp's warm glow creating lovely patterns against the wood panelling as it sways with the ship's movement. Danny drifts off to sleep whereupon he soon stands at the gateway and sees London through one of the windows. He moves closer and feels the pull of the wormhole.

Danny feels the jolt as he returns into his own body. He can hear a rhythmic beeping sound which spurs him on to open his eyes and look towards its source - he sees monitors next to the hospital bed he is lying in. It takes just a moment to work out where he is. He looks at his arms – once again they are the arms of a nine-year-old white boy from England. He sees his reflection in the TV screen and feels a thrill at seeing his own features again – he's home. The door flies open, and the smiling face of a pretty nurse comes towards him, 'Well now, this is a lovely surprise – welcome back, Danny.' Danny can't help smiling back at the beautiful nurse who is dialling a number on her phone. 'Hello Rachel, this is Amelie, I have some good news – guess who just woke up?'

* * * * *

'Get dressed and phone Claire, I'll get the car keys,' my mum says and then the human whirlwind is out of my room and pounding her way back down the stairs. I feel euphoric and incredible relief all in one go – if I could bottle this sensation, I'd be a trillionaire.

Everything is happening so fast. I'm in the car and I realize that this really isn't a dream, all the steps are logical, unlike the nightmare I've just had where one minute I'm at Danny's bedside in hospital and then the next I'm on patrol in a forest in China. This is real, we're probably driving a little over the speed limit - my mum is so happy I can almost feel the joy radiating from her. I'm not sure she's entirely focused, so grip my car seat a bit tighter.

'Danny is awake!' I text Claire. My mind can't seem to sit still. 'C u at the hospital!' Am I losing my mind? Am I unable to tell real life from travelling or just a dream? Mum parks up in the closest staff car park to Danny's ward and we're out and running before the car seems to have really stopped.

Breathless we reach Danny's room and burst in and stop dead. Danny looks up at us with a huge smile and almost drops the ice cream cone in his hand. Amelie the nurse takes it off him before it gets crushed in Mum's all-enfolding embrace. I wait my turn and then grab him in a bear hug, I couldn't be happier, I don't care if a few tears escape. Mum sits on the bed and we rattle off a few questions before I sit down on a chair and feel a nice kind of exhaustion wash over me. It's over. I watch Mum fussing over Danny, jabbering away a hundred miles an hour.

We're soon joined by Claire who also sheds a few tears while giving him a kiss and a hug. Then Doctor Jeffries turns up, followed quickly by the consultants. A little voice in the back of my mind reminds me that one of them might be working for a dodgy organisation. Doctor Jeffries seems slightly distracted, the consultants' smiles seem fake, and if I'm not mistaken, Amelie seems to be a little wary. But then what do I know? When Claire turned up, she seemed a bit awkward with me – I have to keep a check on my paranoia.

'I'm going to see if I can switch my shift – we're going to celebrate with whatever food you fancy, Danny,' my mum says. She then gives Danny another kiss, I get one, then Claire, and then all the staff in the room get a kiss which is quite funny as they aren't sure how to react. After her kissing frenzy, my mum disappears followed closely by the doctors and Amelie.

Claire sits on the bed and I get back to my chair. I look at my brother and can't wait any longer, 'So Danny, tell us all about it.'

I feel chilled to the bone. Danny's adventures have left me stunned - my earlier sense of joy has been replaced by guilt at not being able to protect my brother from such horrifying experiences. Claire looks equally mortified by Danny's brushes with death. She looks unseeingly in Danny's direction before she stands up smiling at him, 'I'm gonna get us some snacks from the vending machine – what do you fancy, Danny?'

'Something chocolate,' my brother's face breaks into a beaming smile.

'I'll be right back,' Claire leaves the room with a skip in her step. I watch the door close then look back at Danny – this is my chance.

'I'm really sorry about that night,' he looks at me confused so I continue, 'you know when I lost my temper with you, and you locked yourself in the toilet.' Danny frowns seemingly struggling to remember the incident. I can see it as if it only happened yesterday – a look of fear on Danny's face as he ran away from me. Me banging on the toilet door and yelling at him that he can't travel anymore because it's too dangerous. That scene has been playing back again and again in my mind filling me with shame, but Danny barely remembers it. I feel a surprising sense of relief - I've been beating myself up about something Danny sees as just the normal rows brothers have. He just looks at me and shrugs as if it was nothing.

Claire returns with a load of snacks which she dumps on the bed. We wait for Danny to choose one then help ourselves. Between mouthfuls of chocolate, I describe my search for him, my escapades in China with Tianyuan, and the build-up to the final battle.

'You're learning kung fu?' Danny asks.

'Yes, from the best teacher there's ever been.' I smile as Danny's eyes open wide with wonder. His reaction spurs me on to describe Claire's idea for identifying each other while we're on our travels. But as I mention gold and turquoise dragonflies, I get a sense of déjà vu which brings back memories of the nightmare I had last night. What am I doing? Talking about adventures when I have no intention of letting my brother travel again.

'I want to go to China with you,' Danny's eyes sparkle with excitement.

'No, Danny, you can't,' I say a bit too abruptly. I see Danny's face drop and don't want to spoil the joy of the moment. 'Once you have rested you can come with me, okay?' I lie. Danny nods. 'But first you need to recuperate.' Danny looks down into his lap and nods again – I'm not convinced. 'You are not going to travel to China, do you understand?' I feel a rage brewing, so I use Tianyuan's meditation methods to calm myself.

'Yes,' he looks so sad I start to feel guilty, again.

Claire comes to the rescue, 'Danny, you can travel once you have recovered. Your body needs to rest before you go on any other adventures, okay?'

Danny nods reluctantly, still looking down at his hands in his lap. Tianyuan's meditation techniques aren't working - I'm getting wound up at the feeling that he's planning to join me in China.

'Danny, look me in the eye and say, "I promise I won't go travelling until you say it's okay."'

Danny looks up at me and takes a moment before repeating the promise. I look at the expression around his eyes – it doesn't reassure me - I've seen that look before. But I don't want to argue and spoil the mood any further.

Mum rushes in and fist pumps the air, 'I've done it, I've switched shifts. So, Danny, what do you fancy for dinner?'

Chapter 15

Tianyuan and I are having a breakfast of millet porridge with sesame paste. It might not look that appetising, but hunger's the best spice, as my father used to say, and I tear into it. But my mind is elsewhere, what am I doing in China now that Danny has returned? I quickly glance at Tianyuan who looks up catching my eye before I continue eating. He's the answer - he's become like family; I've grown to love that walnut face. An image of Han's beautiful mischievous smile springs to mind - my feelings for her are difficult to put into words.

'Lu-wis, you'll continue to serve as my assistant in teaching the recruits kung fu.' They have been divided among kung fu masters from all over China, but Tianyuan was their overall Captain of Training. 'But I'm afraid you'll also have to continue drill and field craft with the other recruits. I know you are eager to find your brother, but I can't excuse you from your duties. If I show you any favouritism, it could generate bad feelings against you and me – and we don't need that.' Tianyuan looks at me, gauging my reaction.

'Very well, Grandfather Teacher.' I haven't worked out how to explain to him that I'm not looking for my brother anymore.

The sound of marching soldiers draws our attention – whoever they are they come to a halt outside our tent. We grab our oak staffs and head out through the tent flap, an officer slams his right fist into the palm of his left hand and bows at forty-five degrees before returning upright to stand to attention.

'I am Captain Lee of the God of War's personal guard.

General Qi Jiguang has returned from a meeting with the governor and requests that you join him immediately in the command tent.'

'Thank you, Captain Lee, please lead the way,' Tianyuan then turns to me, 'Lu-wis, you will accompany me as my steward.' Captain Lee looks at me briefly but doesn't say anything before he marches off briskly.

Things have improved in the few days we've had while waiting for the General's return. When we first rode into the camp we were surprised by what we saw. The rabble who sat around fires or just stood in twos or threes looking dishevelled were a complete contrast to the soldiers training around the camp we'd seen from the hillside. I remember seeing a rare frown crease Tianyuan's forehead as he studied them. As our entourage rode past, these new recruits grew quiet and watched, some with a tangible hostility. The new recruits were civilians from all walks of life - monks, farmers, labourers, fishermen, and even the odd merchant. Their lack of respect really irritated Captain Sun Qi who was on the brink of dishing out a reprimand, when Tianyuan intervened before there was a scene. 'Captain, leave it. These men have evidently been through a lot and are just confused. We'll give them the leadership and purpose needed to knock them into a formidable force.'

Just then, a monk stood in the way of our horses and spat on the floor and slowly and deliberately scratched his behind. Captain Sun Qi's head almost blew off his shoulders with rage at the deliberate insult, but Tianyuan reached out and gripped his shoulder. With a sharp exhale, the Captain released his grip on the hilt of his sabre and sat there trying to contain his fury. The monk was clearly amused by the reaction and then turned with an almost bovine expression in his eyes to Tianyuan.

'So, they've made you the leader of the kung fu masters,' he growled.

'It seems so, Bao, but it has to be officially confirmed by General Qi on his return.'

'Surely the leader of the kung fu masters should be the best fighter among us?' Bao exclaimed to murmurs of agreement from the dozen or so monks stood around him glaring at us.

'He is,' Tianyuan replied, and I couldn't help but laugh at the comeback. The tension ramped up as the atmosphere almost crackled with hatred. Captain Sun Qi had had enough and at a command, sabres rattled out of their scabbards and the cavalry rode their powerful mounts in a way that forced the monks off the path.

I let out a sigh of relief as we rode on, but Captain Sun Qi was evidently still livid, looking back at the rabble a couple of times. 'I can have them flogged and expelled from the camp.'

'Please let me try my approach first,' Tianyuan responded as he looked ahead deep in thought.

As we walk to the command tent a semblance of order and a military attention to detail can be seen in the recruits marching to and fro. However, Bao and his supporters are not making things easy. They are often late, deliberately misinterpret orders, and worse of all, seem to be taking out their resentment of Tianyuan's command on the new recruits during their kung fu training; some are already in sickbay nursing broken bones or severe concussion.

We are led to the largest tent which is situated in the centre of the camp. If the pennants don't give away the fact that there are some important people inside, the size of the guards surrounding it will. They stand statue-still a few paces away from the wall of the command tent, I guess to avoid overhearing their leaders' plans. We march to the entrance where the guards acknowledge our presence by blocking our path with their spears and then returning to attention, all in quick sharp movements.

I follow Captain Lee and Tianyuan into the tent where we stop just inside. As my eyes adjust, I see that there are a number of bareheaded officers leaning over a map on a table intently listening to each other's comments. They are so engrossed that they don't notice us until Captain Lee coughs politely. All the faces at the table turn to look at us. They all look magnificent in their military gear, ornate hard leather chest plates with brightly polished fish scale armour covering thighs, shoulders, and arms. Despite the elaborate designs of dragons, tigers, and such on the hilts of their swords and daggers in their belts, there's no doubt these are functional weapons, razor-sharp and lethal in their hands. There are four veteran officers and one young man. I expect one of the older generals to welcome Grandfather Teacher, but in fact, it's the youngest of the group whose face lights up as he moves towards us.

'Grandfather Teacher, you honour us with your presence,'

'General Qi Jiguang, it is an honour to be of service to you. I am at your command,' Tianyuan responds. There's a friendliness and sparkle in each other's eyes that indicates a deep friendship. Captain Lee steps backwards and signals to me with a nod that I should join the other stewards at the back of the tent, out of the way of the important business being discussed.

'I'm afraid we'll have to catch up later - we have received daunting intelligence from our spies among the wokou pirate forces. Here, let me appraise you of the situation,' the General leads Tianyuan to the map. 'We are here, near the village of Wengjiagang, near the mouth of the delta, at this slight bend in the river. Three pirate clans are aiming to mass their forces here, here, and here.' I can see the general pointing to different areas on the map. 'They might be pirate scum, but they are wily pirate scum. By massing their forces at these three different locations, we can't be sure whether their target is Shanghai or Hangzhou. This means we've had to deplete our forces here so that we can garrison towns that may be in danger. At the same time, we've had to send patrols out far and wide to try and deter them from raiding too far inland.'

Tianyaun is concentrating on the disposition of the enemy forces. 'Where do you think they will join forces?'

'Our sources suggest they will join forces here,' I can see the General pointing near to where a little figurine of a soldier marks our position on the map, 'and proceed to destroy everything in their path on their way to the capital.'

'You mentioned three pirate clans, how many men does that equate to?'

General Qi Jiguang sighs, 'Anywhere in the region of 60,000 men.'

Tianyuan is good at hiding his thoughts and emotions, but the way he looks up from the map and stares at the general says a lot – he doesn't like what he's hearing.

'Yes, I know that sounds bad. But we have been assured that two armies are on their way from Beijing to reinforce us.'

'How long will they take to get here?'

The God of War meets Tianyuan's gaze, 'Probably too long, to be honest. So that means we may well be left with just 1,500 regular forces, which is why we've asked you to train the 1,500 recruits; they need effective martial arts skills as quickly as possible, to give us some sort of chance of holding out till the reinforcements arrive. We can mitigate the disparity in numbers by building a formidable defensive position here.' There's silence as we try to digest the true scale of the seemingly impossible task ahead.

'I assume by the fact that you've based yourself here that you believe the pirates are heading for Hangzhou, not Shanghai?' Tianyuan asks.

'Yes, our spies seem to think so – unless they are double-crossing us. You can only trust them so far – they may have been paid to tell us that to clear the way for a pirate assault on Shanghai. But I have a hunch Hangzhou is indeed their target.' Most people would dismiss 'hunches', but the God of War has built a reputation on his. 'Hangzhou is not only the region's capital, but the most important trading port along this coast. If this alliance, formed by Xu Hai, Chen Dong, and Ye Ma's clans can take the capital, they are in a better position to rampage across the land from a more easily defended stronghold.' I'm trying to get my head around the idea of an army of pirates taking over a capital city; in effect, it would be like them seizing London, Paris, or New York – it's difficult to comprehend. 'This morning we've heard that Chen Dong has already started to amass his forces here, and Xu Hai has sent a vanguard here. Fortunately, the bad weather has held up most of Xu Hai's force on the Goto Islands, and almost all of Ye Ma's fleet is still at his base in Songjiang. Once they get here and join forces, we can expect the pirate horde to be here within a matter of days.'

They continue to discuss the dire situation, then something occurs to me. When I'm back home, I can look up the events that happened here in history books and maybe get an idea of how to help things along in General Qi Jiguang's favour. The quandary is, I don't know if I've gone back in time or am in a parallel universe. So, if my history book says the pirates attacked Hangzhou that's all well and good, but in a parallel universe they may have attacked Shanghai or another of the main cities. Therefore, suggesting they attack a particular city might lead troops away from the real threat. Still, there might be something in the history books that will help diminish our enemy's power.

At the end of the day's training, I'm shattered, but I know that I'll have to travel home tonight in my dreams. I need to find any information that will help in the fight against the pirates - a force possibly thirty times our strength. Our officers try to play down this factor by telling us that we are the best soldiers in the world and can beat any enemy, however much they outnumber us. Some of the soldiers start to really believe this, but I imagine every soldier in every country on Earth has been told that to give them confidence and an edge. This won't be enough to win as things stand. Other officers have tried to play down the threat the pirates pose by saying that our enemy is just an undisciplined rabble. But there are former samurai among them who have devoted their whole lives to honing their fighting skills. The rest will have learnt all about combat in the best classroom any soldier can have - real battle. Nope, I need to get home and use my unique skills to help us win the fight.

* * * * *

The agent trembles while dialling on the encrypted phone, the boss isn't going to like this.

'Report,' comes the command.

'I'm afraid I have some bad news – the boy has woken up. He'll be monitored for the usual 24 to 48 hours and then be discharged from the hospital into the care of the family,' the silence stretches out, just the sound of breathing, slightly heavier than before.

'This is not good. Await instructions.' The phone line goes dead as the agent exhales, hands trembling.

* * * * *

The Boss looks down at a news article:

Four bodies found in burnt-out building

The police have reported that the remains of four people, two adults and two children were found in a burnt-out derelict building on the outskirts of Brenheim near the Black Forest on Monday morning. The building which used to be a school was more recently used by local drug addicts. Initial reports suggest that the fire was deliberately started. Anyone with any information should contact the local police on 555 278 3738.

Source: International Press

They had sent the boy on his mission, but he had died while asleep from who knows what. That was one of the dangers of travelling – you never knew whether you would wake up in peaceful times or in the middle of a war. They'd had to get rid of the whole family to try and avoid too much scrutiny. They'd forced the father to tell friends and family that they were going on a world tour with their remaining child – life was too short! A husband and probably more importantly a father will agree to do and say anything when looking at men clad in black pointing guns at his wife and child. Precautions had been taken so that the bodies would never be identified, so they wouldn't suffer the same issues they'd had with the girl a few weeks back. The news that the boy, Danny, had woken up wasn't good but wasn't really a setback. He could well be a traveller and so the Syndicate would have to kidnap him to find out. If they were careful, he would just become another statistic - one of the many children who disappear daily. The benefits outweigh the risks. The Boss picks up the phone to make the arrangements.

* * * * *

'Come on Ichiro-san, we're going on patrol,' Danny feels his host stirring while he merges with Ichiro's mind. But something is wrong, he has no control of the host's actions or decisions. Ichiro strides over to the water barrel of his own accord. Danny feels like a passenger or spectator - this hasn't happened before. Maybe the strength of the samurai spirit has stopped him from taking control of this host.

Ichiro looks at his reflection in the water. Danny usually loves this moment - examining his new features. However, this time the ferocious intensity of his host Ichiro's stare is frightening - Danny is actually scared of his own reflection. Fortunately, the image disappears as Ichiro plunges his hands into the water and splashes some on his face. He then turns to his boiled leather armour hanging on a pole in the corner of the large tent he shares with three other samurai who are already kitting up. Ichiro starts donning the armour, testing the straps, and ensuring his short sword and beautifully ornate long sword move easily and soundlessly in their scabbards. Danny is unnerved by this, it's like watching a TV screen while someone else is playing a computer game on it.

They walk to the base's canteen along tracks through the wood. Danny sees what appears to be laundry hanging from trees but then realises that they are bodies swaying slightly in the breeze. He doesn't want to look but has no choice when one of the samurai stops to look up at the grisly scene, Ichiro joins him.

'What's the matter?' One of the other samurai asks.

'Isn't it obvious, Kenji? Catching and hanging deserters

is no job for a samurai, it's dishonourable - not the Bushido way.'

'Keep your voice down, Shinsuke, we're only doing this to complete our mission for the clan – but we'll be hanging up next to them if anyone overhears you. Come on Daisuke,' Ichiro says to the first samurai who had stopped.

Danny struggles to get used to being a passenger in his host's mind - every thought Ichiro has is audible to Danny. Memories appear like a montage of clips from films. The recollections are accompanied by raw feelings, mostly of rage with scenes of battles and horrifying images of death and destruction; but the occasional flashbacks of walking through immaculate gardens under the cherry blossom with a beautiful girl called Yoshiko bring an unexpected softness and sense of longing. These mellow feelings are followed by heart-warming images of Ichiro playing with his brother, Daisuke, when they were younger, or training with wooden swords at the village dojo. Ichiro takes a step towards Daisuke and rests a hand on his shoulder. 'Come on brother, we'll leave this hell hole soon enough and regain our honour. You'll be back in Aya's arms, and I'll be with Yoshiko before you know it.'

The group break their study of the dead deserters and head to the canteen where they grab a bowl of thin miso soup and a ladleful of rice. While the four samurai have their breakfast, Danny's mind races. Despite promising Lewis that he wouldn't 'travel' anywhere while he recuperated, Danny couldn't resist the idea of learning kung fu and helping his brother fight the pirates. He had looked forward to seeing the surprise on his brother's face when he strode up to him and mentioned turquoise dragonflies – seeing Lewis's face break into a beaming smile. But his plans have all gone wrong. He is on the enemy's side and not in control of his host.

They patrol through the forest all morning without any incident. The samurai stop to rest in a bowl-shaped shallow hidden by trees. Daisuke walks away downslope through the trees to relieve himself while the others lie down and enjoy a tranquillity not possible at their camp. Rays of sunlight pierce the forest canopy creating a beautiful woodland scene.

All of a sudden, they hear Daisuke shout, 'I give ground to no man, especially monk scum like you.' Ichiro and the other two samurai crawl to the edge of their bowl and peer carefully through some foliage down towards Daisuke who stands in the centre of a path surrounded by Shaolin monks.

One of the monks, the biggest, shouts scornfully, 'You call us scum! You dress like samurai, but you're a pirate – where's the honour in that?' The monk taps his chest and then raises his little finger in front of him, 'I, Bao, of the Wendeng temple, have more honour in my finger than you.' His fellow monks laugh and jeer at Daisuke as they slowly surround him, staves and swords at the ready. Bao quickly glances around but doesn't see anyone, 'Are you alone, scum? Have you lost your gang?'

'My name is Daisuke, and I am samurai. I'll show you the meaning of honour,' with that he draws his long sword and moves slowly and deliberately, trying to gauge who will strike first. 'Know this, Bao, whatever happens here today – I will be avenged.'

Ichiro starts to rise with the aim of running down to help his brother, but Shinsuke clamps him down to the ground with his hand firmly on his shoulder and whispers urgently, 'No, Ichiro, did you not hear Daisuke – that was a message for us – retreat and fight another day. Let him die with honour – there is no way we three will make any difference against 20 Shaolin monks. Your brother wants us to avenge him, not today…but soon.' Shinsuke keeps his hand firmly on Ichiro's shoulder until Danny feels his host relax and slide his half-drawn sword back into its scabbard.

With a nod of the head, Shinsuke indicates to them they should retreat via the opposite side of the bowl. Danny feels a stinging in the eyes as he watches the monks circling Daisuke, laughing and taunting the samurai, knowing he doesn't have a chance. Ichiro vows to kill any monk he ever meets. A sudden shout and leap sees Daisuke behead an overconfident monk and in the same movement he reverses his sword and impales another who is standing too close, but the thud of Bao's staff on Daisuke's head crumples the samurai to the ground and the other monks spring towards their kill.

Chapter 16

My fingertips hover over the keyboard. I need to find any information that might help General Qi Jiguang, but where do I start? I know I was in China, but when? Chinese historical records are divided by different dynasties. I take another spoonful of crunchy nut cornflakes. Okay, I seem to remember someone saying we were in the Ming dynasty, so I've got the time frame, that's a start. General Qi Jiguang will be famous, but how do I spell his name? I've heard the name hundreds of times and seen it written in Chinese, but never in English. Qi could be spelt how it is pronounced, a sort of Chi which sounds like the 'Chee' in cheese, or it sometimes seems to sound like the 'jee' in Jeep – a few taps on the keyboard reveals it's spelt Qi. And this Qi Jiguang matches the period of history – bingo!

    Mum comes downstairs to the kitchen – she's so happy she could burst. We have a quick chat and plan the day – finish breakfast, chill, and then head to the hospital for visiting hours so we can carry on where we left off with Danny last night.

    Okay, back to my mission. When I look up General Qi Jiguang on Wikipedia there are loads of battles – which one am I about to be in? Usually, battles seem to be named after a local village or town. Ah, there it is, Wengjiagang. Now I need to look up what happened in the build-up to the battle to see if there's anything that might help us beat the pirates – where they gathered, their numbers, stuff like that. I look up the names of the enemy. Those names are etched on my mind as I've heard them mentioned again and again quietly around the camp. People don't seem to want to say the name of a feared enemy in a raised voice for some reason, always in a whisper and only among trusted friends.

I type in wokou pirates and the names Ya Me, Xu Hai, and Chen Dong. There's a whole section on the alliance they made to take over a whole swathe of China. And there it is, General Qi Jiguang's name, describing him as one of the main men involved in the fight against them.

I pause. I know I should be trying to find any information that will help the God of War, but the urge to find out whether we win the Battle of Wengjiagang or die is so strong. Maybe it's better not to know? I could just close the laptop and go back to bed, it's the weekend and so it won't matter if I sleep in. But I know I won't be able to sleep. I pluck up enough courage to scroll down to the outcome of the battle and see that General Qi Jiguang won - with the aid of Shaolin monks. Relief floods every part of my body - I actually feel physically lighter.

I hear the phone ring and my mum answering it. Something in my mum's tone draws my attention – it's bad news. I hear my mum put the phone down and then walk slowly to the kitchen. I look up – and know that Danny has gone again before she says anything. She looks like I feel, hollow, not sure if I have the strength to go through the same nightmare again. Was last night going to be the last time Mum, Danny, and I would sit together laughing and enjoying a lovely dinner? I can guess where he's gone – China; the lure of kung fu and pirates was too much for him to resist, as I knew it would be. Now I really do have to go back and get him out of there.

I try to comfort my mother who seems almost catatonic with shock. The doorbell goes – for some reason, I think it could be someone who has more positive news about Danny, so I race to the door and open it to find the nurse, Amelie, looking concerned on our doorstep.

'Hi Lewis, has the hospital phoned you?'

'Yes, we just-' I can't finish the sentence.

'I'm so sorry, Lewis. How's your mum holding up?'

I just shake my head.

'Be strong, Lewis, do whatever you have to do to get your mum through this,' Amelie reaches out and gives my arm a comforting squeeze.

I nod and open the door, 'Please, come in.'

Amelie follows me into the kitchen where my mum looks up and they just stare at each other in silence. My mother walks into Amelie's open arms and just crumples, sobbing uncontrollably into the nurse's shoulder. I'm welling up - I just can't take it anymore. I want to call Claire, but I also just want to be alone. I want to comfort my mum, but I also want to escape this scene. I want to do something but can't think straight.

But there is something I can do – find Danny, so that Mum, my brother, and I can try and get on with our lives again. I need to focus. Danny is in China, that's almost definite, so I need to find him before the battle. Breathing in deeply I head back to the lounge where I wake up my computer screen.

If I can find something which helps General Qi Jiguang, then he'll be more amenable when I ask him for help looking for my brother. I have to set aside the sadness that this morning has suddenly brought, close my ears to the grief going on next door in the kitchen, and concentrate all my remaining energy on getting myself into the God of War's good books.

The focus of the Wikipedia page is on the main events of the battle, so I look at the references to the pirates cited in the text and click on them, which takes me to different articles detailing how the pirates planned to take over that part of China. The hours fly by. Amelie takes Mum for a walk and is gone for ages. Claire phones me again and again, but I can't face her, so I don't answer. A part of me wants to - a hug and soothing words from her would be so nice. But I need to get this done before tonight.

It's a strange feeling reading about the events which took place hundreds of years ago in a far-off land and being able to actually visualize the preparations from my trip last night. I can almost hear the familiar noises of soldiers going about their daily routine, and smell the aromas, both pleasant and unpleasant – wood smoke, food cooking, oiled leather, stale sweat, and the latrines. I'm jumping between then and now. I even spot a few mistakes in the accounts of what happened, but that's to be expected I suppose, as the events have been documented based on minimal surviving records and a lot of speculation.

Hold on! I'm looking at an old map relating to the Battle of Wengjiagang – according to this website page, the site of the battle is on the way to Shanghai. Oh, no! I think we've set up our base in the wrong place… But that doesn't make sense as I know the village near our fort is also called Wengjiagang. Have the history books got it wrong? I'm feeling a bit hot and sweaty at the thought that we've been duped by the pirates. I quickly click on a different website's account of the battle which states the pirates were en route to Hangzhou. Phew! We're in the right place – just some of the historical accounts are wrong. I have to take a deep breath – if I had gone with the first account of the battle then I might have persuaded the God of War to relocate to the Wengjiagang in the north. A mistake like that could have given the pirates everything they wanted, and cost thousands of lives in the process. If I ever have to do something like this again, God forbid, then I'll have to check every detail thoroughly.

After a few hours of looking at the computer screen, the words are no longer registering. I've got what I wanted and now it's just a case of waiting till bedtime when I can travel back to China. Time to close the pages and switch the computer off – but something leaps out from the page I was just reading – I reread it again hoping I've misunderstood it. Maybe this account of the number of casualties on our side is wrong – God, I hope so, otherwise it seems hardly any of us survive. I'll have to put it to the back of my mind, or I won't be able to think straight.

To take my mind off the unnerving revelation I try to think of how I can use what I've learnt. Plans start to take form and so I contemplate how I can feed my ideas into a conversation with Tianyuan – that's going to be tricky. When I think of Grandfather Teacher, I picture those bright intelligent eyes almost aglow in his dark walnut-like face. He seems to be able to spot deception from a mile away. I can just see myself spluttering and struggling to form sentences under his gaze and then just blurting out the whole truth of my situation. I need to keep a cool head – maybe I can get him to think that he has come up with the ideas. If I ask some probing questions about how things usually unfold in the build-up to a battle, then maybe I can just nudge him with words and questions towards the actions we need to take to win.

The day drags on, Mum returns and takes a sleeping tablet before wishing me goodnight and heading upstairs. I clean my teeth, lie down, look over at Danny's empty bed, and switch off my bedside light. Please, God, let me fall asleep and just get on with what I have to do.

I look at Tianyuan going over the training programme in his command tent, the strain is taking its toll. Some of the recruits' martial arts training is falling behind, which has a knock-on effect on their other training. Bao is doing everything possible to undermine Tianyuan – whatever the cost to training and ultimately the whole force's ability to defeat the pirates. Everyone in the camp seems affected - the morale is at an all-time low, which further impedes progress. Tianyuan looks tired, his usual upbeat manner gone, and even his shoulders seem to sag.

I don't want to interrupt Tianyuan's thoughts so let the silence go on, the only sound in the tent is the fizzle of the oil lamp's wick and the distant sound of barrack life - shouted commands, soldiers being drilled on the parade square, marching men and horses going back and forth. I become aware of another sound getting steadily closer, raucous laughter, completely at odds with the deflated atmosphere which has pervaded the camp. As the forced laughter gets closer, I start to recognize some of the voices, they belong to the rival kung fu masters.

A bark of laughter breaks Tianyuan's concentration, he looks up registering the voices and to whom they belong. He lets the scroll of paper roll itself up on the table and mutters, 'Ah, it seems the time has come.' As I watch, he does a few quick stretches, makes sure his robes are securely fastened, straightens up, and then turns to me. 'Whatever happens outside, whatever they say, whatever I do, do not respond or join in – this is my fight.'

'But Grandfather Teacher, you know I cannot do that! Let me help you put these idiots in their place.' I reckon I have learnt enough to hold my own against anyone in a fight and am ready to prove it – I dismiss the little episode I had at the assassin's castle where I froze as a one-off. Actually, a fight with these monks is something I've been looking forward to – I've heard the sly little digs the rabble outside have come out with as I walk by – a constant stream of comments intended to provoke a reaction. To my shame, I haven't offered any of them out, but now I've had enough, and looking at how it has brought Tianyuan's spirits down, I want to fight them.

'No, Lu-wis, please, you must not intervene. Watch and learn. The impact of what happens next will be all the greater if I do this myself.'

'But-'

'No. You are ready in terms of kung fu skills, but there's more to a fight than physical violence. Control your emotions, observe, but do not be drawn in, that's an order,' Tianyuan looks directly into my eyes and there's no doubt he's serious. He stands up straight, then slumps a bit, adding years to his appearance – he's a master of deception as well as kung fu. He starts to walk towards the tent flaps, unarmed and with a slight shuffle.

'Grandfather Teacher, you've forgotten your staff,'

He looks back at me, and with a quick smile, he says, 'No, I haven't. Watch and learn, Lu-wis, watch and learn.'

We emerge from the tent and as our eyes adjust to the sunlight, we can see that there is a large group of monks loitering outside. Silence descends as the group notices us. There are eighteen masters of king fu from the dissenting factions in the camp, all sullen-eyed and moving slowly to surround Tianyuan.

The stand-off draws the attention of passers-by who stop or rush off to get their buddies. Tianyuan just stands there looking each one of the kung fu masters in the eye. They don't seem intimidated by Grandfather Teacher; I suppose the old, unarmed man stooped before them doesn't really look much of a threat.

'We need to talk, Tianyuan,' there's an intake of breath at the rudeness of the address, not using his respected title. As expected, it's Bao who leads this rabble - big, arrogant, and a bully.

'What do you want, Bao? You should be training the recruits.'

'I've decided that your training isn't worthy of someone with my skills, you need to relinquish the title of Captain of Training and let me take over.'

Tianyuan stares at him for a moment and then laughs, which becomes a wheezy cough further sloping his shoulders and causing his body to slump. After he gains control of his cough, Tianyuan tries to straighten up with limited success and looks back at Bao.

'"Your superior skills," you say. I agree, you are superior to me in stupidity and ugliness. You've been scratching your brains so much it's worn away the cloth in the seat of your pants.' The tension ratchets up, there are gasps from the crowd of onlookers that have gathered. Bao's accomplices visibly grip their weapons more firmly in their hands.

Bao takes a moment to respond, 'Leave now old man, and I'll spare you the shame of being completely outfought by me, Bao, your master.'

'Big talk, from a big dumb ass.'

'This is your last chance, Tianyuan, leave with some semblance of pride or stay and be humiliated - let the world see how your skills are no match for mine.'

'I don't think so. These are my terms. You and all your followers will drop your weapons, walk barefoot to the temple at the top of Tayun Mountain, where you will spend the rest of your lives in the snow and cloud praying for forgiveness as a penance for your crimes.'

'Crimes, what crimes?' Bao shouts.

'The crime of allowing people in your charge to not fulfil their potential. The hundreds of recruits who, due to your negligence, are not ready for the impending battle. You will be as guilty of their deaths as the pirates they will face - lives you are willing to sacrifice just to feed your inflated ego.'

'You talk big, old man, but you are nothing, and now I will teach you a lesson in martial arts.'

'No, I don't want to fight you, it would be unfair.' The silence is complete. Nobody can believe that Tianyuan is admitting his inferiority to Bao.

'Ha-ha! Do you hear that, Tianyuan admits my kung fu is superior to his - all of you are witnesses,' he's elated and swirls around to see the reaction of the mass of people that have now gathered around them. But most look confused, they can't believe their ears.

'You misunderstand me. It would not be fair on you, Bao, to fight me without the help of your 17 thugs.' Everything stops. Bao's head whips around to face Tianyuan, puce with rage. His acolytes share his anger at the taunt. To be called a thug is the ultimate insult for a Buddhist monk, a man with no skill, no virtue, a person only out to satisfy themselves at the expense of everyone else.

'You will fight me, here and now, I will defeat you, and then you will carry out your penance on Mount Tayun, never to show your face in civilised society again,' Tianyuan continues.

'You have to beat us first, a dead man can't make decrees,' with these words Bao moves into a fighting stance followed instantly by the other 17 masters, each armed with their weapon of choice, sword, staff, spear, billhook, and whip chains. Tianyuan is unarmed. He calmly appraises his enemy before he suddenly leaps backwards towards the entrance to his tent and unearths the pole holding the flag bearing his rank. The pole is made of steel and is incredibly heavy, but in one swift movement, Tianyuan whips the pole against a nearby wagon taking off the crossbeam holding the flag, so that he can now wield it like a staff.

There's no sound or movement. The onlookers don't seem to be even breathing. As I survey the crowd, I'm alarmed to see that the God of War is among the crowd, surrounded by his imperial bodyguard who have cleared a space for him to watch the events unfold. He doesn't see me as his gaze is focused intently on the confrontation – he whispers something to one of his lieutenants who sprints away, hopefully for help.

Bao looks around and also sees that his commander is present – there's no backing down now, so he leaps forward swirling his staff in circles faster than the eye can follow. He is surprisingly nimble - Tianyuan watches him calmly and at the last moment, before Bao looks like he will connect with his staff, back flips with staff in hand which circles around and connects with the back of Bao's head and that is it. Bao's eyes turn up in their sockets, his knees give way, and he crumples to the floor. Time speeds up, spears and swords thrust at Tianyuan, chains, staffs and billhooks whip in his direction. Tianyuan dances around them, like a dragonfly, he leaps to and fro in random directions striking his enemy on head, chest, groin, and back. Before I fully exhale the breath I've been holding, all his opponents lie either groaning or unconscious on the ground. One of the masters of kung fu tries to crawl away into the crowd, but the God of War nods at two of his men who raise the injured kung fu master roughly to his feet, his head lolling around. The guards tie his arms behind his back and then push him to his knees.

There's silence and then a massive cheer. Tianyuan doesn't acknowledge the crowd, just surveys the scene - bodies lying everywhere. He allows himself the faintest of smiles, then adopts a very contrite and serious expression as he approaches the God of War, kneeling in front of him awaiting his punishment – fighting in camp can hold the death penalty.

'Rise, Tianyuan, Captain of Training.' The God of War reaches out and supports Tianyuan under the elbow until Grandfather Teacher is on his feet. He then turns to address the crowd. 'We have our Captain of Training to thank for showing us that we can win, whatever the odds. We are fighting a noble cause, just as Grandfather Teacher has done here, and we will prevail, just as Grandfather Teacher has done here. We will eradicate all brigands from our lands. The pirates will die. These scum,' he indicates the fallen kung fu masters, 'will walk barefoot into oblivion as Grandfather Teacher has decreed, failure to do so will result in death; they will no longer be addressed as masters of kung fu and their names will be erased from all records. But we will live on forever, never to be forgotten, for the victory we will have over the pirates in the battle ahead.' With his last word, he clasps Tianyuan's hand in his and raises both in the air to a deafening cheer which spreads across the camp. The camp's malaise evaporates - the army is ready to take on anyone, whatever the odds.

* * * * *

'Ichiro-san! Ichiro-san!' Danny feels Ichiro bolt upright from his bedroll, hand already gripping the hilt of his samurai sword - instantly fully alert for danger. Ichiro's memories of his brother Daisuke and Yoshiko pass fleetingly through his mind – Danny watches these images and feels Ichiro's feelings turn from ones of love and fondness to a vicious rage and an unquenchable need for revenge.

Kenji and Shinsuke are also fully alert and in moments all three rush out of the tent into the crisp morning air scanning left and right through the forest and the slowly dissolving mist for any threat. A junior samurai stands panting before them. He bows and looks up with excitement sparkling in his eyes, 'Ichiro-san, a band of eighteen monks have been tracked coming through the forest. They stopped for the night at a clearing on the track to the fishing village we went to two days back.'

'How do you know they are monks?' Kenji asks.

'They've shaved their heads and dyed their robes orange – as Ichiro-san said they would in preparation for battle.'

'This could be some sort of trap, why would a band of monks venture so far from their camp?' Shinsuke asks aloud rubbing his chin.

'Hiroshi and I wondered the same. But while we tracked them, we noticed that they seem to have been in a fight – some are being supported by others because they are carrying injuries. And they don't have any weapons, only branches they've tried to fashion into staffs, but they're little more than sticks.' The junior samurai then looks nervously at Ichiro which doesn't go unnoticed.

'What?' Ichiro asks but has already guessed what the young samurai is holding back.

The junior samurai takes a moment to find his voice, 'Their leader goes by the name of Bao, and fits the description of the monk who killed your brother, big and brash... so sorry.'

Danny can feel the hate-filled fury pumping through Ichiro's veins and then hears the plan of action forming in his host's mind. 'You said there were eighteen monks, but some of them wounded?' The junior samurai nods quickly at Ichiro's question. 'Assemble three sections, we'll need 30 men, half of them archers.' Danny watches the frantic activity through Ichiro's eyes and within moments the samurai are trotting through the woods following the young scout.

They move silently through the forest. Danny looks around to see the demon-face plates of his fellow samurai looking ahead with eyeless sockets and grotesque smiling faces. Figures seem to appear and disappear in the mist as they race through the trees.

A bird call brings them to a halt. The junior samurai responds with the same birdsong and then a samurai appears in front of them. He bows and reports to Ichiro. 'The monks have broken camp and are continuing on their way to the fishing village. They are moving even slower than yesterday because of their injured. If we head in that direction,' he points right, 'we will be able to cut them off.' Without a word they run in the direction suggested keeping the track a few hundred meters away on their left.

Ichiro slows the pace so that the samurai creep forward scanning the forest. A few brusque orders and the samurai disperse to set up an ambush – five archers on either side of the path hidden far enough in the trees not to be seen but within effective bow range. Ten samurai head up the trail ready to seal off any retreat by the monks. Ichiro and nine others wait concealed behind trees near a bend in the track, ready to block the monks' way. Then absolute silence.

The sound of walking, limping and the odd grumble can be heard getting closer. Ichiro peers from behind a tree and then nods at Kenji who draws back the arrow notched in his bow, aims, and releases. The first monk is punched off his feet by the impact – the other monks stand frozen with shock for a moment before arrows rain down on them from both sides. Some turn to flee but see the ethereal figures of ten samurai through the mist blocking their escape. They go to ground leaving ten of their men dead or dying on the path.

'Cease fire!' bellows Ichiro. There's silence as he stands up and then walks slowly down the track towards the monks flanked by Kenji on his right, another arrow notched in his bow ready, and Shinsuke on his left, sword drawn. The other seven samurai form a screen to ensure nobody escapes.

Danny sees the bodies of orange-clad monks dead or breathing their last as his host strides towards the remaining monks who cower behind tree trunks along the side of the track. They don't dare reveal themselves for fear of being shot by the archers. Shinsuke and Ichiro dispatch the quivering monks with quick slashes of their swords, barely breaking stride. Then Ichiro stops as he sees his brother's murderer stand before him. Danny feels Ichiro raise his arm to ensure none of the samurai interfere.

Bao stands up straight, his face sneering as he points his make-shift staff at Ichiro, 'You think-' Ichiro slices off the offending arm below the elbow. The monk pales and looks wide-eyed at the blood pumping out of the stump. Ichiro moves forward and back slashes through Bao's hamstring causing the monk to collapse to the ground. By this time all the samurai have emerged from their hiding places and stand around Bao.

'Leave him for the wolves,' Ichiro commands, and with that, the samurai turn to head back to camp. 'I have avenged you, brother,' Ichiro says looking up to the heavens. Bao looks dumbly at the blood pumping from his arm's stump and at his useless leg and then up at Ichiro who cleans his sword on the monk's orange robes before turning to follow the other samurai. Danny can sense that Ichiro's vendetta against monks isn't quenched. To his horror, he hears Ichiro swear to kill every monk he encounters – and that, Danny realises, means Ichiro, his host, will murder Lewis if they ever meet; and all he'll be able to do is watch as his brother is killed.

Chapter 17

Tianyuan and I are walking to a quiet glade we've been using outside our camp for one-to-one training. This daily routine has really improved my kung fu; having a teacher of his calibre watching my every move and identifying strengths and weaknesses has meant I'll reach master's level in a fraction of the time it would have taken me otherwise. My mind drifts off to all the other skills I could learn in a similar way by travelling and working with the most inspiring people in history or by using them as my hosts. I pull my thoughts back to the present and start a conversation I've rehearsed in my mind repeatedly since I woke up this morning.

'Grandfather Teacher, may I ask a question?'

Tianyuan looks sideways at me as we walk to the glade, 'Of course, Lu-wis, what's on your mind?'

'General Qi Jiguang and all the commanders keep telling us how we will beat the pirate clans and wipe them from the face of the Earth.'

'Yes, so?' Tianyuan looks at me curiously.

'Reports suggest that the pirate clans may have twenty or even thirty times more men than us – and most of them battle-hardened. How can our small army made up of mostly new recruits have a chance against such odds?' Tianyuan looks ahead and a few moments pass in silence as we keep walking, albeit a bit slower.

'In our favour, we have soldiers who are fighting for not just their lives, but the lives of their families. In the past, such a motivation has won battles for armies in similar situations. We have also been training well, our soldiers are now privy to kung fu skills not usually taught in the army or at any temple except to trusted acolytes of many years' service.' I come to a halt and consequently, so does Tianyuan.

'Grandfather Teacher, do you think we can win?' He's looking at me in the way I've been dreading.

'Lu-wis, I'm glad you are thinking with a cool head and not swept up by grand empty words, seeing through all that nonsense will serve you well in life. In answer to your question, yes, I think we can win, but it will be close. We need to use all our cunning and guile to overcome our enemy.' That's my cue.

'How do the pirate leaders feed such an army?'

'That's a good question, Lu-wis.' We've started walking again and I can see Tianyuan seriously pondering over what I've just asked – this is my window of opportunity.

'The clans are sailing from up and down the coast to their meeting point, right?' Tianyuan nods as we walk. 'They must be as worried about food supplies as we are, and so if they heard of a huge shipment of rice coming from somewhere, would they be able to resist trying to capture it?

'Where are you going with this, Lu-wis?'

'Imagine if we let it be known that there was a huge shipment of rice sailing down the coast to resupply us, and the pirates captured it, they would think it a great victory and a good sign of things to come.' Tianyuan doesn't say anything, my prompt to continue. 'What if we poison the rice? Not all of it, leave some of it clean so that if they test it, it's okay. Then, when their camp canteens serve up dinner, they'll all just tuck into it without a thought.'

'Poison.' Tianyuan looks at me with a serious expression, 'How did you come up with such an idea?'

'I thought about it at dinner last night. I was watching the wagons bringing in the precious bags of rice and how even in our camp the food needs to be guarded. We seem to get through wagon loads of food every day, and we're only a fraction of the numbers the pirate lords have to feed. The idea just came to me in my sleep, I guess.' It's not a complete lie, so I am able to look Tianyuan in the eye.

'Hmm,' is all I get which is a bit disappointing. I'm not

sure if that 'Hmm' means it's a stupid idea or that he'll think about it. We've reached the glade and so drop off our knapsacks and warm up with our staffs in opposite corners of our well-trodden training area, our grass dojo.

'Today, Lu-wis, I want to teach you The Lion's Spring and The Crane's Ruse, both are lethal and so I remind you of your promise that you will not teach these moves to anyone.' I'm expecting a response to my idea of poisoning the enemy's food supply, so it takes me a moment to process what Tianyuan has just said.

'Yes, Grandfather Teacher, you have my word.' He turns around and scans the area near us to ensure that no one is spying on us and then shows me the first move in slow motion. He pauses frequently, his body frozen so that he can highlight the position of his feet, knees, hips, the angle of his torso, and the grip on his staff.

We walk back to the camp in silence a few hours later. I'm disappointed with myself, my training wasn't good - my mind wasn't focused because of the lack of reaction I got from Tianyuan to my earlier suggestion. Does he think poisoning is a step too far and breaks some sort of moral code? Or maybe he wants to present the idea as his own to get credit for it. No, he wouldn't do that. I'm so deflated, my mind has started imagining ridiculous scenarios.

My troop are laughing at each other – we've had to shave our heads and die our clothes orange – a tradition among Shaolin monks going to war; it has a practical purpose too – it's easy to identify friend from foe in the chaos of battle. Our field craft instructor, Sergeant Wang, marches forward and barks, 'Dragon troop, fall in'. Immediately, we form up in ranks, stand feet together, hands straight down at our sides, shoulders back, chest forward, eyes looking straight ahead at an imaginary object that keeps our undivided attention.

A quick glance shows that a couple of weeks of drill training has really paid off – the ranks and files are perfectly spaced. Sergeant Wang starts his inspection, checking to see our robes are clean, our boiled leather chest plates polished, and that our personal hygiene is up to scratch. The military is fastidious about such things. The first day it was clear that spitting, touching your face, and not washing or shaving were all big no-nos. If one person is caught out, then we're all in for a 'beasting'. This usually involves running up and down hills with a heavy training spear or sword held above your head, followed by press-ups and other exercises that can result in half the troop throwing up or literally passing out – 15 of our bunch ended up in sick bay the first day. The seven o'clock parade and inspection is usually a good indicator of whether we're in for a bad day or a good one.

Sergeant Wang seems to be making rapid progress along the front rank – a good sign. The true test comes when he inspects Recruit Zhang - a short and slightly overweight teenager. There seems to be nothing we can do to stop him from looking like he's slept in his uniform in a muddy puddle - it's some sort of mystery. I can feel the tension in the air rise as the troop awaits the indicator - are we all to be beasted or are we going to focus on proper military training? My uncle told me that when he was in the Marines, the training was geared to making sure you looked after each other, or to weed out those who weren't suited to military life. Punishing everyone for one person's mistake drove people to work together or, if this didn't work, make life so difficult for the person causing the problem that they gave up and left. However, sometimes some recruits were victimised due to a random dislike by the training team, then there was nothing rational that could be done. The person had to go or everyone would suffer. Recruit Zhang was our indicator, our litmus test.

The seconds stretch out as Sergeant Wang inspects Recruit Zhang up and down, peering in closely to have a good look at his face. 'Did you shave this morning, Recruit Zhang?'

'Yes, Sergeant,'

'Sorry, were you trying to whisper sweet nothings into my ear, Recruit Zhang, I didn't catch what you said.'

This isn't looking good.

'Yes, Sergeant!' Recruit Zhang shouts.

'Did you use a mirror?'

'Yes, Sergeant!'

'Well next time use a razor, it gives a closer shave.'

There's the titter of laughter from some of the recruits behind me and a tangible relaxation of the tension, we seem to be okay.

'If Recruit Zhang is fine for parade, then I'll assume you are all up to scratch this morning.'

I can feel sweat trickling down my back and my arms as we practice anti-cavalry charge manoeuvres using spears on the parade ground. We march, and wheel into formation presenting a wall of spear points in the direction of an imaginary cavalry attack. The front rank is on their knees, the rank behind crouched, and the rear rank with the long spears standing side on - the heavy spears held firmly in both hands and the wooden end of the spear forced into a fresh pothole in the ground. We're motionless as our sergeant moves up and down the line inspecting us and telling the odd soldier here and there to adjust his stance or grip.

A messenger comes running across the parade ground and halts in front of Sergeant Weng. After a brief exchange, the Sergeant scans the ranks and his eyes rest on me.

'Lu-wis, fall out. Report to General Qi Jiguang's command tent.' At that, I can hear loads of muttering in the ranks, everyone is surprised and as curious as I am about the order. 'Silence!' Sergeant Weng barks. 'What are we? A bunch of gossiping fishwives? The next person I hear talking in the ranks will be on latrine duty for the next month.' The prospect of cleaning out the toilets for hours a day clamps everyone's mouths shut. I move my spear carefully out of the formation and look at Weng questioningly, not sure what to do. 'Well, what are you waiting for Lu-wis, get a move on. At the double!'

'Yes, Sergeant,' I trot across the parade ground, return the spear to the rack at the side, and look back at my troop and sergeant. I can feel the curiosity emanating from the group. Sergeant Weng gives me a nod and a wink and so I look at the messenger who then turns and we both 'double' towards the command tent. As I'm trotting towards the

Headquarters, I realize that this might have something to do with the plan I mentioned yesterday to Tianyuan.

Whatever the reason for my summons, this is my best chance of finding Danny. Now that I'm fairly certain he is here in China I thought my search might be made easier by the fact that Danny will hopefully be wearing a dragonfly pendant, like the one I'm wearing. But I've not seen one and so have resorted to just gawping at people to try and spot if any of them have my brother's characteristics – it's impossible. When I meet the General, I'm going to ask for his help, whether it gets me into trouble or not. The messenger and I stop outside the Command Tent.

'Recruit Lu-wis reporting as commanded,' the messenger announces. One of the guards disappears into the tent and returns a moment later indicating with his arm holding up the tent flap that I should enter. I walk forward and stop at the entrance, where I take a moment to let my vision adjust to the dark interior. Inside the tent around the same map table I saw when I first arrived all those weeks ago are General Qi Jiguang, Tianyuan, the camp adjutant, and a man in civvies who looks at me with a grin which I'm not sure is friendly or sly. I march forward and come to a halt five paces in front of General Qi Jiguang.

'Recruit Lewis reporting, sir.'

'At ease, Lu-wis,' the General says. He studies me up and down and then looks directly into my eyes, he seems to be evaluating me in some way or another. 'Grandfather Teacher has told us of your plan, which,' he starts nodding ever so slightly, 'is a good one.' There are smiles all around which is reassuring and injects me with a bit of confidence. 'Tell me Lu-wis, where would you send this shipment of poisoned rice?' He gestures at the table.

I approach the table and study the map, identify the locations of the pirates' clans, and try to remember what I saw when I surfed the net. I see the furthest of them all from our location and recognise the name, Ya Me. I look up and get a nod from Tianyuan, the others are observing me intently. A scribe I hadn't noticed before sits ready in the corner of the tent, his hand hovering over some paper ready to record my thoughts.

'I would let it be known that there's a rice shipment moving in these sea channels here, near Ya Me's forces. He's further away and so if, I mean when he attacks and steals the rice, news of the poisoning is less likely to reach the other pirate clans massing here in time. That might have the added benefit of sowing seeds of doubt in the other pirate clan leaders as to the strength of their alliance.' I don't know where that last idea came from, but it sounds good to me, and to the others gauging by the slight nods of approval I get.

'What do you think?' General Qi Jiguang asks the civilian. I haven't been introduced and reckon that I won't be - this man must be a spy or the leader of a spy network.

'It will take some planning, and probably cost a few sailors' lives, but it's a good one, and so I support the idea.' The civilian says this while staring at me the whole time.

After a moment's silence, General Qi Jiguang nods, 'Do it, get everything you need. But only a handful of people must know about this, we're not the only ones with spies lurking in the shadows. Tell me, Lu-wis, where did you get this idea?'

'Sir, I'm not sure, sir. It might have come from all the history lessons my father gave me.'

'Oh really, and where is your father now?'

'He's gone, sir.' My mind wanders to my father - I look down at the map to hide my feelings. The name Wengjiagang where our camp is marked leaps out at me. The General follows my gaze and then I see him look back at me.

'Tell me, Lu-wis, where would you meet the enemy.'

'Here, sir, at Wengjiagang. There's no better place we could have sited our fort.' I look at the little geographic illustrations and hope I interpret them correctly. 'Time is of the essence. The pirates must be eating through their supplies while they wait for the rest of their forces to arrive, so they'll need to take the most direct route to Hangzhou to replenish their stores. They'll also want to get there before our reinforcements arrive. Trying to go through the marshlands or forests will take an army too long, therefore, they have to come this way. Wengjiagang allows us to block their march along the road or rain down fire on any boats that try to go upriver. Our fort lies on raised land, unlike the other options along their route, which will give us an additional advantage in that our archers will be able to hit the enemy before we come into their range.'

Now all their eyebrows are raised. I'm such a fool, there are bound to be questions about me now. They'll be wondering how a lowly recruit can come up with such a plan, read maps, and be so aware of logistics. The silence stretches out.

'I think we have Sun Tzu reincarnated in our midst.' The comparison of me to the famous master of battle tactics causes a little chuckle around the table. 'If you have any other ideas, Lu-wis, please let us know. It's taken you just seconds to come to the same conclusion which took us days. I'd be a fool not to listen to your thoughts on the upcoming battle when you clearly have a very special gift.'

'Thank you, sir.'

'Return to your troop, Lu-wis.'

'Yes, sir, General, sir.' But I don't move. I came here on my own mission, and I need to stick my neck out now or miss a great opportunity.

'Is there anything else?' The General asks, a mixture of wonder and amusement playing on his face.

'Sir, I was wondering if… if it's not too much trouble, and if you don't mind me asking, and it's not breaking any rules of conduct, and-'

'Spit it out, Lu-wis, what can I do for you?'

'General, sir. I am looking for my brother who I think is in this camp, but it's impossible for me to find him among the thousands here. Could I ask that you include an order for him to go to Grandfather Teacher's tent as soon as possible, in your written camp notices? And if you could get the camp criers to shout it around as well that would be great - just in case my brother can't read, I mean doesn't check the notices.' I look at Tianyuan to see if I have overstepped the line, but his smile indicates I haven't.

'Of course, Lu-wis, family should be reunited before a battle. What's his name?'

'Danny, sir.'

'Danny. What an unusual name.' He then turns to his adjutant, 'Issue the orders,' the adjutant nods and there's silence while they wait for me to leave.

'Thank you, General,' I about-turn and march out of the tent, a huge smile on my face at the prospect of the reunion with Danny. There's also a growing sense of wonder at how easy it is for me to use my travelling skills to impress people of influence. The opportunities out there are limitless when you already know what is going to happen, provided I'm in the right universe. Hmm…

* * * * *

Ichiro surveys the scene. The village is strewn with bodies – orange-clad monks, but mostly pirates and a few samurai. This does not bode well. There were only around 20 monks who came to rescue the village – as planned. Chen Dong has correctly, in Ichiro's opinion, ordered bands of pirates to ravage the land far and wide forcing General Qi Jiguang to send out patrols to try and save the local population. And in the process, weakening the strength of his garrison at the fort.

Ichiro organised this ambush. It should have been a rout, thirty samurai, 200 of the pirate rabble, and the villagers press-ganged into joining the pirate horde versus 20 monks. Another of Chen Dong's ideas – give the local men a choice of joining the pirate army or being executed along with their families. So the ranks were swelling with untrained locals with a dubious level of allegiance to the pirate clans – not a good idea in Ichiro's opinion.

Danny hears Kenji joining his host, nothing is said, they just survey the carnage. Ichiro's thoughts are once again audible to Danny who can also sense an element of doubt creeping into his host's mind. The monks were dead, but so were over a hundred of his force. If the monks fight like that behind defences at the fort, then they are going to be in for a long, drawn-out battle. The pirates will win, Ichiro is sure of that, with odds of 30 to 1 they have to win, but it will cost them.

He'll have to think of a way to deploy his samurai in the final battle so that they will live to take vengeance on their real enemy – the Japanese clan that beat theirs in a costly battle by breaking the Bushido code, showing no respect for honour.

A cry of pain draws their attention. Ichiro and Kenji walk to the sound. There are two pirates on their knees leaning over an injured monk. They seem to be cutting at something. Ichiro looks over and sees the mutilation that the two have already carried out and immediately draws his sword and thrusts it down into the monk's chest, putting him out of his misery.

'Animals!' Kenji nods agreement but draws Ichiro away.

The tattooed Mike looks at the retreating samurai, 'What's his problem?'

Emma shrugs, 'Let them clear up and head off – I'm pretty sure I heard a monk groaning over there by the animal pen. Just think, anyone of these monks could be Lewis.'

Mike beams at the idea, 'I guess we'll find out if he's dead when we get back to London.'

'Yeah, we will – just try not to look too happy when you hear the news.' Emma looks quickly around before continuing. 'We'll just hang back and let them leave so we can carry on. We'll get back to the main camp by nightfall – nobody will notice that we've gone for a bit.' Mike nods, liking the idea.

Ichiro looks back once more at the two and realises one is a girl. He shakes his head in disgust. 'Who are they?'

Kenji looks back, 'They were nobodies until a few weeks back, but then their exploits have started to become the talk of the camp,' he spits as if getting rid of a bad taste in his mouth. 'They've had tattoos of a skull and crossbones on their arms, I don't know if they had them together or that was what got them to team up. Anyway, you know how it is, the pirates love to make a name for themselves.'

'The sooner we've got what we need, the sooner we

can head back to Japan, I'm sick of this place,' Ichiro says under his breath. Kenji nods agreement. Just then Shinsuke turns up looking worried.

'There's hardly any food in this village – certainly not enough to bolster our dwindling supplies,' Shinsuke says with a sigh.

'Just more evidence of our leaders' incompetence. Who organises a campaign of this size without enough food to keep us going? Like I say, the sooner we leave China, the better.' The two samurai nod agreement. 'Let's get back to camp.' The samurai round up their forces, signal when they are ready, and head back to their base.

Chapter 18

I can't stop feeling pretty happy with myself as I look over the battlements that we've been building over the last month at Wengjiagang. Tianyuan told me before it was announced to the rest of the camp that my plan has worked: Ya Me's clan has had to return to their base at Songjiang badly battered with thousands dead and even more fighting for their lives after eating the poisoned shipment of rice they captured. Also, Xu Hai and the main body of his force haven't been able to join their vanguard near here as they were blown off course and so their fleet has had to return to their base. This seems to corroborate what I've read in my research, that Ya Me and Xu Hai didn't make the battle, so it seems fair to assume I am in my world and not a parallel universe.

One issue that is troubling though is that the scale of the conflict doesn't correlate with what I've read - historical records suggest that we win a much smaller battle. But I also remember reading that General Qi Jiguang played down his triumphs in order to avoid too much acclamation: if a general became too popular in those times, they were often executed on jumped-up charges of treason.

An uninvited thought brings me down. Despite the notices and the camp's criers ordering Danny to report to Tianyuan's tent, he hasn't turned up, which must mean that my brother isn't here. A shiver runs down my spine as I remember that horrendous dream where I killed Danny whose host was a samurai warrior. Surely he can't be among the pirate clans, can he? If my brother is here, will he survive the battle? Will I survive the battle? I try not to think about the fact that according to my research, only around 50 of our side survive – but, maybe that account, like so many others, was wrong. What else can I do? Can I do something to stop us from losing so many men?

Looking across the battlements gives me a little hope. A huge palisade wall made of timbers sunk into the ground forms a five-meter-high barrier around our camp, which lies on a small hill alongside the river on my left. The marshland on my right protects us from that direction, it's almost impossible to walk across, especially under a hail of arrows. So the pirates will have to come at us head-on out of the forest five hundred meters away.

I scan the ground ahead; the soldiers are working tirelessly to build the final defences. A man-made moat surrounds our camp which looks harmless enough except for the fact that the muddy water conceals thousands of sharpened stakes. In front of the moat are line after line of more sharpened bamboo barriers pointing outwards. Here and there groups of soldiers are camouflaging the lily pits – holes in the ground with yet more sharpened stakes buried in the bottom of them. It all looks pretty good, however, there is one drawback with this location, especially at this time of year – the area is prone to fog which limits visibility to less than a few meters at times.

Birds burst from the trees to my front – something has spooked them. The lookouts have also noticed this and start frantically clanging gongs - pandemonium ensues as orders seem to rebound off the palisade walls. Soldiers sprint to return to the safety that the fort provides. Oxen are whipped mercilessly to pull barricades of wooden spikes across the road, blocking it off, before they too lumber towards the safety of the camp.

Out of the forests stream thousands upon thousands of pirates. My earlier positivity vanishes as I see their numbers. This can't be right. I count the surprisingly well-ordered formations of around 500 hundred men. There are already twenty of them, so ten thousand enemy and they are still pouring out of the forest. There are so many of them that they have to march forward to within 200 hundred meters of us to make room for the remainder of their army. They stretch out left and right as far as the marshland and river allows until the whole area in front of us is filled with pirates. I'm so engrossed in the scene before me that I haven't noticed that General Qi Jiguang stands on my left and Tianyuan on my right.

'It looks like your spies were right, General, sixty thousand men,' Tianyuan says calmly. Grandfather Teacher told me about the reports – locals have been press-ganged into joining, and bands from other pirate clans have also enlisted hoping to get a share of the plunder when they reach the wealthy city of Hangzhou.

'Yes, it appears so. But thankfully no siege equipment, at least not yet.'

I look back and forth at them; they seem completely unperturbed by the sight. General Qi Jiguang looks at me and sees the unease etched on my face, 'Thanks to you, Lu-wis, we're not facing thousands more. Did the enemy scouts take the bait you left them?'

'Yes, sir. Our wagon drivers made sure that they looked taken by surprise and fled on the ponies we left them. The pirate scouts saw the barrels of baijiu and in their delight, didn't even bother to chase our men. 50,000 litres of unrefined spirits with a little extra added to them thanks to Grandfather Teacher - they'll wake up for battle tomorrow with the worst hangovers of their lives.' I was pretty happy with this additional plan I'd read about somewhere – leaving lots of alcohol for an enemy to capture and then allowing human nature to take its course. Tomorrow, due to the effects of the strong Chinese spirit known as baijiu, the enemy should be groggy and slow with splitting headaches - therefore unable to fight effectively. Looking over at the fairly disciplined ranks of the pirates I feel doubt gnawing in the back of my mind. 'They look better ordered than I expected, General, do you think they'll be allowed to drink?'

'Don't worry, Lu-wis, they look quite disciplined, but this is all for show – to intimidate us. They can barely keep order without executing a number of their ranks on a daily basis. Besides, it's tradition to allow the rank and file to drink the night before a battle – it numbs their fear and makes them feel invincible. That is until the fighting starts and reality sets in, then they'll wish they had taken up a nice quiet life as a farmer or teacher a million miles from here.' We've been joined by most of the officers at that point who all nod sagely at General Qi's wisdom.

'You've come up with some excellent ideas, Lu-wis,' he then addresses all the officers who encircle us hanging on his every word. 'We keep these "tactics" secret, gentlemen, we may win this battle, but we have a war ahead of us, and anything that helps us gain the upper hand needs to be known only by us. Therefore, there will be no mercy shown – kill every last one of them.' I look at the General slack-jawed while all the officers bow punching out their salutes to show acknowledgement - Danny is quite possibly among the enemy. How am I going to find him and save him before one of our soldiers carries out the General's orders?

The General looks at me, 'If you come up with any other bright ideas, do let me know.'

'Um ah, yes, sir,' is all I can manage. Tianyuan looks at me with a smile on his face then rests a comforting hand on my shoulder and gives it a squeeze. He seems to be enjoying this, the crazy old git.

Suddenly the enemy forces part along the forest road to allow a large group of men through. It's their leader, Chen Dong, his 'officers' and his personal guard, all dressed in armour of the highest quality. I now see that the rest of the pirate horde is dressed in whatever armour or clothing they have been able to steal from their victims, ranging from pieces of fine mail to just rags or furs. On closer inspection, our enemy is starting to look more like the rabble the God of War referred to earlier. I look along the battlements and see the disciplined ranks of our soldiers in their uniform red or orange tunics and armour and my confidence lifts.

My attention is drawn back to the pirate leader and his party - they are pulling men who are hooded which causes them to stumble frequently as they are drawn forward by ropes tied to their wrists. When they reach the front, Chen Dong looks directly at us while his men force the hooded men to kneel in a line before us. A nod from their corpulent leader results in the hoods being whipped away, and then the prisoners' heads are pulled back to ensure we can see them clearly. I hear muttering and curses along the battlements as our soldiers recognise the prisoners. They are scouts from one of our patrols sent out to warn us of the enemy's approach. The look of pleading on their gagged faces tears at my soul - the way their captors dance around them laughing, knowing what is about to happen, freezes the blood in my veins.

'Should the men be watching this?' the adjutant standing behind General Qi Jiguang asks.

'The men need to see what awaits them if we lose,' the General responds.

'We need to do something to restore our troops' morale,' Tianyuan states.

As we watch, Chen Dong eyes us with a smirk on his jowly face. He raises and lowers his arm which is the signal for his men to murder the prisoners. I almost vomit at the gruesome spectacle, which I realise is exactly the reaction the pirate leader wants.

'Surrender, and I will let you live. Or die like your fellow soldiers here,' Chen Dong bellows while looking along our men manning the walls. 'You have until tomorrow morning to decide.' With those last words, he turns and starts issuing orders to the men around him.

'So gracious of him,' whispers the adjutant.

'Spread the word - we fight. If we surrender, the pirates will kill us all anyway,' General Qi Jiguang orders him.

'Yes, sir. Shall I keep the men stood to?'

'No, just double the guard, the men will need to rest as much as possible now, before the battle starts. The pirates will be busy setting up camp and collecting bushels of wood to bridge our defences. There won't be any attack till tomorrow morning.'

* * * * *

'I hear Chen Dong has said no prisoners,' Mike whispers to Emma as they watch the soldiers being executed in front of the fort.

'Yup, with odds of 20 – 1, tomorrow should be interesting,' Emma's eyes gleam with anticipation.

'Have you tried this alcohol?' Mike hands over a wineskin of the captured baijiu. Emma, whose attention is on Chen Dong coming back through a channel in the assembled ranks of pirates, takes a swig and immediately coughs and splutters. Mike laughs at his sister's reaction – the grimace makes her look like a bulldog chewing a wasp. His laughter dries up in an instant as they both become aware that Chen Dong has stopped and is looking at them.

The dark feral-like eyes study the twins and spot the skull and crossbones tattoos on their forearms. The twins don't know what to say or do and so just stand there looking at the ground. Chen Dong's bodyguard eye them suspiciously, their hands grip the hilts of their swords a little more firmly – ready for any sign of treachery.

'Nice tattoos, I like the design. Make a note of them – I want our army to have banners in this style.' One of his entourage bows pulls out a scroll and an ink pot from his satchel, and immediately starts making a copy of the design. 'Send it to our artisans - I expect to have banners ready for our victory parade as we enter Hangzhou.'

'Yes, my lord,' the scribe nods repeatedly as he sketches the design and then sprinkles sand on the ink to dry it. After one look into the faces of each of the twins and not a word to them, he continues walking back towards the forest.

The twins exhale as they watch their leader move away. Mike frowns, 'Thanks for nothing.' He grabs the wineskin from Emma and takes a quick mouthful. 'He didn't even acknowledge our existence - tosser!'

'Keep your voice down,' Emma says, glancing around quickly to ensure nobody overheard her brother. 'What did you expect?' She takes a sip from the wineskin, winces, and then whispers, 'Who cares what he thinks? We're better than any of these scum. We come, we have our fun, and then we go, that's it.'

* * * * *

I haven't slept well. Nor do I think has anyone within the fort. You'd have to have ice in your veins to be able to sleep before a battle, but you'd have had to be deaf as well last night because of the drunken singing and shouting coming from the pirate camp. I've climbed the ladder to look down on the enemy from our palisade as doing something is preferable to lying on my bedroll just waiting for the inevitable morning call to arms. The darkness is turning to grey as dawn approaches, but a heavy fog makes visibility impossible; I can just make out the blurry glow of enemy campfires every now and again as the fog thins and thickens. Something starts niggling at the back of my mind. Something I've read about in my history books, and then it comes to me – I clamber down the ladder - one element of a plan after another leaps to mind as I run towards the camp headquarters, sidestepping anyone who suddenly appears out of the fog.

'I need to see General Qi Jiguang.' I say to the two guards between gasps for breath.

'The General is resting,' one of the guards replies without even looking at me.

'What do you think the General will do when he hears you prevented us from delivering the pirates a fatal blow?' I ask calmly, looking straight into his eyes. He turns to the other guard who just shrugs, and then he looks back at me, weighing up the possible outcomes.

'Wait here,' he turns and enters the tent. He is probably as surprised as me to hear General Qi Jiguang wide awake and prepared for battle. I hear a command to send me in, and so the guard opens the tent flap and begrudgingly lets me through.

'Lu-wis, what brings you here?' He examines my expression and continues, 'You have a plan, don't you?'

'Yes, General, but it requires the whole camp to be called to arms immediately, and quietly.'

'What do you propose?'

I tell the General of my plan - he considers it for just a few seconds and then gives orders to the bleary-eyed clerics on duty who dash here and there. And the camp is roused.

A few moments later we arrive at the main gate. Officers wait in a huddle, anticipation and excitement vying with anxiety at what to expect. The men are being massed in ranks, corporals and sergeants checking their troops, making them jump up and down to ensure all their kit is securely fastened and won't make any noise that will give us away. Bowstrings are being fastened and quivers of arrows distributed, all in complete silence.

'Gentlemen, it's time to take the initiative. We will use the fog to hide our advance to the furthest of our outside defences. On my command, all soldiers will release arrows, and continue to release extending their aim by five paces each time.' Just then the head of the scouts appears.

'Sir, all is quiet in the enemy camp. Their guards are half asleep – they are certainly not patrolling.'

'Good. Right, march your men out, each man holds the shoulder of the man in front with his left hand. Follow the scouts and make sure they are all facing the right direction before they fire. Once you have emptied your quivers, march your men back in the same way.'

'Sir, shouldn't we at least leave a rear guard to defend the fort, just in case?' The adjutant is uncomfortable with this breach of military protocol.

'Not this time, let's hammer them using every soldier we have.' The general then looks at each man in turn. 'We have a chance here to fatally wound the enemy, time is of the essence, proceed.'

Three thousand men walk carefully out into the dense fog. To my ears we are making a racket, men stumbling all around me, but we eventually get to our objective and stop. The order to 'Face left' is whispered down the line. 'Prepare arrows' is the next command. I pick the arrows out of my quiver one by one and gently press the arrowheads into the ground by my right foot so that I can easily grab them. My heart is racing, a drumbeat in my ears, I can feel the pulse in my fingers where I'm pulling back the bow cord. 'Nock and aim 40 paces.' I place an arrow and bring the bow up at the appropriate angle for a forty-metre shot.

'Release!' The order is instantly followed by the

thrumming of bowstrings and the whoosh of three thousand arrows flying in unison towards the enemy. A moment later screams come from out of the fog. I focus on my duty, nock the arrow, change the angle by five meters, release, and repeat, and repeat. Screams, shouts, and the sound of panic coming from the enemy lines contrasts starkly with the silence from our ranks as we rain down death on the pirates. My hand reaches out for another arrow but finds just empty air. I've shot them all and so have the men around me judging by the whispering going up and down the ranks. 'Right turn' is the next command whereupon we turn back towards the way we came and feel out into the fog for the man in front and clamp a hand down on his left shoulder. The men stumble back to the fort quicker as the fear of a counterattack grows in our minds. Despite the fog, we are back within the safety of our palisade walls in a few minutes.

* * * * *

The screams and clanging of cymbals and iron bars wake the twins from their drunken slumber. It takes a moment to get their bearings before they grab their weapons and scramble out of their tent just as arrows pierce the tent's leather skin as if it were made of paper. They look at each other, confused and scared. They can't see anything through the fog, just dark shadows rushing around, accompanied by shouting, shrieking, and cries for help. And the constant whoosh of arrows flying through the air hitting targets all around them.

'Head for the-' Emma hears Mike's voice cut off, followed by the sound of him dropping to his knees. Mike's eyes are as wide as saucers as his fingers fumble around the shaft of an arrow protruding out of his chin. It has passed through his lower jaw and then lodged deep into his neck. Emma screams and kneels down beside her brother unable to understand the gurgling sounds emanating from him. Tears well up in his eyes. She tries to cradle his head but two thuds thump into her back driving her to the ground. She gets up on all fours, her stomach feels like it's ripping apart - the agony causes her head to spin. Gritting her teeth, she looks at the arrowheads protruding from a bloody gory mess that was her stomach. Mike makes a mewling noise at the sight. They both start to cry, unnoticed in the mayhem around them. Clearly, they are not going to get any help, their cries became wails, which soon became barely audible whimpers.

A few moments later back in England, Mike dies in his sleep for no apparent reason. In the morning, Emma is rushed to hospital barely clinging on to life.

Chaos continues as the bands of pirates fight each other in their drunken stupor. Some lash out at anything that moves, they fight until they are exhausted. Horns sound repeatedly, echoing eerily through the fog, ordering them to stand down. Eventually, just the pitiful moans of the dying can be heard.

*****

'Stand to!' The order comes and men rush off to their positions to await the anticipated pirate assault. The sky lightens but only to a lighter grey, the fog still lies heavy around the fort. We listen out for any movement, any sound of an enemy advance. Bundles of arrows lie at our feet, next to spears and our swords, all in the order we'll need the weapons as the pirates breach our defences.

We hear screams nearby - a pirate must have fallen into one of the lily pits. Then the fog wall just in front of us seems to rip to shreds as thousands of men charge at us, screaming their battle cries - or just screaming. 'Fire at will!' comes the command - we all aim and fire, aim and fire, but there are too many of them. My fingertips are bleeding from the rapid fire of arrows. and then I see the first pirate reach the base of the palisade. He's followed quickly by others carrying ladders and shields. Now we endure a barrage of arrows coming our way with the odd spear as the pirates try to clear the palisade walls so their men can scale our defences. Cries of pain come from all around me as our soldiers topple to the ground below. There's no time to think. Just fight. Spear the pirates climbing the ladders. Throw rocks, hurl anything – we must stop them from getting into the fort.

I hear the order for the fire arrows to be shot. Arcs of flame fly from our positions towards a tar-filled trench on the outside of the moat. Immediately a wall of fire races across our front silhouetting the pirates against a blazing backdrop, even from this distance I can feel the heat. The sound of shrill screams pierces the air as the pirates seem to dance in their agony creating a grotesque depiction of hell. The fire burns away the pirates' will to fight, they turn and race back to their own lines. The ones trapped between the fire and our walls are shown the same mercy they showed our scouts.

Dawn has come and gone; we have been fighting off attack after attack for hours. The fog is starting to clear revealing a scene of carnage. The ground must be carpeted with thousands of dead and dying pirates. Just beyond our defences, directly in front of us, the fog parts like the curtains at the opening of a stage play at the theatre, revealing the pirate leader surrounded by his commanders – there seem to be fewer of them.

'If you surrender now, we will let you live!' I hear a voice shout from our battlements and look left to see General Qi Jiguang. He is flanked by Tianyuan and the adjutant who can't hide a wry smile. 'You have until tomorrow morning to decide.' We've earned ourselves another day to prepare while the pirates reorganise themselves.

The morale in the camp is indescribable: we have dealt a severe blow to the pirates' army, thousands dead and thousands more injured. Our losses were minimal, 23 dead and 68 injured. I try not to think of the battle like a score sheet, but the need to think that we can win against such odds forces us to think in that way.

I'm relieved at the fact that I didn't freeze with fear during the battle as I did that time when I faced the Imam at the assassin's castle.

The constant sound of cries and pleas for help from the

pirate injured on the battlefield brings me back to earth. It gnaws at my soul, but then I force myself to close out the sounds. These very same pirates have committed unspeakable atrocities for years, I tell myself – no, I *order* myself not to feel any pity for them.

But the scene does trigger something I can't quite put my finger on – some memory or possibly a scene from a film I once saw. It's like there's an idea screaming at me from the back of my mind, but I can't hear it. I look at the almost spectral sight before me – the figures walking and wailing through the fog and then it comes to me. I dash towards the General before the plan has formulated completely in my mind. The General sees me approaching and stops talking to those around him as he scrutinises my face.

'Lu-wis, if you have another plan, then I think we'll have to swap uniforms, and you be the general,' The officers around him chuckle.

'I do, General, it's risky, but it could win the battle in one morning.' Their faces turn serious - I have their attention. They all know about my input in the poisoning of Ya Me's clan and can see the evidence of my successful battle tactics by just looking over the parapet at the blanket of dead and dying pirates.

'Come with me,' the General says, leading the way to the command tent.

Chapter 19

I've been trying to put my plan into words to 'sell' it to the General. 'We need to send some men out tonight to retrieve around 200 of the pirates' bodies,' I can see eyebrows arching left, right and centre. However, the God of War and Tianyuan just stare at me waiting for me to continue. I explain what they need to do and then move on to another part of the plan. 'As soon as it's dark, the packs of monks will have to cross the river upstream by boat and then float downstream so that they can recross the river behind the enemy lines. They'll be armed with their weapon of choice and the dragon's teeth harnesses.'

    Weeks ago, I drew my design for the throwing knives' webbing which I got from the assassins' castle. Tianyuan liked the way the fan-like shape of the webbing across the shoulder blades allowed a person to fling up to six knives accurately within a couple of seconds. So all of the Shaolin monks have been training with them and the wrist harnesses. It's an incredible sight to see steel knives flashing in the sunlight like a swarm of silver hornets embedding themselves into wooden targets with pirates painted on them.

    'The calvary will mass most of their squadrons behind the fort so that when they are given the signal they can appear on the battlefield at the gallop. Then they will sweep through from here to here.' I indicate where they will form up on the map - all eyes glued and trying to keep up with how all the different elements of the battle plan will come together. 'Meanwhile, we'll need most of the archers manning the palisade here,' I gesture again at the map, 'so that they can concentrate their fire here where the cavalry will "herd" the pirates.' There's silence. I think if I didn't have a record of success with my earlier strategies, I would be thrown out of the command tent. I start to feel riddled with doubt – where did I get this idea? Was it really from a history book or was it from a far-fetched film? However, as mad as my plan is, the officers hold their tongues, but can't hide the scepticism from their eyes.

'Grandfather Teacher, you will lead the negotiations at the head of ten Masters of kung fu. Your exploits have become legendary, almost mystical, and are well known even among the pirates, so we need to work with that reputation.' Tianyuan raises an eyebrow. 'Believe me, Grandfather Teacher, because the pirates are so superstitious, they will be watching you closely for any hint of your supernatural powers.

'The pirates will see you and ten monks, unarmed except for your staffs – you'll have the dragon's teeth concealed under your orange robes. Chen Dong will probably expect you to negotiate terms for our surrender. That is when you give them this ultimatum.' I relay exactly word for word what Tianyuan has to say, then emphasise, 'Make sure you are loud and clear, so even the pirates as far back as the forest hear you. I'm sorry Grandfather Teacher, but I'm putting your life in extreme danger by asking you to do this. You'll be vulnerable until you give the signal.'

'All our lives are in extreme danger whatever role we have tomorrow – don't worry about me.' His nonchalant response in the face of his high-risk mission seals it – none of the officers can now query the plan without losing face.

General Qi Jiguang gets each officer to repeat their orders and then asks them questions about how they will deal with unexpected scenarios. The God of War then confirms signals and timings and sends us away to get my plan underway - some of the officers give me unreadable looks as they leave the tent.

* * * * *

Ichiro and his samurai brothers look around

dispassionately at the carnage the pirates have suffered. They hadn't partaken in the drinking the night before, instead, they had found a quiet glade within the forest to pray to their ancestors for victory and honour; even if they were fighting for barbarians, they could still uphold the Bushido code.

When the screams started and the sound of fighting erupted across the camp, they stayed at the edge of the forest. When Chen Dong ordered an ill-advised attack in a knee-jerk reaction, they stayed put. They watched as anger took over from sense and thousands upon thousands of pirates hurled themselves at the palisade. When the fire arrows lit the trench of oil capturing a mass of their army in a kill zone, they just shook their heads at the stupidity of it all.

Now, the following morning they survey the scene. Walking among the dead, disturbing crows having a grisly breakfast, they can piece together what had happened. It started with a clever night assault by enemy archers showering their camp with tens of thousands of arrows – it looked like the farmer who owned the field would be harvesting arrows rather than wheat. Then, the chaos and the impenetrable fog resulted in different bands of pirates clashing with each other – they form the circles of dead which gives the battlefield a grim pattern - culminating in bodies piled high against the palisade walls. Ichiro and his men walk slowly through the scene ignoring the shouts of the pirate commanders trying to get the army to form up in battle lines.

Something catches Ichiro's eye; he nudges a dead pirate's arm with his foot then stoops down and tears off a brooch from the victim's chest. He studies it, nods approval, and then drives the dragonfly badge into the blue-boiled leather of his chest armour. The other samurai look at Ichiro's chest and grunt noises of admiration.

A horn is blown within the fort drawing their attention to the main gates which open slowly. An old orange-clad monk emerges from the fort's main gate leading 10 others, one of them waving a leafy branch in the air to show they want to parley.

'Something's not right here. Coming out to parley before the blood fury has cooled. They're up to something,' one of the samurai remarks.

'We must still outnumber them at least 10 – 1. And now they don't have the fog to hide behind, what can they do?' another responds.

'Hmm, you're right, they are up to something,' Ichiro acknowledges the first speaker scanning the treeline a hundred yards away for threats, then the marsh area and the riverbank. 'Keep your eyes peeled. We'll slowly withdraw to the edge of the forest. It's time to end our alliance with these savages.' He looks up at the fortress and knows there is something wrong with it but just can't put his finger on it. He scans the men manning the palisade from left to right and then sees it. 'Look,' he says nodding in the direction of the enemy stronghold. His men stop scanning here and there and focus on the palisade walls. 'Their archers are concentrated towards the river end of the fortress. Yes, they are up to something, and this,' he gestures at the monks who are waiting for Chen Dong and his entourage to reach them, 'is just a diversion. Time to go.'

The samurai approach Chen Dong's elite guards who are stationed at the forest's edge to stop any of the pirate army from deserting.

'Where are you lot going? Haven't you heard? We're going to attack during the parley?' the guard commander snarls. Looking back across the battlefield they can see messengers run around the camp, calling out 'Prepare for battle' every few paces. The pirate horde are edging closer to the fortress. Nobody breathes as the elite guard eye the samurai suspiciously, easing their swords slowly out of their scabbards.

Ichiro looks the man straight in the eye, 'We're on a mission for Chen Dong.'

'Let's see the order,' the commander holds out his open palm.

'He didn't have time to write anything down, but if you want, you can go and ask him,' Ichiro gestures towards where the parley is about to take place. Chen Dong and his quickly assembled commanders have almost reached the monks who stand five on either side of Tianyuan.

The guard commander looks from where the parley is about to take place, back at the 30 samurai and then the vastly superior numbers of his men lining the treeline. Was it worth the hassle? They might genuinely be on a mission for their leader…

'I'll be checking with Chen Dong after the attack, don't you worry.'

'Fine,' Ichiro answers and then leads the samurai through the ranks of pirates into the forest. They walk carefully through the trees alert for any danger. A fist is raised in the air by Kenji out in front resulting in the men going to ground, peering from behind tree trunks. Ichiro scans the dense forest on his left and then sees it, a flash of orange moving stealthily through the wood. Then another, and another. There's a band of around ten monks moving carefully towards the treeline, obviously to attack the pirates from behind. He looks to the right and sees another band doing the same. Ichiro's lip curls into a snarl - Danny can only hope they'll be far away from this place before the battle starts and so reduce the possibility of him coming face-to-face with Lewis. Ichiro remembers his oath to his ancestors and instinctively grips his sword more tightly, but they have a mission, steal Chen Dong's treasure and get back to Japan to fund their clan's revenge on their arch-enemy. He waits until the monks have crept past on both sides then signals his men to continue towards the pirate army's baggage train.

* * * * *

Danny lies asleep in his hospital bed oblivious to the tension in the air around him. Four medical staff stand around in his room here to do a job, but reluctant to do it in front of the others. Amelie is changing the intravenous drip bag feeding into Danny's forearm while listening to the consultants talking with Doctor Jeffries.

Doctor Jeffries flips the file containing Danny's records shut and returns it to the little envelope-shaped basket at the foot of the boy's bed.

'How is your research going, doctors, any progress?'

'Yes, we've had a few ideas, but we need to check their feasibility,' Doctor Davies responds while Doctor McCormack nods in agreement. 'How about our patient here, how is he doing?'

Doctor Jeffries takes his time replying, 'There doesn't seem to be any change and it's difficult to make head or tail of the data. Those random episodes where there are spikes in the heart rate and blood pressure - it's impossible to work out the cause.'

'Indeed,' the doctors nod sympathetically.

Amelie glances out of the window and sees a van pulling into the parking spaces reserved for hospital transfers. She recognises the two men who get out of the front and then open the back to pull out a trolley bed which they wheel towards the entrance. 'It's time,' Amelie thinks to herself. She slips her hand into the pocket in her uniform and presses a button. Immediately, Doctor Jeffries's pager goes off. He takes it out, reads it, frowns, and then looks up.

'Sorry, if you'll excuse me,' he says to the consultants ending their awkward conversation.

'Sure, actually we have to get going as well,' Doctor Davies says, and so Amelie is left alone in the room.

She looks down at the boy sleeping peacefully in the bed, 'Sorry about this, Danny.' Amelie then retrieves a little bag she hid in Danny's room weeks ago for this eventuality. She checks quickly up and down the corridor, Doctor Jeffries seems to be agitated about something on the phone by the ward sister's desk. 'Okay, time to get to work,' Amelie says to herself. She then takes out some make-up and proceeds to darken under Danny's eyes and then does the same below his cheekbones. She brushes his hair in a way that gives it volume and then takes a step back to appraise her work. 'Yes,' she thinks to herself and nods approvingly at the boy who looks thinner in the face, and quite ill.

Just then, an upset Doctor Jeffries returns, 'That was a waste of time – some glitch in the system – nobody actually paged me,' he frowns, looking on edge.

'Excuse me, doctor, you might be interested in something I've noticed in Danny's charts,' Amelie says, blocking Doctor Jeffries's view of Danny's new makeover. 'The spikes we've had over the last few days seem to show some kind of trend,' Amelie retrieves Danny's records from the foot of the bed. Doctor Jeffries looks at Amelie curiously as she opens the file and turns her back on Danny. He automatically stands alongside her, so he'll be able to see what the nurse has spotted. She turns to the page with the graph showing the last two weeks' results.

Amelie traces the results along the graph with her pen and checks to see that the doctor is paying attention. She is relieved to see that he is focused on the gentle movement of the ballpoint's nib. 'You can see the heart rate here,' she says softly, 'it appears to be steady, up and down, up and down, no real change,' her lilting French accent is quiet, the doctor leans in to hear more clearly, following the nib of the pen tracing out the regular line marking Danny's heartbeat. 'The heartbeat just keeps going up and down, looking at it can make you feel drowsy, really tired. It would be nice just to lie down, wouldn't it? Just a moment to close your eyes, then you'll feel refreshed.' The doctor nods, eyes heavy, focused on Amelie's nib moving up and down. The nurse's voice continues in soothing tones until, 'When I count down to one you can sleep, three, two, one, sleep,' the last word comes out a whisper, at which point Doctor Jeffries's eyes close, as he falls into a trance.

'Who are you working for?' Amelie asks.

'The Syndicate,' the hypnotised Doctor Jeffries answers.

'Is that who you've been sneaking off to speak to on that funny little phone of yours?'

'Yes.'

'What do they want?'

'We're supposed to inform the Boss if we have any patients with Danny's characteristics – activity during sleep and an improvement in muscle tone - possible travellers.'

Amelie resists the urge to slap Doctor Jeffries - things must carry on at this hospital without the Syndicate realising they've been detected. 'I will tell you what you have seen here at the hospital, so you can report back to your boss. The boy,

Danny, has recovered. He woke up this morning and has gone through the usual confusion experienced by people recovering from a coma. Danny has muscle atrophy; his muscles have lost definition and size as a result of being inactive in bed for so long. These suggest that he has not been "active" in his dreams, so he is not a traveller – previous results were wrong due to an issue with the equipment. Do you understand?'

'Yes,' Doctor Jeffries nods.

'You will recommend closing Danny's file, concluding that no further action is required, he is not a person of interest. What are your conclusions about Danny and what will you recommend?'

'Danny is not a person of interest, no further surveillance of the patient is required,' the doctor says and repeats the reasons why.

'Okay, when I count back up to three, you will wake up, leave the room, and then make your report. One, two, three,' Amelie watches as Doctor Jeffries blinks a few times, a little confused but then takes in his surroundings and seems to be back to his normal self.

'Thank you, Amelie, I'm glad to see Danny has recovered. I'll go now and make my report and notify the necessary people.' He smiles vacantly, turns on his heel, and leaves the room.

As Amelie watches the doctor walk away down the corridor, she sees two porters pushing an empty trolley bed towards her from the opposite direction while one of them checks some details on a piece of paper. 'Excuse me,' she says to the porters, 'can I help you?'

'Yes, thanks. There's a patient transfer order, um,' the one porter consults his papers, and sees that they are outside the right room. 'He's being transferred to a private medical facility,' the porter peers through the small window.

Amelie thinks quickly on her feet and responds casually, 'I'm afraid you've had a wasted journey. The patient has woken up and will be discharged later on today. Doctor Jeffries,' she nods towards the doctor who is talking on his phone in a quiet corner of the ward, 'is arranging everything.'

One of the porters eyes her suspiciously, 'Come and have a look at our star patient, he's nodded off again but he's been doing that all morning.' She opens the door to let the porters in and hopes her amateur make-up job will do the trick.

'Wow, he looks terrible!' the lead porter says.

'Shhh!' Amelie puts a finger to her lips, 'Please, keep it down, the patient might subconsciously be aware of anything being said.' She continues in a whisper, 'But you are right, he's lost a lot of weight - it's going to take a lot of time and effort to get fit again.'

The porters nod before taking one last look at Danny and moving back into the corridor. 'Okay, we'll need to get this paperwork updated and signed off,' the lead porter indicates the forms on the trolley.

'Of course, if you're quick you'll catch Doctor Jeffries before he continues on his rounds. Again, sorry you've had a wasted journey.'

'No problem,' the lead porter says, 'thanks for your help.' With that, the porters wheel the trolley towards Doctor Jeffries. There's a brief discussion and all three look back at Amelie stood outside Danny's room, then the Doctor takes the paperwork, scribbles a few notes, and signs it. Amelie breathes out as she watches the porters leave the ward. She shoulders the door open and looks down at Danny asleep – unaware of how close he was to getting kidnapped. Amelie takes out some make-up remover and returns the boy to his healthy-looking self. She considers the situation: the leader of the Syndicate will receive reports from two different sources that Danny is not a traveller which is clear from his condition.

She looks down at the boy and breathes out a sigh of relief – that was close. She'd seen the porters coming for Danny when she'd travelled in time, but the details weren't clear as her host was one of the little girls drugged up on medication on this paediatric ward. The wormhole had then closed so she wasn't able to find out anything else – just that Danny was in danger.

Amelie touches the butterfly pendant on her blouse bringing back fond memories of her time travelling with Terry, her travelling companion and love of her life. He had disappeared two years ago. He could be floating around anywhere - nothing is certain which means there is always hope. She caresses her pendant - the butterfly is their identification symbol. Working on the ward at the hospital gave her the chance to help other 'travellers' as well as keep an eye out for Terry. 'One day, Terry, one day…'

Chapter 20

I hear the first horn sound from the fort, so signal to my pack of monks to get ready to advance to contact – military lingo for moving to a position where we can engage the enemy. Thankfully, we've had an uneventful night getting to our current location in the forest two hundred meters from the tree line behind the pirate army. But the last 24 hours have taken their toll – I'm exhausted and so are the others judging by the bags under their eyes and their struggle to stay focused. I take out the wineskin that Tianyuan gave me and to each of the monk packs. I uncork it and take a whiff – it smells a bit like the energy drinks we have back in London. Grandfather Teacher wisely foresaw how tired we would be and so produced this tonic which will give us an injection of energy, but he warned us not to use it too soon as once its effects wore off, it will be impossible to stay awake. Energy surges through my body – the other monks look suddenly alert and fresh – ready for anything. We move stealthily through the wood until we're ten meters from open ground, where we crouch behind bushes or tree trunks and wait. This is where my plan succeeds and we win a decisive victory or fails and we all die.

* * * * *

The attention of everyone is on Tianyuan and his fellow monks who watch as Chen Dong and his commanders come to a halt a few paces away from them. Chen Dong just stares at Grandfather Teacher as his forces slowly form up and inch closer to the fortress. 'You have a nerve coming out here to parley, monk, when your archers have been firing at our men trying to retrieve our wounded,' he gestures to the area around them where the odd groan can still be heard from the mass of bodies.

'A fool fights with a code of honour when his enemy uses that code as a weapon against him,' Tianyuan replies.

'What do you want, monk?'

'We seek your terms for surrender.'

Chen processes what he's just heard and then barks out a laugh in triumph, 'I'll give you terms, first-'

'You misunderstand me, Chen,' Tianyuan interrupts, 'we will tell you what terms we will agree to… for your surrender.' Chen's gimlet eyes shine in his reddening face, but he quickly calms himself and turns to his commanders giving them a subtle nod. He then turns back to the monk and raises his arm, but before a command or signal can be given, the old monk's voice roars across the battlefield – the sheer volume coming from that little old man surprises everyone.

'Before you do anything rash, and remember we are under the rules of parley, know this Chen,' the monk pauses, there's complete silence as everyone listens to the mad monk, 'I have powers that I will unleash-'

'You, have powers!' yells Chen scornfully, 'You don't scare me! We outnumber you 15 – 1-'

'You should be afraid!' Tianyuan's voice drowns out Chen's who gawps at him, he lowers his arm slowly – confusing his commanders – it's not clear if it's the signal to attack. 'I have the power to unleash the hounds of hell on you and your men – they won't stop until they have satisfied their hunger for your souls.' Even Chen feels a tingle of fear. He's about to compose himself and raise his arm again to order the attack when the monk continues, 'I curse you and all those who remain on the battlefield.' He lifts his staff into the air whereupon a horn sounds a deep mournful note, 'Rise!' Tianyuan bellows.

There is utter silence – no one moves. The enemy unconsciously holds their breath as they look around to see if anything will happen. Chen laughs mockingly at the apparent failure of the monk's sorcery, then a cry of 'look!' silences everyone. There is movement among the dead who lie in line with the monks, just in front of Chen and his commanders. An arm stretches then shoots out straight, grasping a sword which lies beside the dead man's body. His torso then lurches upright, and his bloody head turns to look at the pirate horde. There is a tangible intake of breath from everyone. Then another corpse moves – a leg straightens, bends, then straightens again, before this body too turns to kneel ready to pounce towards the brigands. More of the dead begin to move, all bloody from their lethal wounds and all facing towards the pirates. The silence is broken by cries of alarm followed quickly by the sound of movement as weapons are dropped and men begin to bolt towards the forest.

'Hold!' Chen howls at his fleeing army, 'Kill any man who deserts!' he commands. The ranks of his elite guard at the treeline start cutting down the deserting pirates, they in turn fight back with a rabid ferocity, blinded by fear in their eagerness to get away from the cursed battlefield.

Chen Dong and his inner circle of commanders survey their fleeing army, a few of his commanders roar at the officers to restore order and form up the men to attack the fort, while Chen just glares at Tianyuan. The old monk just stares back at the pirate commander five meters in front of him – a glint in his eye which Chen interprets as a look of mockery.

'You monk sc-' Chen shouts but is cut off as Tianyuan leaps forward driving his staff straight out in front of him at arm's length ending with a clump - the dead Chen slumps to the floor.

'You talk too much,' Tianyuan says to the corpse as Chen's commanders look on stunned. Before they can gather themselves or draw their weapons a group of the walking dead, who have crept up behind them, kill them quickly and efficiently. One pirate manages to swing his sword at them yelling incoherently but sinks to the ground with a chest showing off the dragon's teeth blades the monks have strapped to their backs.

The sight of their leader and commanders so easily dispatched breaks the resolve of the pirates who stood firm and almost formed up for the assault on the fort. They drop their weapons and look around for the best way to flee this hell. In front they see a line of the walking dead facing them - searching for new souls to feast on. To the right is the river, to the left the marshy ground, and behind them a battle rages as the elite guard fight an army of deserters. They look back to Tianyuan who waves his staff. Horns sound and red dragon banners are waved high in the air from the fort's towers. A chill runs through them – they all know that these flags mean that their enemy will take no prisoners.

The ground rumbles as a mass of cavalry gallop from behind the fort until they reach the forest where they stop and the files of horsemen turn to form three ranks of calvary facing the pirates, blocking off any escape across the marsh. Horses neigh and chomp at their bits, stamping the ground in their eagerness to leap forward. Troops of archers trot out of the main gate in perfect formation, then line up to face the enemy.

The river is their only escape. An eerie silence descends on that part of the battlefield before a horn sounds from the fort and the cavalry start to move at a walk, then a canter. There are wails and shouts as the pirates turn like a murmuration of starlings towards the river, trampling their comrades to death in their desperation to escape. The archers start raining down volley after volley of arrows into the fleeing pirate army. Here is where the hours of training and discipline show - the cavalry form a perfect line as they charge, the archers change their arc of fire accordingly, the arrows falling further into the heart of the enemy who are now fighting each other to escape the slaughter. The pirates wade out into the river but soon get stuck in the muddy riverbed blocking those behind. But more keep joining creating a mass of static targets for the archers and the cavalry, who sheathe their sabres and grab their recurve bows – every arrow finds a target.

* * * * *

Ichiro and his band converge on a clearing where Chen has left his most loyal guards to protect his treasure hoard. The 80 or so pirates stare towards the sound of battle with increasing anxiety, fidgeting with their weapons, looking questioningly at each other. Their previous confidence in an overwhelming victory has been evaporating steadily during the course of the morning as the screams coming from so near indicate that the fighting was occurring in among their positions rather than at the fort. Then they witness their own men fleeing almost mad with fear into the forest. And now a group of around 30 samurai stand before them. Their captain walks towards the samurai leader.

'What's happening out there?' the pirate commander demands.

'Chen has lost the battle; his army is surrounded and being annihilated as we speak – it's a rout.' Ichiro answers. Danny realises that is host is deliberately trying to unsettle the pirates guarding Chen's fortune to make what comes next a little easier.

'Don't mock me, samurai! There's no way their small brigade could overwhelm our greater numbers,' the guard commander growls, clenching his sword more firmly in its scabbard.

'I don't mock you – look at the faces of your brothers running away from the battle.' As if on cue, three pirates run into the clearing and stop abruptly, looking left to right but not seeing – a craziness in their eyes. All they seem to register is that people block this path of escape so, almost frothing at the mouths, they run around the edge of the clearing to the far side and continue running for their lives. The pirate guards watch their former shipmates fleeing into the woods – not willing to believe their own eyes – the samurai can't be telling the truth!

The whisper of samurai swords being unsheathed is the only warning – within a heartbeat, a score of the guards, including the commander lie dead around the wagons. But these are Chen's most trusted and feared men – they won't go down without a fight and within a moment each one has found a samurai to fight, their greater numbers forcing some of the samurai to defend against two or three adversaries.

The guard commander's lieutenants launch themselves at Ichiro who dances between them and turns raising his sword above his head, pointing behind him, ready. His feet move subtly as he faces his two opponents. The air is filled with the sound of swords clashing against swords, shouted threats, grunts, and cries of pain, but Ichiro filters out the distraction so he can focus on his own fight. One of the pirates edges away trying to get behind the samurai. But Ichiro moves so that he can keep one on his left and the other on his right. He seems to be looking at no one, but in his mind's eye, he can see their battleground, each step the pirates take registers. One of the pirates leaps forward slashing down with his sword which Ichiro easily sidesteps and in the same fluid movement brings his own sword up, forming a lopsided O in the air - the sword completes the circle by slashing into the back of the pirate who crumples to the floor. Before the other pirate can recover from the shock of seeing his comrade fall, he looks down to see Ichiro's sword burst through his belly. He too slides to the ground.

  Ichiro takes a moment, using all his senses to feel the battle around him. The samurai have outclassed the pirate rabble but have suffered due to being so outnumbered. They've lost 12 men, and seven are carrying injuries.

  'Kenji, see to the injured. Shinsuke, take two men and sift through the treasure – take only the bags of jewels, leave the heavy stuff. Akira, we'll create a funeral pyre out of the wagons. Empty them, lay our fallen on them, and soak them in oil. Hurry, we leave in two minutes. The 10 unscathed samurai dash here and there carrying out their orders. Two samurai saddle up the horses which are tethered to the wagons. Ichiro surveys the forest for signs of danger. They don't have long.

  'Ichiro-san, we are ready,' Akira reports indicating the wagons now filled with the fallen samurai. The samurai form a half circle in front of the wagons, heads bowed, a hum starts up in their throats, barely perceptible at first but gathering in volume as Ichiro lights the oil and flames erupt from the three wagons, the smoke billows upwards guiding the souls of the fallen warriors to their rightful place in the afterlife. The humming stops, silent prayers are made.

  'Time to leave,' Ichiro breaks the silence. The samurai

turn to the horses - it becomes clear that they are three short. They have fifteen horses, seven of which have their wounded tied to the saddles or lying across them. Without any hesitation Ichiro breaks the conundrum, 'Kenji, take the men and meet us at the rendezvous. Don't wait more than 24 hours – take the treasure to our clan leader.' Kenji looks like he might protest but sees Ichiro's expression and bows. 'Shinsuke, Akira, are you ready for a run?'

The two samurai smile back and give a quick nod. The men rush to their horses while Ichiro and his two runners check each other's gear, tightening straps and laces.

'See you at the rendezvous,' Kenji bows to Ichiro before wheeling his horse around and leading the mounted men into the forest at a gallop. Ichiro waits a moment, takes a deep breath, and then breaks into a run with Shinsuke and Akira flanking him.

* * * * *

I watch as the pirate elite guard cut down the mass of deserters. But even though most of their assailants are unarmed, their numbers prove too strong, and soon pirates start breaking through the line. That's our cue to attack. My pack of monks form a wedge and charge out of the forest – our throwing knives announce our arrival slicing paths through the enemy. The pirates either stand in our way and die or flee between the deadly orange wedges pouring out of the tree line. They run past us frantic with fear, we turn to chase them into the woods – their exposed backs making easy targets for our dragon's teeth which we can sometimes collect without barely breaking stride. Their flight for freedom becomes even more desperate when they hear the horns of our cavalry joining the hunt.

My plan has worked. The pirates experienced the same paralysing fright I had when I thought I faced the supernatural Imam at the assassin's castle: seeing their dead rising from the ground and facing them ready to attack unhinged them – how could they kill the already dead? The pirate army disintegrated in front of our eyes and now it seems just too easy to throw knives at our enemy's backs as they try to escape the slaughter.

I see plumes of smoke rising from somewhere ahead – that must be the baggage train, food, supplies, and most likely the loot Chen has amassed while pillaging the country. A slight change of direction takes us to what isn't actually the pirate baggage train as it's too small. I stop at the edge of the clearing - corpses lie everywhere – another skirmish has already taken place. There are around 80 dead guards strewn around the scene with surgical-type sword wounds to their bodies – from samurai swords. The samurai contingent of the pirate horde must have cut their losses and run. Looking at the spilt gold still trickling out of some torn sacks next to the wagons, they must have decided to take their share of Chen's treasure with them.

My pack of monks spread out, checking warily for signs of an ambush. No one is alive. One of my men draws my attention to the deliberately lit carts which on further inspection are actually funeral pyres for the fallen samurai. Then the horse tracks – a band of 15 samurai have fled on horses, but there are three sets of footprints which head off in the same direction. The length of the stride and heel imprints suggest that they are running - not sprinting.

There's a king's ransom still left in the carts. What do I do? If I leave this undefended some of it's going to get stolen – again. War is expensive, the God of War will appreciate this treasure to help pay for the war effort. I decide to leave five monks guarding it, send two monks back to the fort to request a guard of troops to protect the treasure – which leaves three of us to run down the samurai – three against three – I don't like it, but the treasure will help wipe these scum off the face of the Earth. The samurai on horseback have already escaped our trap. But samurai are proud – they won't dare mention that they ran away from a battle where they were routed by a force thirty times smaller than their own. The God of War's tactics are safe. But the three samurai on foot can be punished for their crimes.

With a nod in the direction of the footprints, I signal the chase. We trot along their trail – it's easy to follow as in their haste they haven't had time to disguise their tracks. I judge that they aren't going to set an ambush as they are desperate to get away, so we break into a sprint.

I slide to a halt as one of my monks is impaled by a sword which appears at the end of an arm on a body that has leapt out from behind a tree. Then there's a scream – or rather a challenging shout. My other monk is frozen and takes a step back with the force of the challenge – like being punched in the chest. The samurai withdraws his outstretched arm, palm facing the monk at the same time as the sword arm appears and cuts down my last man. I manage to duck and leap back and to the left from a samurai who has appeared on my right from behind another tree, screaming the same challenge. I'm lucky – he is not as adept at Kiaijutsu as his comrades.

Tianyuan has instructed me in all manner of martial arts, but this is one of the strangest - especially the use of one of their techniques: using the 'spirit cry' to immobilise the enemy. I've often seen soldiers training and being encouraged to shout as they practice attacking the enemy, but never really thought about it. Tianyuan taught me there's more to it than just show or rage. Some samurai still practice Kiaijutsu where they believe they can use the power of their ki or life force as a weapon. Stories have been told of experts of this martial art being able to stun their enemy with a shout – some even believe that they can kill – channelling their life force in a scream which ruptures the enemy's internal organs. I thought of it as just a fascinating story – but here is the reality, two of my men dead, one of them initially stunned by kiai, and me only alive not because of my skills, but because my opponent wasn't that good at it.

The three samurai see only me left - one of them gets complacent. He sees the dragon's teeth webbing on the back of my friend and crouches down to take a closer look – I throw my last two knives into the gap between his helmet and body armour. Now there are only two samurai left and they aren't complacent anymore. I draw my sword and back away so I can keep both samurai in my vision.

There's something about the leader, I can sense the hate emanating from beneath the ghoulish mask. The only indicator that he's watching me is the slight movement of his helmet as I back away – the demon mask's deep dark soulless eye sockets hide his eyes. The rest of his body remains static in its blue lacquered boiled leather. The other samurai moves his feet gently to the side, matching my moves.

I register movement and instinctively leap to the side as a sword from the leader slices down where I stood less than a second before, he continues scything his sword at all angles where my body should be but Tianyuan's training, muscle memory, and fear keep me a hair's breadth from death.

The action is so frantic that the other samurai can't get a killing blow in – the trees help me here. The leader and I weave our way around trunks and duck and dive below branches exchanging blows – the ring of metal pierces the forest. I sense before I see that the other samurai is behind me and in one movement dive backwards swinging my sword so that it catches him in the thigh severing his femoral artery – he'll be dead within three minutes, and he knows it. He looks at the wound and then at me before his legs give way and he drops to the floor.

There's no time to think, I duck just as a sword almost gives me a haircut. In the leader's eagerness to kill me, he has made a mistake – he lashed out without thinking where his sword strike will end up – an elementary error – the sword gets stuck in the tree trunk behind me. I slash with my sword connecting with his chest. He falls to his knees. Looks up at me, and that's when I see the dragonfly pin on his chest. The strength leaves my body as nausea, fear, and dread leave me dumbstruck. No this can't be happening. 'Danny?' I can only whisper.

The jerk of his head looking up at me answers my question. Tears are flowing down my face unbidden as I kneel down, 'Lewis, is that you?' comes the question between gasps for breath – Danny is in charge of the host – the samurai's spirit must have been wounded in the fight. I can only manage a nod. 'Thank God, Thank God. We've found each other. Everything will be okay, won't it?' His hand reaches out – searching the air for mine – I grip it tightly. A spasm of pain racks his whole body.

'Don't talk, we'll get you fixed.' I can save him – I must save him. Right, think straight. Find the wound and apply pressure, dress it, stop the bleeding – 'There'll be patrols from our army following our pursuit into the forest, so help will be here soon, Danny. Stay with me.' I take off his helmet, it's a Japanese face that looks back at me, but the expression and character in the eyes are definitely Danny's. I stifle a sob as I remove his armour and rip strips of cloth off my robe to wrap tightly around the chest wound. It's not frothing or hissing so I don't think I've punctured his lung. But the blood keeps seeping through the bandage – something is terribly wrong. I rest Danny up against the tree trunk in a hollow formed by roots on either side. The wound is on his right, so I gently lower his left side into my lap, elevating the wounded side. His eyes are flickering. 'Danny, stay with me, don't go to sleep.' Danny just looks up at me with a love and adoration in his eyes that cracks my heart in two - I can't stop the tears streaming down my face. 'Stay with me Danny, please, stay with me.' I have to keep us both awake until help arrives. I must stay awake. I must stay awake.

I wake up in my own bed. Something feels wrong. There's a palpable anxiety lurking in the back of my mind. I look across to Danny's empty bed and it floods back to me. I fell asleep – I feel physically sick – I've let Danny down once again. And from this there's no return or future opportunity for me to make amends – Danny was dying in my arms. The phone's shrill ring pierces the air – my mum calls, 'I'll get it.' I hear mutterings and low one-syllable responses from my mum. I leap out of bed and take the stairs three steps at a time to get to the hallway where my mother stands motionless.

* * * * *

Tianyuan's relentless search for Lu-wis and his pack finally reaps a reward. There are two dead monks and two dead samurai lying around the forest floor. Lu-wis has an injured samurai unconscious in his lap. They are both asleep or possibly dead. Lu-wis is slumped over, cradling the samurai's head. Judging by the amount of blood that has seeped through the orange bandages Lu-wis must have applied, the samurai doesn't have long. But the orders are clear, all the enemy are to be executed on sight. Tianyuan calls the medic to make sure Lu-wis is ok. He wakes from a stupor – one of those now familiar gormless looks on his face as if he doesn't know who he is or where he is. Very strange. He looks down at the samurai uncomprehendingly. Tianyuan walks over, 'Are you okay?' a look of concern furrowing his brow.

It takes Lu-wis a moment to answer as he looks around taking in his surroundings. 'Umm, yes, Grandfather Teacher.'

The medics gently pull Lu-wis away from the bleeding samurai. Tianyuan gives a nod to the monk who holds his sword ready to rid the world of one more pirate samurai. The monk raises his sword, lowers it to Danny's neck to get the right angle, then lifts it for the killing strike.

*****

'Mum, who was that? I look at my mum's face – her face looks gaunt and the sparkle seems to have finally left that once joyful face.

'Lewis, I'm sorry.'

'What Mum?' I ask quietly. 'Who was that? What's happened?' Deep down I know who it was and what has happened. But I don't want to acknowledge it.

My mum takes a deep breath and whispers, 'That was the hospital. Danny's vitals are weakening. They said we should get there as soon as possible,' she finally breaks down in tears.

*****

Something catches Tianyuan's eye on the samurai's blue lacquered chest armour, he looks across at Lewis who is still dazed and spots a similar pin on his chest. What is that advice he's always giving people – 'It's important to observe what we can't see as well as that which we can – there's a link here which might suggest…

* * * * *

I prepare myself as we walk through the corridor towards Danny's ward. I look at my mum and wonder if my face looks as drawn, if my eyes reflect that same sense of emptiness, sorrow, and raw pain in their far-away look. We walk in a trance, through the ward's door, down to Danny's room. And stop. I look at Mum and she looks back at me, both resigned to the grief that awaits us on the other side of the door. Mum pushes the door open and stops abruptly.

There's the sound of a woman laughing. I'm confused. Then I hear Danny's laugh, a little subdued but still his laugh. I follow Mum quickly into the room, Amelie sees us, breaks into a big smile, and moves to reveal Danny who looks up at us with a wonderful smile mixed with relief and if I'm not mistaken, a bit of sheepishness. No words are necessary – we have a big family hug and stay in each other's warm embrace.

I let go of Danny at the same time as Mum, tears streaming down our faces. We chat and laugh at nothing, my mum strokes Danny's arm while I feel a sense of relief that allows me to breathe normally for the first time in what seems like ages. Time passes before Amelie gently reminds us that Danny needs his rest. We stand up and look down at him lying there smiling back at us.

'Don't go anywhere,' I say to my brother. Mum laughs thinking I'm joking around as she looks at her son in a hospital bed all wired up to monitors and an intravenous drip. Danny sees the seriousness in my look and nods understanding. Mum kisses him on the forehead, tucks him in and then we leave, happy, but with that niggling feeling of dread – neither of us wants Danny to go to sleep, just in case we have to go through all this again.

* * * * *

'Stop!' yells Tianyuan. The sword's momentum takes the sword down, but the monk manages to shift the angle of the blade so that it imbeds itself in the nearby tree root.

* * * * *

The God of War watches the aftermath of the rout. His men are helping the injured, checking the defences and starting to pile wood in pyres to burn the dead. Those who have a moment to spare stare vacantly at nothing, trying to come to terms with everything they have seen in the last 48 hours. To his left one of the actors who played the role of a pirate zombie coming back from the dead chats quickly with some of his friends who are cleaning off the grisly makeup. They see one of their friends from another troop approaching swiftly, lost in thought. When he nears the group of soldiers, the zombie leaps in front of him screaming and waving his sword in the air. His oppo yelps and jumps out of his skin generating a roar of laughter from the surrounding soldiers. The victim hurls abuse at the group before he too reluctantly starts to laugh. General Qi and his officers chuckle at the soldiers who are bubbling over with the thrill of surviving the battle – of just being alive.

'This has been an incredible victory - and won with remarkably few losses on our side – it's a shame no one will ever hear of it.' The God of War looks around his officers who look confused initially, but one by one their jaws set as they nod understanding. News of the rout of the pirates at Wengjiagang would fill the hearts of the people with joy and hope. However, the ruling politicians would see anyone involved in such a victory as a threat to their hold on power - and they could be more deadly than the wokou pirates.

Epilogue

Cato watches the dolphins entertain the crew as they race either side of the bow, leaping through the air, diving, and doing the odd trick in between. Their trills trigger images of times gone by. There are distant memories of his family dying from the pestilence which tore through his village two days' ride from Carthage. After his neighbours had helped bury his family, he remembers lying down, all alone, and wishing he had died with them. Then events flew by as if they were someone else's memories: there were flashes of Carthage, ships, battles, images of faces – some friendly, some fierce. Cato wonders if the mind made everything a blur as a sort of coping mechanism to deal with bereavement and despair.

'Captain Danny, we should be in Ostia soon, shall I get the ritual ready?'

Cato turns around at his nickname, Danny. He had picked it up during those times when he seemed to be going through life in a dream. He liked it and so kept the name.

'Aye, go ahead.'

He also went by his adoptive family's name – Cato. The legate and his wife had welcomed him into his family as the son they'd always wanted. They seemed to understand that he didn't want to follow the usual route into the senate via a military career – he'd seen enough bloodshed already for a lifetime. No, he would make his name in trade and benefit from the wealth that generated, and consequently, the status that brought in Rome's high society.

He looks back along the deck as the crew, his crew, ready themselves to thank Neptune for another safe voyage before they reach Rome's main port of Ostia. The men are in good spirits, their cargo will add to the fortunes they have already made while in his service. You can see the light of expectation in their eyes, some are thinking of getting back to their families, the others are ready to party. He will go back to his family.

His boatswain passes him an amphora of wine. A hush descends on the deck, the only noise coming from the rigging being stretched and released as the onshore wind fills the sails in the direction of the port.

'Oh great Neptune, we thank you for taking care of us on this voyage. As with all voyages, your protection allows us to live a good life and keep our families hale and hearty.' Danny takes out the stopper from the double-handled jug and tips a little wine into the sea. 'Thank you, benevolent Neptune, we are always at your service.' The crew echo his last words and pass amphorae around, each pouring a libation into the sea and taking a gulp of wine for themselves, trying to suppress the excitement building up at the prospect of getting into port.

Danny lets out a sigh of contentment. Tonight, he'll be home with his wife and three children, feasting in their new villa on the Palatine. He still can't believe he lived in one of the wealthiest parts of Rome, on a hill with a view and a breeze. Danny feels excitement bubbling up inside him. Last night he'd had another one of his dreams where a new innovation came to him. His successful maritime merchant business seems to be vying with his innovative ideas to make him rich. Danny's ideas have built him a reputation as someone who can apply his mind to all aspects of life. Strange how his dreams kept on giving and giving.

'Ostia ahoy', a shout from the lookout breaks his train of thought. Time to get busy, docking a ship in the world's busiest port demanded one hundred percent concentration.

* * * * *

Dido winces as the soapy water seems to find every cut and sore on her calloused hands. But she continues to knead the laundry in case the slaves' overseer sees her slacking and uses it as an excuse to beat her again.

Her heart feels heavy as she remembers earlier that day seeing Danny in the marketplace. He'd evidently done well judging by his entourage of guards, slaves, and most painfully of all, wife and children. What might have been? She didn't begrudge him – he'd saved their lives on that ship all those years ago. Even if it had resulted in them being imprisoned, that wasn't his fault.

Those were awful times: her father had died when his heart had finally given in while they waited for a ransom to be paid or a prisoner exchange. Thankfully he didn't live to hear that his beloved Carthage was no more – razed to the ground by the Roman general, Scipio. Their fate was then sealed – a life of slavery. Maybe it was Tanit's punishment for her sister's actions which had resulted in the innocent Danny being sold into slavery. He hadn't recognised her in her slave garb carrying baskets of food for their master's kitchens. She mustn't think about it, or she'll start crying again.

The sound of a pot hitting the ground and shattering draws her attention to her sister. Oh no, she's done it again. When they were in the cells Jezebel's haughty and selfish manner had incensed their cellmates. They simmered away waiting for an opportunity to take their revenge on Jezebel for her attitude, and at the same time, for all the ills that had befallen them. It came after their father died. One night, they crept up, gagged her, beat her, cut up her face, blinded her in one eye, and broke her nose. Now it was painful to look at the quivering wreck that was her sister. The slave overseer is looking down angrily between the broken shards of the pot and Jezebel - she's going to be flogged again. Dido looks up to the heavens, 'Please merciful Tanit, save us from this nightmare.'

* * * * *

Lu-wis walks back from the meeting with the region's village elders. 'Elder' seems a bit of a misnomer for him, as he had only just celebrated his twenty-eighth year, but his position had been awarded as a sign of respect for everything he had done for his country and its people in the service of General Qi Jiguang and Tianyuan. A far cry from his early days. He has vague recollections of working from dawn till dusk with his family in the rice paddies. Despite the hardship, his mother and father had always done whatever they could to make life for him and his brothers as enjoyable as possible: sometimes they would work longer hours toiling away on their farm so that he and his brothers could go hunting or fishing; and the children always got the best cuts of meat, and the nicest vegetables.

Then, one day, he woke up with a throbbing head and the smell of smoke. Lu-wis tried not to think too often about that day when his world turned upside-down, it seemed to weaken his Chi. But out of respect for his family, he would never forget. The pirates had come during the night and turned his village into hell on Earth. Murder, screams, fire, and incredible loss. He was the only survivor, left for dead due to the bloody head injury he had sustained. Not only did he feel the terrible pain of grief, but also an overwhelming sense of guilt for being the only survivor of that night.

He remembers wandering the land, living in the forests, and then, everything became weird. It was as if he were a member of an audience watching a play about him – renamed Lu-wis instead of his birthname Shuo - the scenes of battle, his growing love for Han, and his friendship with General Qi Jiguang and Tianyuan unfolding before his eyes. Even if he didn't feel as if he was in control of his actions at that time, he had won the respect of the people, including the God of War. He still felt a little guilty for accepting praise for all his exploits while he was in that trance-like state, but who was he to argue? People had seen him do remarkable things, and the stories of his successes had helped to inspire them to finally defeat the Wokou pirates.

Lu-wis has been given rewards beyond his wildest dreams: land, gold, a pension, and a position as an advisor to the region's Imperial Council – a very lucrative post. But the most valuable gift of all was receiving Tianyuan's consent to marry Han. His wife brings him such happiness his heart actually aches when he's away from her. He will never tire of looking into her eyes. He always has a skip in his step on his way home from wherever looking forward to being in her company, and now the additional company of their first child, a baby boy called An, which meant peace.

He stops to look up at the starlit night. The soothing breeze carries the lovely fragrance of Jasmin which competes with the aroma of the various evening meals being cooked - sweet and sour pork, marinated vegetables, spicy chicken, honey cakes - his mouth waters. What a wonderful evening. Studying the stars with a smile on his face, he feels the unusual urge to utter two simple words to the heavens, 'Thank you.'

* * * * *

Emma wakes up in her padded cell – she's been sectioned under the Mental Health Act due to her crazy behaviour – randomly lashing out, blabbering on about battles with pirates, preaching extracts of sermons, barking orders in German, and muttering in incomprehensible languages. She looks wildly at the white walls, unable to process recent events.

* * * * *

The Boss is about to move the file on the boy, Danny, to the Syndicate's database to be stored and probably never opened again. However, there's something stopping him from clicking on the mouse to complete the action. It's clear from the reports that Danny isn't a traveller, but he's the only candidate they've found who is still alive. The Syndicate's bosses are piling the pressure on him to find a traveller and therefore help their organisation re-establish its power and wealth. Is it worth getting one of his agents to double-check? Hmm...

* * * * *

Our scrum half grabs the rugby ball from the back of

the scrum and passes it to me which I quickly chip over the advancing opposition's defensive line. Their fullback and left-wing race towards their own try-line to try and retrieve the ball before me. The ball bounces high in the air – we all leap to grab it, but I get there first, snatch the ball out of the air, break through their tackles, and sprint the last few meters before diving across the line for my third try in the Schools' Regional Final. The crowd go wild, except for the opposition supporters and Claire and Amelie who glance at each other with the look of long-suffering parents watching their children misbehaving again.

They'd had the same look last night at our school's end-of-year concert. I understand that they are worried about drawing unwanted and possibly dangerous attention to us, but Danny and I are recovering from some shocking experiences. So I've decided to be realistic, as Claire suggested ages ago, and let Danny travel, but on condition that we travel only to more recent safer times. We've been having a lot of fun, which takes our minds off those ordeals.

My friends are in the band that played last night – the lead guitarist had broken his arm, so I suggested that Danny fill in for him. My schoolmates had looked at me as if to say, 'You've gotta be kidding, right?' but I managed to persuade them to let my brother come to their rehearsal in my friend's garage. Danny looked a bit nervous, especially when he saw some neighbours in their 50s, who were stood around a car, watching, shaking their heads, oozing contempt. But when my brother started to play AC/DC's Thunderstruck the reaction was incredible – the neighbours stood temporarily dumbstruck, beer cans halfway to open mouths; they turned out to be closet headbangers – getting into it as if they were at a concert. My mates, energised by the reaction of the older blokes, joined in and completed the track. It was awesome! After a lot of whooping and applause the older guys wandered off into one of the houses leaving my mates buzzing. They'll be the first to admit that they are geeks and looked it - they started playfighting which ended up with them wrestling on the floor – Tianyuan would not have been impressed by their fighting skills.

When my brother got onto the stage last night, he looked a little shy and out of place – a junior schoolboy playing at a high school concert. The crowded school hall was silent except for the sound of sniggering coming from here and there. But then my brother started with the same song - the crowd went from stunned to wild - it was superb; especially when my brother put on the schoolboy cap I'd given him just before – he started dancing up and down the stage in his schoolboy shorts and blazer just like the guy from AC/DC. Now, as he watches me play rugby, loads of students and even teachers go up to him to congratulate him on his performance – he's the Man.

His rendition of Queen's Don't Stop Me Now has been playing in my mind throughout the rugby game – inspiring me. But when I look at my brother, smiling, sitting next to my mother who is also enjoying the praise from an endless stream of people, I can't help but worry. How is Danny really coping with all the horrors he's lived through? A word from my German class comes to mind - *Weltschmerz* – it means world pain or world-weariness. Those battle scenes haunt me, leaving me out of sorts. I dread to think how all that has affected him?

When he remembers his time with Dido, does he feel like I do when I think of Han? I now know what they mean by having your heart broken. Danny and I checked out the history books to try and figure out what might have happened to Dido. Just after his experiences over there, the Roman, General Scipio, finally conquered Rome's archenemy - the Carthaginian Empire. That would mean that Dido would have most likely been sold into slavery.

I study Danny while our full-back takes the conversion which will be the last play of the game. Is he up to something? He's only mentioned Dido that one time. He talked about her with a far-off look in his eyes which disturbs me – they'd evidently grown really close on that voyage, but he hasn't mentioned anything since. Maybe this is an example of what Tianyuan warned me about – to always notice the things you can't see and hear as well as those which you can – is Danny planning to save Dido?

My thoughts return to Han and Tianyuan: the wormhole to China closed, so I'll probably never see them again. I wonder what happened to them. I wish I'd had a chance to say goodbye, but that's the problem with travelling, you never know if you'll see newly made friends again once you go to sleep.

The referee blows the final whistle and so the spectators come onto the pitch. I'm missing Han terribly… I see Claire coming over – I'm lucky to have a friend like her; I tried telling her that the other day, but I realize just how bad I am at expressing myself – she seemed a little annoyed and went all quiet.

Mum and Amelie are walking towards me smiling – they've become firm friends. Mum doesn't realise it, but this is particularly good news for Danny and me as Amelie is also a traveller. She has been able to fill in some of the gaps about dream travelling – she's confirmed that we can assimilate any of our host's skills providing we have the physical and mental capacity. Amelie's expression darkens as she sees me exchange my rugby top with my opposite number. My physique is pretty chiselled, even if I do say so myself, which obviously means I haven't heeded her warning about dream travellers' jet lag – an incredible fatigue you can experience from overdoing your night-time exploits. But the thrill of travelling is too hard to resist - we've really enjoyed residing in some of the world's greatest rugby players, guitarists, and others – the benefits of which are clear from our successes over the last 24 hours.

I avoid looking at Amelie and see Danny walking towards me beaming – a wonderful sight, completely at odds with the intensity of the other night. He asked if we could use our skills to rescue Dad – I didn't know, but it got me wondering. Then he really blew my mind by asking whether we could live forever by just moving from host to host. I couldn't answer that either but suggested that we ask Amelie. Hmm, I'll have to remind Danny that we have to keep an eye out on our travels for someone wearing a butterfly accessory – it could be Terry, Amelie's long-lost love.

* * * * *

Ryan doesn't think he'll ever get used to the sweltering heat or the biting insects. A moment's respite gives him an opportunity to survey his dismal surroundings. He looks down the line of men waiting for their ladle of water before continuing their work in the mine. He is the only white person here now. His two colleagues, who were captured with him on the aid mission in what seems like a lifetime ago, died from a combination of disease and exhaustion.

The thought of his wife and two boys keeps him going. One day he will see them again, he'll give Rachel and the boys a big hug and never let go. He wonders how Lewis and Danny are faring. They are tough resilient boys, so he's sure they're doing okay and that the whole family will be pulling together to get them through these difficult times. One day, he will see them again. He doesn't know how, but he will.

The lash of a whip is the signal to get back down into the mine. He gathers up his pick and sorghum basket then takes one last glance at the edge of the jungle in the distance. Yes, he'll see them again, one day.

Historical notes

The Punic Wars

There were three Punic Wars between 264 and 146 BC. Initially, the Carthaginians fought to retain their territory on the island of Sicily against the expanding Roman empire. The Carthaginian navy had dominated the Western Mediterranean, but the indomitable Romans gradually built a navy to match the Carthaginians and with innovations such as the corvus began to encroach further and further into Carthaginian waters and lands. The corvus, meaning crow or raven in Latin, was a platform with a beak which would securely hook a Roman vessel alongside a Carthaginian ship. The Romans were then able to storm onto the enemy's boat and form up in an infantry battle formation which won them their empire.

In the Second Punic War Hannibal famously marched his army and elephants across the Alps to almost cause the fall of the Roman Empire. Hannibal beat the Romans at the battles of Trebia (218 BC) and Lake Trasimene (217 BC) but showed his true military genius at Cannae (216 BC) where he vanquished an army almost twice the size of his Carthaginian forces. In desperation, the Roman Senate (governing assembly) changed the age of conscription so that almost any man who could stand was drafted to fill the ranks of its decimated forces. Hannibal's reputation was such that many Romans went to great lengths to avoid being conscripted – breaking legs and even cutting off thumbs so they couldn't hold a sword. However, for reasons which dismayed his generals and advisors and continue to get historians scratching their heads, when Hannibal could have sacked Rome and therefore changed history, he didn't. It was as if his mind had been taken over by a different person…

The Romans had no qualms about doing the same in the Third Punic War when General Scipio besieged Carthage. His forces eventually razed the city to the ground and salted the lands so that they became infertile. Dido and her sister Jezebel really had/have no chance of rescue from that quarter…

China's conflict with the Wokou pirates

For centuries the wokou pirates raided the Chinese and Korean coastlines. Wokou translates as Japanese or dwarf pirates, but this seems to be a misnomer as they were predominantly made up of Chinese, some Japanese samurai or ronin, criminals from all over Asia, and a spattering of Portuguese.

In 16th century China the Ming dynasty tried to tighten its political control which involved trade bans. Since this included a ban on maritime trade it caused the knock-on effect of a reduced navy which consequently couldn't cope with increased piracy in the region. At the same time, there were Mongol raids to the north which culminated in a siege of Beijing. Enter Qi Jiquang: the young soldier happened to be there for a martial imperial examination. He and all his compatriots had to help defend the city where Qi Jiguang made a name for himself through his actions and ingenuity.

The rising star became Assistant Regional Military Commissioner of Shandong in 1553 whose main role was to try and eradicate the pirate menace – a duty he fulfilled despite the odds. Here I have used a bit of artistic licence with events, dates, and participants. There was a pirate alliance between Xu Hai, Chen Dong, and Ye Ma whose goal was to take over the cities of Hangzhou and then Nanjing – this would be the equivalent of pirates taking over modern-day London and Paris. Xu Hai's pirates were blown off course and had to return to the Goto Islands. Ye Ma's force did intercept a poisoned shipment of rice and wine which had a catastrophic impact forcing him and his remaining men to retreat to their base in Songjiang. The Ming leaders were responsible for this – I'm not sure Lewis was involved in the planning! Neither am I sure that General Qi Jiquang, whose father was a renowned martial arts expert, directly hired the services of the Shaolin master Tianyuan. But legend has it that 'Grandfather Teacher' did defeat the disgruntled kung fu masters of 18 other temples who wanted to lead the kung fu training of the Ming troops. Incidentally, around this time monks could get married and didn't always wear orange robes, but the rules were changing. What is certain is that General Qi Jiquang with the help of General Yu Dayou finally defeated the last remnants of the wokou pirates on the island of Nan'ao in 1565.

Some historians believe that the perceptive General Qi Jiquang was aware that receiving too many accolades for his military accomplishments would be dangerous – possibly fatal. Therefore, I have exaggerated the conflict at Wengjiagang in order to reflect General Qi Jiquang's wish to play down the extent of his victories. As with any regime anywhere in the world at any time, there were/are people in the shadows waiting to try and steal power and wealth by any means. Political manoeuvrings resulted in General Qi Jiquang eventually being sent to a quiet corner of the empire where he lived out his remaining years.

A final note on my description of the Chinese countryside – I know that bluebells don't grow in China! In fact, half the world's population of the plant grow in the UK. However, bluebells carpeting a forest floor in early spring is one of my favourite scenes, so I used a bit of artistic licence and introduced them to China.

Alamut Castle: one of the castles of the Assassins

I was fortunate to have the opportunity to visit this castle around 130 miles north of Tehran on the way to the Caspian Sea. It had a reputation as being impregnable which is easily comprehended as you walk, as Lewis describes, single file on the only path which traverses the boulder-shaped top of the mountain. Its situation gave the castle its name, Alamut, which means eagle's nest.

Apparently, the castle used to have wonderful gardens, an eclectic library, and laboratories where all sorts of experiments were carried out – all above ground by the way, not in underground rooms as I have written. However, it is better known as the most infamous of the assassins' castles where it was the base for elite mercenaries whose services were used by any who had enough gold to pay.

They seem to have gone a mission too far in 1256 when they accepted a contract to kill Genghis Khan's grandson, Hulegu Khan, whose forces were sweeping across Asia. The unassailable castle was besieged by the Mongols whose fierce reputation persuaded the occupants to surrender.

There are many accounts of the Mongols' brutality. In 1258, the Mongols besieged Baghdad where they allegedly executed the city's population of around a million. Some historians believe these numbers were exaggerated due to anti-Mongolian propaganda. However, research suggests that the world's population was reduced by 10% during the Mongols' quest to conquer the world – which they apparently believed was their sacred duty to their god, Tengri. Therefore, it seems fair to assume that some of the alleged atrocities actually occurred. I hope Lewis and Danny don't end up in those times…

ABOUT THE AUTHOR

After years of working overseas, the author eventually succumbed to *hiraeth* – a Welsh word which describes a yearning or longing to be back home. And he loves it.

Printed in Great Britain
by Amazon